ORDER OF LIGHT

S BOLANOS

CHAOTIC NEUTRAL PRESS LLC

SERIES

<u>Contemporary Lines</u>

Ulwich Preparatory Academy

Fall

Winter

Spring

Oak Haven Romances

One Brave Thing

All the Hype

CONTENTS

Where there is darkness, there is light, and the light will prevail.

CHAPTER 1

HERE WE GO AGAIN

ALEXI

Walking into Battle Tactics on the first day of fall semester was just as surreal as it had been in summer. I glanced to the side and smiled. Only *this* time, Matt and I weren't at odds. We were... dating. My heart gave a happy skip and I couldn't help but wonder how long it would keep doing that whenever I thought about Matt and me together. My guess? Forever.

I waved to some of our classmates—Ellie and Yaren were already deep into gossiping, while Louise and Roland pretended the other didn't exist. An entire class of Shadow Demons. I doubted that would ever stop surprising me either. Though it seemed we were still waiting for a few people.

My smile broadened as Matt and I walked nearly hand-in-hand to our usual corner of the room, where it seemed some fresh faces had also clustered. Or it *could* have been hand-in-hand if Matt hadn't been too busy sulking.

"I still don't see why Battle Tactics has to be so ridiculously early now," he complained from behind crossed arms, his adorable pout on full display. A morning person, Matt was not.

"It's really not that bad." For all the fuss he was putting up, I didn't think it was really about having to wake up earlier. Unlike the previous semester when we'd shared every class, presumably for our own safety, we only had two classes together this term. I was also fairly confident that Matt would die before admitting he was anxious about navigating courses on his own. Except he wouldn't be. "You know, just because we don't share the same schedule doesn't mean we can't still study together."

His sullen expression softened with a glimmer of hope. "Yeah?"

"Of course. Who else is going to make sure you're taking notes and not just doodling?" I raised an eyebrow to forestall the argument I could already see brewing.

He laughed and rewarded me with one of his stunning smiles that had become so frequent these last few weeks.

Personally, I could have done with more of a reprieve than two weeks between semesters. It would have been nice to visit home. But spending time together without things being weird—well, *less* weird—had been nice. And all the cuddles. I was a big fan of all the couch cuddles...when I got them. I was about to ruffle Matt's hair and tease him some more when he pointed behind me.

"Do we know that guy?"

I turned to see who he was talking about and a young man with deep umber skin and twisted locks that hung just past his ears waved. "Uh... no."

"Think he's another TA? I feel like Vera's wearing her usual ones out."

I glanced at Matt. "Why don't we find out?" We moved towards the young man in his pale purple tucked shirt and crisply pressed slacks. I sensed a kindred spirit. I'd dressed remarkably similar on my first day. "Hi, you must be new."

The young man gave a deprecating chuckle and rubbed the back of his neck. "Is it that obvious?"

"No," I said at the same time Matt replied, "Yeah." The three of us shared a laugh. When it died out, I extended my hand. "I'm Alexi. This is Matt, my—"

"Roommate," Matt filled in before I could finish. I darted a glance at him, but he wasn't paying attention.

The young man shifted to take Matt's equally extended hand. "I'm Gilles," he said, with an emphasized Z sound at the beginning. "I was actually supposed to be here for the summer semester, but I, uh... How you say, *chickened* out."

I nodded in understanding at his abashed smile. "This *is* kind of unprecedented. So many Shadow Demons together in one place? And the legendary Vera herself?"

"Will she really be here?" Gilles' gaze darted about the room, his face a mix of awe and trepidation.

Matt snorted. "If we're lucky. Or not." He shrugged. "Depends on how you look at it. So, Gille," Matt began, over-emphasizing the pronunciation, "where are you from?"

Like myself, Gilles was clearly trying not to laugh at Matt's butchered attempt at his name. "Do not worry, the name is French, which is where I'm from, France. You are American, no?"

Matt squinted and I could tell he was trying to decide if he should take offense at the assumption. Before he could decide he should, I intervened.

"What part of France?"

Gilles rocked back on his heels. "I grew up on the outskirts of Paris with my papa."

Matt's face brightened. "Paris-Paris? Eiffel Tower, the Louvre, and everything?"

"Oui. Arc de Triomphe, Montmartre, and the Seine too," Gilles added with a wide smile that revealed dimples.

"That's amazing! Have you been to the Louvre? Of course, you have. Better question, is it as great in person as it looks in books? What's your favorite piece?" Matt's enthusiasm took me aback and Gilles appeared overwhelmed.

I crossed my arms and scowled at him. "Hey, where was all this curiosity when I told you I was from the UK?"

"*You* said you were from a small village in the middle of nowhere," he said with a wry twist of his lips. "If you'd have said London…"

I let out an indignant squawk, and both Matt and Gilles erupted into laughter. Before I could formulate an appropriate scathing response, Matt bumped me with his shoulder.

"If you want me to grill you about your town, I will."

I deflated. "Okay, you win. There's really not much to tell. It's a plain, old boring English village, filled with the usual array of busybodies."

Matt rolled his eyes. "Please. *Anywhere* is better than Nebraska."

"You two are obviously great roommates. Hopefully, I am so lucky." Gilles smiled and Matt shifted.

"Do you know who you're bunking with yet?"

Gilles took on an intense look of concentration. "I believe their name is Miel?"

Matt and I shared a look, then Matt said exactly what I was thinking. "That's weird. Wasn't Miel rooming with Sebastian?"

I glanced around the room for Sebastian. When I still didn't find him, I shrugged. "Maybe he dropped the class?"

Before we could speculate further, the class door opened and the TA, Anne, walked in. She waved to several of us as she made her way to the front of the room. An expectant hush fell over us. Then Anne cleared her throat.

"Welcome back, everyone. As I'm sure you've noticed by now, we have several new students." She smiled encouragingly at a few, including Gilles. "Unfortunately, Ms. Scry will not be here to greet you personally today. She is currently away on... business." Anne's face tensed, her smile slipping slightly, before she pulled it back into place. "I'd like to take this opportunity to set expectations for this semester's Battle Tactics course. Out of consideration for our newest students, we will devote the first couple of weeks to review, beginning with guided meditation."

A collective groan from everyone *except* the new students filled the room.

"I know, I know," Anne said with a placating gesture. "Promise it won't be as extended as before. Vera has made it clear that once everyone is on the same page, so to speak, your studies will accelerate drastically."

I frowned and looked at Matt. He hiked a shoulder, but that did nothing to mediate my sudden concern. My hand flew into the air.

"Don't," Matt hissed under his breath.

"Yes, Mr. Roman. You had a question?" Anne asked with a knowing smile.

I let my hand fall and ignored Matt's exasperated huff. "I don't mean to sound rude, but why? What's the urgency?"

Anne shifted her weight, clutching her ever-present clipboard a little tighter. "I'm not sure 'urgency' is quite the right word."

"Then what?"

"For fuck's sake, Roman. Who gives a shit?" George grumbled from across the room.

Matt took a step forward, already snarling, and I shot him a look that our new friend definitely didn't miss. Matt stopped, but I noticed his fists didn't unclench, nor did his shoulders relax.

I dropped my voice to be for his ears alone. "Could you two refrain from getting into it for *one* day?"

He scowled at me, but didn't advance further.

"*As* I was saying," Anne said, speaking louder to regain everyone's attention, "your studies will accelerate as your requirement to take Battle Tactics will have been met. Does that address your concerns, Mr. Roman?"

A hope I hadn't thought to entertain blossomed in my chest. I wouldn't have to keep taking a class where I was required to fight? "Yes, Anne, it does. Thank you." Giddiness fizzed in my chest as I turned to face Matt with what was assuredly an ecstatic grin. "Did you hear that?" I whispered.

The way his crystal blue eyes reflected his smile only added to my fizzy feeling. "Yeah. I did. You don't have to be so damn happy about it, though."

"Now, before you all start celebrating too much, I'd like to emphasize the imperativeness of passing this course. Retaking will not be an option. Should you fail Battle Tactics, your scholarship will be revoked, you will be expelled from the university, and you will not be permitted to return."

"Yikes. That's severe," Gilles said softly, a sentiment echoed by new and existing students. Even Matt looked a touch anxious.

"Honestly, it's not much different from the proclamation Vera made over the summer. Though Anne is being a lot nicer about it," I clarified.

Gilles grimaced. "*That's* the nice version? I'd hate to hear the not nice one."

Matt's tension faded. "Don't worry, you probably will. Vera's big into scare tactics. But she's not all *that* bad."

Gilles looked at Matt like he'd lost his damn mind and I couldn't help but laugh.

"I can't believe I'm agreeing, but he's right. She likes to look all terrible, but once you know her a little better, she's not much different from the rest of us." The admission was worth it for the pleased smile that touched Matt's lips. A quick glance around showed we'd missed the back end of whatever else Anne had said and our peers were now settling into comfortable positions on the floor. "We should probably get on with it as well," I said.

"I really hate meditation," Matt griped as he lowered himself to sit on the floor beside me.

Gilles settled into a seated position and looked at us expectantly. "Now what?"

"Just wait for it," Matt mumbled.

Right on cue, the sound of waves crashing on a shore drifted through the room. "Picture a lake in your mind's eye. A dark, inky lake with a smooth surface and endless depths. This is your essence, your darkness defined…"

Matt rolled his eyes, then closed them. I followed suit with significantly less attitude.

I wonder how long it will take him to fall asleep.

CHAPTER 2

A NEW SCHEDULE

MATT

I already didn't like the new class schedule. Demon History II was first thing in the morning, which was an obscene time to expect anyone to function. The only plus was that Battle Tactics was right after. Of course that meant you were also a sweaty mess for the rest of your classes. But the worst part was that they were the only two classes Alex, and I shared. Half of the time we couldn't even have lunch together because one of us was running off. The bottom line was it sucked. It was a good thing that I stopped going to the 'bruiser club' as Alex called it too; there just wasn't enough time or energy for it. My only concern was that they would eventually track me down, anyway. It was a constant fear anytime I stepped out of the dorm and was on my own, but thus far, there hadn't been a single sign of either Otto or Neese.

The campus was a blaze of amber as I trudged toward Starling Hall. It had only been a week of fall semester and my back already ached from all the books I was carrying. Part of me couldn't help but wonder if my back really was sore or if it was purely psychological because I was so grumpy about the extra class. Not that I had a right to be grumpy, considering I'd voluntarily signed up for it. By the time I made it to the dorm, I was more than a little tempted to shadow inside rather than climb the stairs, but I didn't trust the backpack to make the trip. My shadowing skills may have improved, but they were still inconsistent.

I walked into our dorm and dropped my bag unceremoniously to the floor. It made a heavy thump before toppling to its side, reinforcing my belief that it really was getting heavier by the day. Maybe a witch had put a curse on it. There were more than a few in my classes. That would be just my luck.

Unsurprisingly, Alex was already there and working on some assignment at the table. His dark hair swept across his forehead in stunning contrast to his flawless cool olive complexion. He looked up and smiled. "Hey, you," he said, the greeting touched by a slight British accent. The way his emerald eyes lit up made my stomach flutter.

I still wasn't sure what to make of the feelings. I'd never been attracted to a man before, but then, I'd also never had the liberty to be attracted to anyone. As uncertain as I was, there was no denying I was into Alex—*really* into Alex. Truth be told, not much had really changed since he'd agreed to date me, except he was noticeably more relaxed... and I was getting in fewer fights.

"I'm going to say it again. This totally stinks. Why do you get to be out of classes before me? It's not fair."

"Might have something to do with the fact that they also start before yours," he said, setting down his work.

"They wouldn't if we were taking the same classes," I griped under my breath. In all fairness, I *had* opted to take different courses from him.

"Oh, I don't know. I kind of like it."

I narrowed my eyes at him.

He laughed as he walked toward me, making my stomach flutter again and my skin tingle in anticipation. "It certainly makes that I get to this more special." His fingers slid around my neck and my breath caught. He hesitated only a moment before he leaned down to press his lips against mine.

All the tension in my shoulders loosened. Even my back stopped aching. Much as I hated my schedule, this was probably the best part of it, even though I had to wait all day for it. I kissed him back, tasting his lips like they were the sweetest treat I'd ever had. Yes, this was definitely the best part of my day, though his fixation on taking it easy was borderline making me manic. I had no idea when I'd become addicted to Alexi Roman, but he always left me craving more.

Alex pressed harder, and I took a reflexive step back to keep my balance, gasping when the wall brought me up short. He took advantage of my surprise to kiss me deeper, his tongue teasing past my lips, his wonderfully soft mouth holding me entranced. It always amazed me how confident he was. I, however, still didn't know what to do with my hands. They opened and closed by my side. I wanted more, *needed* it. I just wasn't sure how to go about it.

Fuck it all.

Throwing my doubts right out the window, I slid my hands around his waist. The rightness of it settled into my bones, making me light-headed. I pulled him closer, pressing his lithe, muscular frame against me, and deepened the kiss without waiting for an invitation. There was a soft moan, though I wasn't sure who from. It didn't matter. I could do this forever. I tugged on his lip and slipped into the heat that sprung to life anytime we kissed.

He pulled back slightly and looked at me with a grin that made me want to pull him close again.

"What?" I asked, pretending to be equally confident. Thinking about what I was doing usually ruined everything.

"Nothing," he said, his smile growing. He looped his arms around my neck and claimed my mouth again.

I completely melted into it. This was more than he'd given me since this whole thing started, and I hungrily ate it up. I tightened my arms around him, determined to keep him close where I could savor how amazing he tasted. This was incredible, perfect—and it still wasn't enough. I needed more.

He sighed into me, heightening the buzz already clouding my head. Then he leaned back again and released a soft laugh. "Easy there. Slow, remember?"

Yeah, I was too far down the rabbit hole for that. "I can do slow," I responded, my voice low. I slipped my hand beneath his shirt and trailed my fingers across his lower back. His breath caught and heat flashed in his eyes. Maybe I wasn't the only one desperate for more.

"Night, Matt," he said breathlessly as he reached around to place my hand far from its wandering. "Anyone ever tell you you're nothing but trouble?"

"It might have been mentioned a few times." I gave him a crooked grin. It was definitely more than a couple.

"I bet it has." He brushed his lips against mine in a chaste kiss, then pulled away before I could steal more. "What would you say to hanging out this Friday? We could stay in, watch a movie?"

I couldn't contain my smile. "Alex, are you asking me out?"

"If I am?" He teased me with the possibility of another kiss.

"Then I only have one question."

He quirked an eyebrow.

"Are we getting Chinese or pizza?"

He laughed, stepping back and venturing towards his abandoned homework on the breakfast table. I could have groaned with frustration. He was an insufferable tease. "What would you prefer?" he asked as he resumed his seat.

"Chinese, definitely."

"Done." He pointed at the chair pulled out beside him. "Now get over here so you can actually have free time on Friday."

I rolled my eyes. "Everything is always school with you."

"School is important. What kind of homework have you accumulated?"

"You say that like you assume I haven't done any of it," I scoffed as I dragged my ridiculously heavy bag to the round table.

"Have you?" He had me there.

I plopped down and pulled out my books.

"Are the classes going well?"

"Eh." I shrugged. "Math is easy enough. I can't believe you didn't have to take the next course, though."

"It's not my fault I tested out."

"If I'd known that was an option, I might have tried harder," I complained, not for the first time.

"And now you see why it's important to pay attention during class and not just doodle the whole time," he teased.

I thought about the sketch I'd started during the summer semester—our first semester together at Arminius—when I'd started having weird feelings about my awkward roommate. It was almost done, but there were still a few details I was working on. I wanted it to be perfect. It had to be the longest I'd ever worked on any project.

"What else?" he prompted as I took out a few notebooks.

"They aren't all sketches," I said, belatedly defending myself.

He snagged probably the only folder that was predominantly drawings and gave me a look as he flipped through. "Oh, really?"

"One class." I snatched it back.

He let me have it and grabbed another one. "What's this class?" He gazed at the page curiously.

I shifted to get a better look. "That's Advanced Spells."

"You took the class?"

I rolled my shoulders uncomfortably. "Of course. You said I should."

He looked just as surprised by the admission as finding out I was taking the class. "How's it going?"

"Well, I guess. Most of the stuff so far is pretty basic in concept, though the execution seems far more complicated than necessary. I suspect it's one of those things that it's easier done than explained."

"What do you mean? What kind of magic are you learning?"

"It's still all shadow magic, kind of like our version of things that other people can do. Like manifesting something out of shadow and getting it to hold its form without constant concentration or creating a portal. Hiding a portal," I added as an afterthought.

"That all sounds really complicated."

"But it isn't. You just have to know what you're doing." I shrugged again. The irony, of course, was that I rarely felt like I knew what I was doing, especially where Alex was concerned. "What?" I asked when I realized he was staring.

"You never cease to amaze me. I can't get you to admit to being able to shadow half the time, and here you are, telling me that shadow spells are easy. Matt, only higher levels can even hope to master shadow spells. I bet you're top of your class."

I squirmed beneath his intense gaze. Alex was the smart one, not me. "Why do you say that?"

"Because, aside from Vera, I'm pretty sure you are the strongest shadow demon on campus."

I barked a laugh. "That's preposterous. There are plenty of others better than I am. I mean, look at you. Besides, the entire class isn't demonic. I think some are just there for research."

He shook his head, clearly exasperated. "I don't know how many times I'm going to have to tell you before you finally believe me. You are a more powerful demon than I am."

"You don't know that," I insisted.

"Yes, I do. I can sense it." He dropped his gaze to where he was playing with the edge of some papers. "Turns out that might actually be my specialty."

"Specialty? We have those?"

Like flipping a switch, Alex brightened, momentarily stealing my breath with the passion shining in his eyes. "Yeah, I learned about it in my Powers class. Like witches, some demons have areas they excel in. So, like a witch might have a gift for scrying or weather magic, a demon could be sensitive to power levels or exceptionally good at shadow walking. The higher up you go in levels, the more likely that you have more than one specialty."

"If you say so. If yours is sensing power levels, then what's mine? Besides getting into trouble," I added.

He chuckled. "That's definitely one of them. Who knows? Personally, I also think you're fantastic at shadowing. You seem to do it without thinking most of the time. But maybe you're also a natural at shadow magic."

"I don't shadow *all* the time."

"Maybe not in class, but when we're alone, you do. It's almost instinctive. That day I left; you said you knew. How?"

"That's obvious, because you weren't here anymore." I didn't enjoy having to think about that day. I'd been terrified my insecurities around my attraction to him had royally screwed everything up. That not only would I never get to understand these feelings, but that I'd also sabotaged the best and only friendship I'd ever had. Even a couple weeks later, I was still nervous he'd change his mind and disappear altogether without a word, no matter what he said to the contrary.

"But how did you *know*?" he pressed. "It's not like you saw me leave. The only way you would have known was by sensing the shift in my shadow presence. Instead of seeing me leave the dorm, you *felt* it."

"That still doesn't make sense. I'm not doing anything special."

"You've got to be the most stubborn person. Alright, homework can wait for a minute. I'm going to prove my point." He pushed away from the table and stood with his hands on his hips.

"We're not going to arm wrestle again, are we?" Not that I would object to getting to touch him again, even if it was for a silly game. He laughed like I figured he would. Strange to think that first interaction was only a few months ago.

"No, we're not going to wrestle. I'm pretty sure at least one of us wouldn't survive that," he replied with a smirk. "I'm going to shadow out and I want you to find me."

"Alex, really? Hide and seek? Always the kid games with you," I teased, though some of those "kid games," were my favorite memories.

"Shut up and just try it." In the blink of an eye, he faded all to black and was gone.

Damn it.

I looked around anxiously, expecting him to pop out at any moment and say boo. "Alex, this is stupid. Come on, cut it out," I said into the seemingly vacant space.

He walked out of the cabinets still the color of midnight. "Not until you actually try. Quit being so bullheaded." Once more, he vanished.

I ground my teeth.

Why can't we sit here and do homework like normal people?

I blew out a frustrated breath and attempted to focus. He hadn't gone far before. Maybe I could guess where he'd be and get lucky. I stood and walked toward the fridge. But the closer I got, the more wrong it felt. I frowned. Maybe he'd spirited away to his room. That was definitely something I could get behind. I eagerly adjusted my course, but as I got closer to his door, that also felt wrong.

What the hell?

I stopped halfway to his door and considered what I could sense. The shared living/dining/kitchen area was quiet beyond the sound of my breathing. Beyond our sanctuary, I could hear the muffled steps of someone walking down the hall. There, in the back of my mind, I could just make out the strange sensation of someone else. Close. The more I focused on it, the more it *felt* like Alex. I zeroed in on the source. I walked towards the center of the living room, then halted by the coffee table. Before I could second guess myself, I reached into the couch and pulled Alex out by his arm.

He grinned ear to ear as he returned to normal. "I told you, you could do it."

"But I didn't..."

"Now do it again." He disappeared.

"I thought we were supposed to be doing homework?" No response.

He's absolutely insufferable when he wants to prove he's right about something.

I tried to relax and get back to the state that I'd just been in, but the focus wouldn't come.

This is ridiculous. I just want to sit down and be with my friend. That's all. Why does he always have to make things so damn difficult? Isn't it bad enough that he gets to start chilling out for the day early? I knew I shouldn't have signed up for that extra class. If he's going to be pulling stunts like this, I'll never get to spend any real time with him.

My exasperation was only getting in the way. He said that this was no different from Shadow Magic. You just had to know what you were doing. But I didn't. I didn't know how any of this worked. Spells were easy. They came with instructions and rules. This was more like making it up as you went. I felt something move to my right by the front door and dismissed it. No way it was Alex. He was in the kitchen.

My eyes widened, and I turned in place. Alex was in the kitchen. Why was I so sure that he wasn't by the front door? Because I could sense him, just like the night he left.

"You can come out now. I know you're in there," I said, staring at the corner where the fridge stuck out. Sure enough, out he stepped.

"You really should have more faith in yourself. It's almost like you're intentionally ignoring all the things that make you a Shadow Demon."

I shook my head again, almost as discouraged as when we'd started this weird game. "I just don't understand how any of this works."

"Do you have to understand how your arm bends in order to catch something?" He tossed an apple from the bowl on the counter at me.

I snatched it out of the air. "Of course not."

"Or how your feet grip the ground in order to walk?" He took an exaggerated step toward me.

I placed the apple on the table. "You're being silly now."

He smiled in response and walked closer still. "What about this?" He was officially way too close.

I watched him warily. Alex had a unique ability to unsettle me. I never seemed to know what he was going to do next.

"Do you have to know how your lips work in order to kiss?" He didn't wait for another flippant response. His mouth closed on mine and I forgot what I was going to say. I wanted to wrap my arms around him like I had before, but he didn't give me the chance. After a single brief kiss, he was back at the table, looking exceptionally smug.

Insufferable tease.

"If this is how homework is always going to go with you, we're never going to get anything done," I griped, taking out the last of my notes and joining him. He laughed and picked up his pen to keep working. I shook my head and followed suit.

CHAPTER 3

DATE NIGHT

A

Friday couldn't come soon enough. Perhaps it was a little childish to be as excited as I was about the date, considering we technically lived together, but I couldn't contain myself. If the week took any longer, I was going to find some spell to speed up time. It wouldn't be anything big or major or, hell, even life altering—we'd already covered most of that—just something small and simple, sweet. The big deal was that he'd said yes, had even contributed to the plan. That reminded me, I had no idea what kind of Chinese Matt would like. Of course, I knew pretty much everything else about his eating habits, so I felt safe enough guessing.

By the time the day finally bothered to roll around, I was a frantic mess. There was a good chance I'd over-ordered on the food, though I didn't see anything wrong with having options. Food and movies taken care of, all that was left was to make sure I didn't go over the top. I stopped my flurried dance around the dorm and took a deep breath.

If I made a big deal about this, I was liable to freak him out, and that was the last thing I wanted. Things were going fairly well, except, of course, for that he still hesitated with just about everything except for kissing—that was only half the time. I checked the time.

Shit, he'll be here soon.

I raced into my room and peeled off my shirt, which was sticking to me from my frenzied whirl around the dorm. I dismissed three shirts in quick succession before pausing and letting out a heavy breath.

Why am I stressing about this? Matt will probably just wear the same thing he wore to class today.

I ran my hands through my hair, unsure of what to do.

I'm definitely over-thinking this.

The shirt on top of the drawer won, and I zipped into the bathroom to freshen up. The sound of the door caught my attention, and I stopped fighting with my hair. Per usual, it was doing whatever it wanted. I scrambled out into the living room, where Matt eyed me warily.

"Hey." The greeting pitched high, and I struggled not to wince. It hadn't been *that* long since I dated.

Sweet merciful heavens, pull it together.

I cleared my throat and fought for composure. "How was class?"

He chuckled. "I'll tell you in a minute. I want to change first. They really should have showers by the training rooms. There isn't enough time to come back here *and* have lunch. Give me just a sec."

I took advantage of the delay to calm my nerves.

The only thing different about tonight is the fact that we are calling it a date. We hang out all the time.

Except, almost all of our previous attempts to hang out have ended in epic fallouts.

I shook my head to dispel the doubt and ran my hands through my hair, then immediately set to flattening it back down.

"You okay?" Matt asked, reappearing in fresh clothes. Night, he was stunning. The jeans accentuated his muscular legs and the gray t-shirt made his blue eyes practically glow.

I dropped my hands. "I'm fine." It didn't sound very believable to me, but at least my voice didn't crack. *This is only weird if you make it weir.* I took a deep breath and visualized all the tension leaving my body. Feeling much calmer, I asked again, "How was your day?"

He rolled his eyes. "Ridiculous. So, of course, today of all days, I had to get to my first class after Battle Tactics early. There was a signup sheet, and I was not about to have to choose from the bottom of the list." He walked towards the kitchen. The food was still sitting in the delivery sacks, and he began unpacking as he continued. "Anyway, so I race over for that only to find out that class had been moved thanks to a burst pipe. Then I had to scramble to another building that I swear was clear across campus in order not to miss sign up at all. All I have to say is thank Nyx we can shadow. Otherwise, bottom of the list right here." He pointed to himself with a comical scowl that highlighted his natural pout.

I joined him, grabbing plates and silverware from the cupboards. "Did you make it?"

He snorted. "Barely." He finished unpacking the last box and opened the lids. "Oh, you magical creature."

"What?"

"I'm starving." He looked at me with those puppy eyes that had gotten me in more trouble than could ever be considered fair.

I chuckled. "You're always hungry."

"You don't understand. When I say raced over, I mean I ate nothing at all."

I leaned against the counter, snagging an egg roll. "Then I'm glad I over ordered."

"You mean some of this is for you, too?" I choked on my bite and he laughed. "So, what are we watching?"

I shrugged. "There are a few options." I indicated the counter covered in movies.

He swiped the half-eaten roll right out of my hand. "You choose. Whatever you want to watch is fine by me."

I frowned as he devoured the last of my snack and turned to inspect the gathered options. While I'd hoped for a little more input, I wasn't about to make a fuss over something so small as choosing a movie. If he really didn't like it, he'd say something.

Who am I kidding? If he doesn't like it, he'll carry that secret to the grave.

I mentally shook my head and chose an adventure film that promised to have a bit of everything. Playing it safe was pretty much all I had since he hadn't offered a preference.

"Alright, movie picked. Now all I need is a—plate," I finished abruptly when he passed me a bowl already prepped. It even had a fresh egg roll. I stared at the dish in disbelief and back up at him.

How did he know this is what I would have?

He winked and relieved me of the movie. I followed numbly behind and joined him on the couch. As the movie began, I wondered if I should say something. So far, this date was anything but typical. That probably shouldn't have surprised me. This was Matt, after all.

It didn't take long for us to polish off dinner. Without a word, he collected both of our plates and came back with some water. When he sat back down, I used shadow to hit the last of the lights.

"Nice," he commented, sounding impressed.

"I've been practicing." I stretched out and crossed my ankles on the coffee table, letting my arm span the back of the couch.

In hardly anytime at all, I was sucked back into the movie. Matt, on the other hand, couldn't seem to find a comfortable position. I was about to tease him for not being able to sit still when he shifted to be right next to me. Granted, it wasn't a large couch, but there was no reason he had to be close enough to touch.

When he finally stopped fidgeting, I reached my fingers forward to brush the feathery hairs on the back of his head. That was definitely one thing I liked about this arrangement. I could touch Matt's hair anytime the fancy struck me, which was pretty much all the time. He shifted his leg and ended up leaning on me. I was immensely grateful that he was too busy looking ahead to see me grinning like an idiot. Now that he was closer, it was easier to play with his hair.

I loved his hair; it was soft like down and never seemed to be out of place. He sighed and rested his head on my shoulder. As if by magic, all of his nervous energy went right out of him. Eventually, I gave up his hair in order to finish wrapping my arm around him and languidly trailed my fingers along his arm. A part of me could not believe this moment was happening. The other part wanted me to stop jinxing it.

The movie wound down, and I realized he hadn't moved at all in quite some time. I glanced down at him. The thin light from the screen revealed he'd passed out. He really was the most beautiful thing. I stroked the side of his cheek with my free hand and he started awake.

He blinked bleary eyed, then saw me looking at him. "What did I miss?" he asked in a hushed voice.

"Most of the movie."

"Sorry," he said, shifting slightly, but not changing his situation.

"It's okay," I responded in an equally quiet tone, still caressing his cheek. If he wasn't going to make me stop, then I had no intention of doing so. I enjoyed touching him.

He stared back at me with those gorgeous blues. Even dreamy-eyed, they were enough to give me butterflies. Unexpectedly, he leaned forward and planted a soft kiss that lingered on my lips. I cupped his face and kissed him back, reveling in the drawn out slowness of it. He may have been half asleep, but he was still an incredible kisser.

I was getting the distinct impression Matt really enjoyed kissing, not even liked it so much as lived for it. He'd probably go on forever if I let him. The slow burn of the kiss continued to build until I had to consciously dial it back. It would be far too easy to drown in Matt with kisses like that. I brushed a finger across his eyelashes. "We should probably go to bed," I whispered.

He looked properly put out at the notion. He glanced over at his door, then back at me. "But I'd rather stay here." My heart swelled at the blunt honesty. Matt wasn't one for flowery words or appeasement. What he said, he meant.

"You could always sleep in my room," I suggested.

Doubt and indecision instantly clouded his eyes. He opened his mouth as if to say something, then closed it.

I gave him a small smile. "Would it have been an easier decision if I hadn't asked?"

"Probably," he admitted, shifting to a more upright position. I let him go and chose not to let the cold of his absence bother me. He had to move sometime. He looked towards his room again. "I really don't want to go to bed, though."

"Here, I have an idea," I said, smacking him lightly on the arm. "Get up."

"What?"

"You heard me. Get up." I gestured emphatically to hurry him along.

He stood, albeit reluctantly.

"Go put your pajamas on."

"Why?"

"I told you, I have an idea. Just do it." He begrudgingly did, and I quickly followed my own directions, returning with a pillow and an extra blanket.

"Alright, what's this great idea?" he asked when he reappeared, stretching his arms above his head and lifting the hem of his shirt to reveal a peep of pale skin.

I stubbornly squashed the urge to tell him to lose the nightshirt altogether and while we were at it, forget the movie. There was a litany of "date-like" things we could that did *not* involve pajamas.

"Something wrong?" he asked, his brow furrowing when I waited too long to respond.

"I meant to tell you to bring a pillow."

He tilted his head. "What for?"

"We're going to have ourselves a good old-fashioned sleepover." I moved to push the couch back, but he stopped me. My cheek twitched at being thwarted. "What?"

A darkness flitted behind his eyes. "I'm not sleeping on the floor. Honestly, after all this moving around, I'm not even tired anymore. What do you say we put on another movie?" he suggested, already walking into the kitchen to grab one.

"You couldn't even stay awake during the first one."

"That was because I'd just eaten. I've had a power nap. I'm better now." He could say that as optimistically as he wanted, he wasn't fooling me. Matt could sleep standing up after running a marathon.

"You say so," I said, trying not to grumble, and resumed my seat. To my dismay, he sat at the other end. I was debating whether or not to go over there when his legs swung onto my lap, effectively trapping me. It was like he could read minds. At a loss for what to do with my hands, I rested them on his legs. His movie selection seemed to be similar to the first in theme except more astronaut than pirate. As I predicted, he didn't even make it twenty minutes. One minute he was wide awake, the next, he was out like a light. I chuckled to myself and carefully shifted his legs to the ground.

"Hmm," he mumbled in his sleep. I took a moment to appreciate the pure innocence of it, then sighed to myself and grabbed his hands. He reflexively gripped mine, which helped me pull him up.

"Come on."

"But I don't want to," he groaned, his eyes still firmly closed.

I gave a quiet laugh. "That's great, but you're already asleep." His only response was to moan noncommittally. "Here we go." I got him the rest of the way to his feet and began guiding him to his room. I used shadow to open the door and turn on the lamp. At the side of the bed, I pulled back the covers and gently coaxed him in. I'd almost made it to the door when his voice drifted out of the cocoon of blankets.

"Wait."

"What is it?" I asked, returning to turn off the lamp, then walked around to the other side of the bed.

"Don't go," he said, his eyes still firmly closed.

My heart felt like it was going to burst. I pulled my shirt over my head and fought the covers for the right to get under them. At last, I loosened them enough to slide in beside him. "I'm not going anywhere," I whispered, wrapping an arm around him.

"Promise?" The request was barely even audible.

"I won't leave you. Promise." I placed a kiss on the exposed skin by his collar. He grabbed my arm and pulled me closer. I wrapped myself around him, grateful that he still had a shirt on. It wasn't quite the evening I'd hoped for, but I was hard pressed to complain. I placed another kiss on his neck and he sighed in his sleep, snuggling back against me.

If only he could be more like this awake.

Someday, I thought, the scent of sage strong in my nose. *Someday.*

CHAPTER 4

KISS ME STUPID

M

I stretched awake, feeling more rested than I had in ages, maybe ever. Part of me wondered if it had anything to do with dreaming that I'd been sleeping with Alex, though normally when I dreamed of Alex there was a lot more kissing involved. But it was hard to complain when I felt so *good*. Abruptly, I realized I was still wearing my night shirt.

Guess I was more tired than I thought.

I yawned wide enough to crack my jaw, then shuffled into the bathroom to brush my teeth. It still baffled me that some people didn't *want* to do that every morning. I ran my tongue over my teeth, enjoying the minty tingle, and made my way out to the main space. It came as no surprise that Alex was not only up, but already bustling about the kitchen. Morning people.

Alex glanced at me over his shoulder from where he was standing at the counter with a peculiar look in his eye that I was *not* awake enough to decipher. "Good morning, sleepyhead."

Sadly, the teasing greeting didn't give me anymore to go on. I stretched again to wake up my muscles and be a more functioning zombie. "How long have you been up?"

"Longer than I would have liked." Again, there was a distinct note of something else. He turned around and leaned against the counter. "How did you sleep?"

"Really well," I replied honestly, still a bit surprised.

"That's good to hear," he said, clearly trying to suppress a smile.

"What's up with you? Am I missing something?" Seriously, morning people.

His eyebrow lifted in a graceful arc, and the smile he was clearly fighting tugged at the corner of his mouth. "You mean you don't remember?"

"Remember what?" I shuffled from foot to foot, my anxiety increasing. Did the date not go well?

"We slept together, Matt." He flashed a wicked smile, then he laughed, no doubt in response to the look of utter shock on my face, and stepped in close. "Don't worry, Matt, that's all we did. Sleep. I even behaved myself." The way he said it made it sound like that was out of character for him, but he'd never been anything less than the perfect gentleman with me.

"Really?" My sleepy fog stubbornly refused to dissipate so I could make sense of what was going on. We'd slept together? Like, in the same bed?

"You didn't really give me much choice. I take it you don't remember making me promise not to go." I'd done what? He considered me, a hint of concern dimming his almost smile.

Suppose there was nothing for it now. "Guess that explains my dream," I admitted.

Both of his eyebrows shot up. "Oh really? Do tell."

"That was it. We were sleeping." It was possible there was more, but that was all I could remember. I glanced around absently, not really sure where to go from there. Passing out with ease around Alex was becoming somewhat of a theme.

"Hey."

I glanced at him long enough to note his obvious concern. Embarrassment tingled on my skin far less pleasant than the toothpaste had in my mouth. Was it even possible for me not to botch every evening with Alex? First the drinking shenanigans. Now, sleeping? What the hell was wrong with me?

"Hey, look at me." He grabbed my shoulder, and I reluctantly met his gaze. His brows knit together as he searched my face. "There's no need to be upset. I was only teasing. I promise nothing happened."

I dropped his gaze. How could he be so damn understanding? I ruined it. Given my history of ruining most things, that probably shouldn't have surprised me, but I wanted to do better for Alex.

"Tell me what's bothering you."

At the command, the truth popped out before I could temper it. "I fell asleep. Twice." I gave him a level look. "I'm a terrible date."

"Is that all? I thought the parts where you were awake went quite well. Some parts where you were asleep too," he added, tipping my chin up to look at him.

The urge to kiss him burned through me, but I held back, still uncertain. What I wanted and what was right rarely coincided in this world. Thankfully, he made the choice for me, his lips barely even brushing mine. He stayed like that until the feel of our breath mingling pushed me over the edge. I wrapped my arms wrapped around his waist and pulled him close. The feel of his body against mine was everything, and I held tighter, tangling my fingers in his hair as I claimed his mouth. He made a sound of muffled surprise, followed by a moan. Then his hands were on my back and the kiss got deeper. The heat of it was like an inferno threatening to burn us both where we stood. He pulled back and I reluctantly let him go. It wasn't enough, it would never be enough.

"I swear, Matt, one of these days you're going to kiss me stupid," he said, every bit as short of breath as me.

I wanted to trace the path his tongue took over his lips, but hesitated. He pulled back every time. I didn't know what that meant, and I already felt like I was treading water in the deep end most of the time. Was I doing something wrong? I never said I was any *good* at dating and I had exactly zero experience dating a man.

Humor danced in his eyes as he took a step back, removing himself from my arms. "What should we do today?"

I shrugged my shoulders, and he rolled his eyes.

"Come on. It's Saturday. You're already caught up with your assignments and you have the whole weekend to do whatever you like."

What I liked was spending time with him, but that felt weird to say. I wracked my brain for something we could do together, preferably something he would enjoy, too. The corner of a large tomb poking out from beneath some papers on the coffee table. I'd found it when I was trying to apologize for my horrible behavior a few weeks ago. He *did* seem excited about that. Not surprising, since it involved the author of his favorite book.

"What'll it be?" he encouraged. "We could explore town, wander campus, watch another movie."

"We could always work on translating more of Volume Six. We haven't really had a chance to do that." Though exploring the neighboring town of Sieben Hügel did sound interesting. I'd been so busy with the fight club before, I'd only ever made it to the fringes of town.

Alex's smile warmed me from the inside and helped me feel like I'd suggested something halfway decent. "See, that wasn't so hard. You get dressed, then we can go to the library. I'm curious about this mysterious magic lamp of yours."

It wasn't until then that I realized he was already dressed. He was the picture of Saturday comfort in low-slung jeans that barely rested on his hips and a dark green shirt.

"Get dressed, Matt," he said with a look that felt like I was being stripped down right there.

I flushed and quickly scurried back into my room to do as I was told, where I almost put on the clothes from the day before. Finally, I was something resembling decent. I grabbed his book about the mysterious knight and the massive book from the table, then joined him by the door. Technically, I'd finished the knight book a while ago, but every time I went to return it, I remembered the bookmark was still in it. I needed to finish that already.

"Okay, let's go," I said, after shoving everything into my backpack and zipping it.

His lips twitched like he wanted to laugh. "Lead the way." He stepped aside for me to go first.

We stopped by the dining hall for a late breakfast and then wandered to the library. It was already fuller than the last time I'd been here and I worried if I could find the lamp again. This place looked way different with the multicolored light from the stained-glass windows filling the space instead of muted darkness.

"What are you looking for?" Alex asked after we'd been standing in the same spot for a couple of minutes.

"The librarian. The last time I was here, she just sort of showed up. It was really dark when we got the book and she took me over to the lamp. I'm not sure where it is," I admitted.

He looked thoughtful a moment, then started walking with purpose across the library.

"Where are you going?" I asked, trailing after him. The overly loud question earned me several reproachful glares, including one from Alex. I quickened my pace so I wouldn't have to talk so loud.

"We're just going to retrace your steps. We'll start at the table you put your things at."

"How do you know which table I used?" I asked, mystified.

"You're a creature of habit, Matt."

"Oh." Sure enough, we stopped at the same table I'd used for my last visit, which, now that he mentioned it, was pretty much every visit. Someone was already sitting at it though, so he continued walking a little farther.

"Then from here you went to the restricted section? Do you remember which way you started?"

"I think it was this way," I said, retaking the lead. I knew I was right when I felt a sense of dread fall over me. Not far ahead was the sign that declared we were approaching the restricted section. Despite the morning light, the area still felt dark and oppressive. My previous impression that this was knowledge that did not want to be found solidified. I walked closer to the stacks, each step a struggle as the sense of overwhelming apprehension intensified. Suddenly, I realized Alex had stopped several feet back.

"I don't know how you did it, Matt. I'm nowhere near the stacks, and I don't want to get any closer. This is a horrible feeling. I didn't realize the barrier extended so far out."

"Like I said before," I glanced over my shoulder at him, "I needed to get the book for you." It was just a fact. I'd been desperate for anything to make up for my behavior, and I knew that getting that information would at least help. I shifted my shoulders beneath the weight of his assessing stare and eagerly moved on to the next leg of the journey. We didn't need to actually go *into* the restricted section; we already had what we needed. "After we got the book, I'm pretty sure we went this way."

Once more, I took the lead and walked across the space. Hardly anyone was up here. Of course, with an avoidance spell like that to contend with, who could blame them? We rounded a stack and found two rows of identical reading desks with accompanying lamps.

"Yes," I said a little too loudly, but there was no one to scold us.

"Well done." Alex clapped me on the shoulder, then swiped a chair from another table and pulled it up next to the one I'd already taken.

I pulled out his book while he placed Volume six on the table. Just like before, the lamp slowly came to life. He hadn't opened it yet and when the light touched the cover, something unexpected happened. It was almost like time was reversing. The aged binding became supple, the edges crisp and unworn. What I'd thought was flaked leather turned out to be the remains of a picture. As the image came back to life, it revealed a horrific battle scene, complete with knights, banners, and blood. A *lot* of blood. At the bottom of the picture in scrolling letters it read: *All Evil must die and to the depths returned.* I looked at Alex.

The wonder shining on his face crumpled a bit when he read the line. "Why does everyone think we're evil?"

I wanted to comfort him, but wasn't sure how. Did I say something? Wrap an arm around him? Take his hand? In my hesitation, the moment vanished.

He opened the book and the ancient Latin within transformed into something we could read and understand. Unlike when I'd last used the lamp, though, some words couldn't seem to decide what they should be.

I pointed to one. "Do you think it's because we're from different places? Is it confused?"

Alex's shine returned, and he shifted closer to the desk. "That's actually an intriguing point. I wonder what would happen if two people who didn't speak the same language used the lamp at the same time."

I let that tumble around my brain that for a moment, then let it go. That mystery wasn't why we were here. "Do you think there are other pictures?"

"Probably, but we should start at the beginning before we get ahead of ourselves. This book may contain the answers we've been looking for, but it won't do us any good if we skip around and miss them."

"You and your logic," I said begrudgingly as I withdrew my hand. What harm would it really do to flip through and see? We could always go back and read.

"One of us has to at least try to approach this scholastically."

I looked at Alex, taking in his sense of reverence as he lightly traced the calligraphy. Hope and a small touch of pride swelled in my chest. I'd done it. I'd found something to amend for my crimes.

He glanced up and did a double take. "What?"

I shook my head and returned my attention to the book. This wasn't the place to tell him how stunning his eyes were when he was excited or how graceful I thought his long fingers were. Especially not how much I wanted to feel those long fingers on me. "There are so many names. None of them look like demons, though."

"That's not too surprising. This looks more like a history written by humans, not by other supernaturals."

I pulled out the notes I'd taken on my last visit. "But doesn't it say that they held the power to harness light? That sounds pretty supernatural to me."

Alex shrugged. "Maybe? They could have had supernatural connections. This was a different world. *Before* supernaturals went into hiding." He paused as if reconsidering. "Or at least I think it is. No one can really say when *all* supes went into hiding, since each species did it independently."

We really were just feeling our way in the dark with this. What had begun as an innocent project to uncover the identity of Alex's nameless knight had instead unearthed plenty of other secrets. The involvement of Shadow Demons. The existence of a family whose sole purpose was genocide. A forbidden affair. A war against Shadow Demons that wasn't in any history book. And now, what appeared to be a conspiracy to cover it all up.

Alex sat back, and I mirrored him. "What I don't understand is how there was a war at all. I can understand that back then there were substantially more Shadow Demons, but how could they ever have worked together to mount a defense? There couldn't possibly be enough willing to cooperate."

"What do you mean?"

He tapped his bottom lip, looking pensive. "Well, historically, Shadow Demons are known for their apathy. We don't care to get involved with the rest of the world. We're just not social like that."

I smothered a snort. "What are you talking about? You're one of the most social people I know."

He leveled a look at me. "Being social with you is not really the same thing, Matt."

"Whatever you say." He didn't have to see it to make it true. All he had to do was walk into a room and he had friends. He fell into conversations naturally, always knew what to say, how to act. That sounded like the definition of social to me. I turned the page to let the next translate. "How do you think all of this started?" I asked, scanning what appeared to be a battle strategy.

"My guess is that someone pissed off the wrong person. That's always how things like this start. Hey, look," he said.

I followed where his finger led. There was our knight's name—Matthias Warde. "That's not possible. He couldn't have possibly been born yet. How could he be mentioned so soon? Also, in your book it says that his family has been fighting the darkness for as long as he could remember. He should have been born in the middle of this war, not fully grown at the beginning." Was it possible we had everything wrong? Just great. All those hours of research wasted.

"We'll have to read more to find out then, won't we?" he added snidely. I gave him a face, and he shook his head, returning to the book. "Let's see... This says the Wardes led the campaign to eliminate darkness once and for all. That at least coincides with what we've established so far, but I think you're right. There's no way this guy is the same as our knight. Just look at how he's described. A ruthless leader who rallied his family and recruited others to the cause? That doesn't sound at all like our wavering knight." He did that lip tap again, which was incredibly distracting. "Maybe Matthias is a family name that gets passed down. Could be his grandson or even great grandson."

"I suppose that's possible." Then a wild idea occurred to me. "Random thought."

"What?" Alex asked. Faced with his open curiosity, I suddenly doubted the wisdom of sharing my idea. What if he thought it was ridiculous or it upset him?

"Um... You said you never knew your father, right?"

His dark brows pinched together. "Yeah, what of it?"

"What if you're some long-lost relative and *that's* why you have the book?"

He shook his head. "The odds of that are minuscule. Besides, while I've had this book a long time, it wasn't exactly something that was left for me. My mom found it on her quest to gather any resources she could that referenced Shadow Demons."

"Oh, well, never mind." I sagged in my chair. It had been a silly idea, anyway.

"Hey." He nudged my arm. "It *would* be cool, though. To be the long-lost progeny of a knight belonging to an ancient order."

I straightened. "Would that make you a knight by default?"

"I don't think it works that way," he said with a laugh. "Alright, come on, let's get back to this. I still want to know how or why these Shadow Demons got involved in anything that qualified as an all-out war."

We hunkered down, reading the book page by page in our tiny pool of light. Our heads were so close in order to see that it felt like swirls of lavender were spiraling around me. The world seemed to fade away as we devoured history that appeared to have been lost for centuries.

I thought again about how it felt like the books in the restricted section didn't want to be found. Was there a reason they were guarded like that? Hidden in some nameless section by a virtually impassable barrier? But I'd gotten past it. I glanced at Alex out of the corner of my eye. It was amazing what you could do with the right motivation.

Suddenly, all the hair on the back of my neck stood up. I'd had enough hard knocks and ugly surprises in my life to trust the sensation without question—Someone was watching us. I sat up and looked around. The immediate area appeared every bit as abandoned as it had been when we first arrived. As I searched the stacks around us for any sign of life, the feeling intensified. Someone or *something* was definitely out there.

Alex straightened beside me, curiosity plain on his face. Before he could speak, I held up my hand to silence him. After a minute of suffering quietly, he finally whispered, "What's wrong?"

"I thought... I could have sworn..." The feeling was slipping away like mist through my fingers. "It felt like someone was watching us."

"It is a library, Matt. We're not exactly the only people here." He had a point, but I still couldn't shake the feeling it was not that simple. You remembered the lessons you learned the hard way. Letting down your guard could prove not only dangerous, but fatal.

"I don't like sitting out in the open like this." Without waiting for a response, I reached out and closed the book. "We'll should find another way to translate the pages. Something that doesn't rely on the lamps."

Alex glanced around before he leaned close. "You don't think it's..."

"It's what?" I asked, sensing his unease.

"You said that you'd gotten... *snatched* before." Ah, *that*. He thought it might be Neese or Otto come to drag me back to the fight club.

"No, they wouldn't come here. Besides, it didn't feel like any of them. Are you ready to go?" I asked, though he was already zipping up his bag.

As we made our way out of the library, the feeling of eyes following us returned. I quickened my pace, eager to be away from the invasive gaze.

CHAPTER 5

COMMUNICATION

A

I finished clearing the table, then swung my bag onto my shoulder. "You sure you won't be late for Advanced Spells?" Matt and I didn't get to eat together very often now that our schedules weren't identical. To say I missed it would be an understatement. Fortunately, the dining hall was near the heart of campus.

"I'll be fine. Even if I'm a few minutes late, Professor Gwendolyn is pretty lenient. Except when it comes to assignment sign-ups." He glowered at the table and I held back a laugh.

"I take it you weren't able to switch?"

He let out a heavy sigh and grumbled, "No."

I pressed a knuckle against my mouth to keep the determined laughter at bay. It was hard *not* to adore how emphatic Matt could be. For all his efforts when we'd met to be aloof and mysterious, all I had to do was ask to know exactly what he was feeling. "Dare I ask what you got stuck with?"

"A report of the social development of supernatural communities. So, like a shit ton of research."

My smile slipped free despite my best efforts. "And we both know research is one of your absolute favorite things to do."

"Shut up." He shoved me and I caught his arms.

"I'm sure it won't be all *that* bad."

"Pft. It is when I could have been making a diorama." He scowled, showing off his spectacular pout.

I used my grip on his arms to pull him closer with the intention of kissing that delectable pout until he forgot all about his writing assignment. We were less than a foot apart when he threw on the brakes.

"I should really get going." He ducked his head and extricated his arms, then stepped back.

My heart sank, and I pushed away the burning urge to steal my kiss anyway, reminding myself that this was all new for him. Though, perhaps we were overdue for a conversation about PDA. I missed being able to hold my boyfriend's hand and exchange sweet kisses when we parted. Matt had said he'd need time to adjust, had even admitted that he'd stumble occasionally, but surely those acts were small enough to be inconsequential.

"Anyway... I'll see you back at the dorm?"

"Of course, but I'll be late. I have a tutoring session followed by our weekly tutor's meeting."

A cloud briefly darkened his usually light features. "Right. I better get to class. Professor Gwendolyn doesn't like it when we're late."

I frowned at the contradiction to his earlier statement, but he'd already turned away. "I enjoyed having lunch together," I called after him.

He paused and glanced back, a hint of his usual spark dancing in his perfect blue eyes. "Me too."

My shoulders slumped as I watched him walk away. He'd die before admitting it, but he hated beating me back to the dorm, like he didn't trust I'd come back if I wasn't already there. "What's it going to take for you to relax and trust me?"

"Make an invisible friend or talking to yourself?"

I glanced to the side at the familiar voice. "Ha ha, Rubio. Just musing aloud." I crossed my arms and returned my attention to where Matt was becoming a distant, shadowy outline. Rubio bumped my shoulder, and I turned to follow him back into the dining hall.

"How was lunch with your roommate?" he asked once he'd grabbed a tray and found a seat.

I sighed and continued scratching at a spot on the table. "Exactly that—lunch with my *roommate*."

Rubio grimaced. "What happened to the whole giving things a go?"

"We are." I straightened enough to rest my elbows on the table. "Or, at least, I think we are."

"Hate to break it to you, but dating really isn't that hard."

"I *know*. It's honestly not all that different from what we were doing before. Just with a lot more—"

"Nookie," Rubio filled in with a lascivious grin complete with wiggling eyebrows.

I couldn't help but laugh. "I was gonna go with kissing, because we haven't gotten anywhere *near* anything else."

Rubio looked like I'd smacked him in the face with his sandwich. "What about groping?"

"Nope."

"Skins?"

"All clothing has remained very much on," I grumbled.

It didn't seem possible for Rubio to look more scandalized. "At least tell me you've kissed with tongue."

"*That* we have done—before, and a little now, though not as much as I would like."

Rubio abandoned his lunch and leaned forward. "Um, why?"

Okay, that was fair. "Because I don't want him to feel rushed. That last thing I want to do is push too hard and scare him off. We went through so much to get *here*. What if I screw it up?"

"Alexi, as your friend and incubus confidant, I'm here to tell you that waiting will only get you so far. If you don't tell him what you want, how is he supposed to know? He's a Shadow Demon, not a mind reader." He squinted at me. "Right? That's not a thing y'all do?"

"No, we're *not* mind readers. Which would come in super handy right about now. Besides, I'm not the only one not communicating."

"It's not a contest," he deadpanned. "Try talking to him."

"We talk."

Rubio sat back, his lunch completely forgotten, and crossed his arms. "Yeah? You talk about sex? Your relationship? Expectations?"

I shifted in my seat and prayed my face wasn't red.

"Alexi..." he said, his voice dipping low and a hair menacing.

I winced and darted my gaze up to meet his surprisingly judgmental one. "Yeah?"

"Have you *ever* talked about any of that with your previous boyfriends?"

"No?"

He threw up his hands. "Communicating expectations is the cornerstone of successful relationships."

"Says the guy who doesn't believe in relationships," I countered.

"Irrelevant." He waved a dismissive hand before reacquiring his half-eaten sandwich. "I don't have to believe in committed relationships to know how they work. The point is communicating is important."

"Try telling that to Matt. Getting information out of him is like trying to pry open a vault with a licorice string." I let out a huff and sat back, imitating Rubio's earlier pose. "You make it sound like I haven't tried to talk to him at all. And, sure, I maybe haven't gone into *those* particulars, but it doesn't mean we haven't talked at all."

"I'm listening," he said around a mouthful of food.

"Okay, so we had our first date-date last week. And while it wasn't a total disaster, I wouldn't exactly call it a roaring success." I leaned forward, animatedly gesturing as I worked myself up. "We stayed in and watched a movie. I ordered the takeout he requested, but that was literally the most input I got from him. And while there was cuddling, he fell asleep. Twice!" I held up two fingers for emphasis, surprising myself with how upset I actually was.

Rubio took his time licking his fingers clean and then wiping his hands before responding. "So, what I'm hearing is that he's really comfortable with you."

"I don't want him to be comfortable with me. I want him to be touching me!" My hand clapped down so hard over my mouth it made a bubble sound. I stared at Rubio looking smug as a witch, shocked at my outburst. "I... That came out... That's not..." I gave up after a few false starts with no idea how to finish them.

"You, my friend, reek of sexual frustration."

"I do not! Wait, you can *smell* that?"

"Sense it, smell it, feel it. Makes my skin itch and my nose burn. You should be glad I value our friendship so much or I'd be putting you in some seriously compromising positions." He gave me a pointed look, and I had to take a minute to absorb that.

"First off, that's kind of creepy."

He shrugged. "That's why I try to avoid mentioning it. Most people get uncomfortable when they learn you can sense their arousal."

"Yeah... second, I'm sorry. I didn't mean to be making you uncomfortable. If I'd known—"

"You'd what?" His eyebrows lifted. "Bang your roommate like you've been wanting to do for the last three months?"

I dropped my hand, temporarily at a loss. "Well, damn."

He sighed and shifted in his chair. "There's nothing to apologize for, Alexi. You feel the way you feel and you're entitled to do so without a nosy incubus getting involved. Besides, we're on a campus full of horny college students. Trust me, the smell is *everywhere*," he added with a grin that bordered on a smirk.

"Wait a second. Is that why you offered to sleep with me?"

Rubio threw his head back and laughed loud enough to attract the attention of the entire dining hall. He wiped tears from the corners of his eyes when he finally sobered. "You're a trip. No, I *offered* because you're attractive and I could see us hitting it off."

"Oh."

His smirk came back. "I *kept* offering because you clearly weren't doing anything about your attraction to your roommate."

"Rubio!"

He held up his hands defensively and laughed again. "What? I'm your friend *and* an incubus. What did you expect me to do?"

I crossed my arms with a huff and rolled my eyes. "You really know how to kill a guy's ego, you know that?"

"I know how to do a lot of things with a guy's... ego. If you're looking for some tips, I'm happy to share." Rubio's smile was nothing short of feral.

A laugh bubbled free. "Okay, I walked right into that."

"You absolutely did. But the offer stands. And, seriously, talk to your boyfriend. Bottling things up isn't healthy." He held up a hand. "Yes, that doubled as another sex joke and actual advice. Now, on to business. How are you feeling about the tutoring assignments with your course schedule?"

"I thought we were going to be covering this at the meeting tonight."

"We'll touch on it, but I was hoping to have it be a short meeting. That's why I've been making time to touch base with everyone beforehand. If there are any conflicts, then we can look at swapping clients at the meeting."

Admittedly, that was really smart, talking to the tutors one-on-one to get honest feedback before bringing any adjustments to the group, but he wasn't fooling me. "You have plans," I deadpanned.

"You wound me." He placed a hand over his heart and gave me a pitiful look. "Do you really think I'd rearrange my entire schedule and try to get the weekly tutoring meeting canceled just so I could get laid?"

"Yes."

"Okay, yeah, I would. I ran into a cecaelia at a party last semester and she hit me up. In all fairness, I did try to find a better time, but her schedule is a little more limited since she's transferring to another school."

"You could have said no."

"And give up an experience with tentacles! It's like you don't know me at all. Much as I like the group, consider yourselves collateral. If I can get out of that meeting, then I am." He rubbed his hands together, positively emanating glee. "I have a suspicion we're going to need several hours. Don't worry, I'll tell you all about it."

"Please don't."

"Suit yourself. Never know, might discover you had a kink you didn't know about. I've seen how your kind operates. Shadow could just as easily become tentacles." He wiggled his eyebrows suggestively.

"Ugh, that's an image I'm never getting out of my brain."

"You're welcome."

CHAPTER 6

DATING ADVICE

M

No way was I going back to the dorm while Alex had his tutoring stuff. I'd just end up wandering around the living space driving myself nuts wondering if *Rubio* or one of Alex's clients were getting handsy with him. Nope. Not happening. What I needed was a distraction.

Almost immediately, I heard Alex's voice in my head encouraging me to work on class assignments, namely that ridiculous research paper I'd gotten saddled with. I kicked at a rock that had found its way to the sidewalk. I'd meant to ask him about helping me with the paper. Truth be told, whether or not I needed the help, I... missed it. Studying felt so much easier when he was around. Besides, research was his specialty, not mine.

But was that weird? Could the person you were dating *also* tutor you? It sounded like a silly question, even in my head. What was the big deal? Then again, Alex hadn't brought up studying together at all since the fall semester had started. He'd actually taken on more hours of tutoring. And that meant more hours of being on my own. Definitely needed that distraction.

I made my way toward the pool hall. With any luck, Sam and Lucas would be there and I could kill a few hours pretending not to obsessively think about Alex. I considered attempting to shadow walk there—I could always use the practice—but opted to take the long way to eat up as much time as possible.

Garbled voices, laughter, and the sound of balls cracking together hit me in the face when I pushed open the graffiti-covered door of the bar. I searched the tables for any sign of my friends, but came up empty. Deflated, I made my way to the bar, though I had no intention of drinking. Getting drunk lost most of its appeal when I no longer needed the liquid courage, not to mention that "courage" had nearly lost me Alex all together.

I was about to snag a stool when a familiar voice caught my attention. After a little hunting, I discovered Sam struggling to contain laughter—and clearly losing. Surprisingly, the witch was his normal skinny blond self and *not* impersonating another attractive patron.

He glanced at me from where he stood a few feet from the bar as I approached and gave me a head nod in greeting before returning his focus to whatever was cracking him up by the crowded counter.

I leaned closer and raised my voice to be heard over the din. "Where's Lucas?"

Sam pointed toward the counter and bit his knuckle in another hopeless attempt to subdue his laughter.

It took a few seconds of squinting to realize that the back of the nearest person to us, who was currently leaning halfway over the counter to flirt with the bartender, was actually Lucas. "Um, what's going on?"

"*Someone*, Hera bless their soul, gave him moonshine after his run earlier tonight."

I did a double take. "He's *drunk*? I didn't even know werewolves could get drunk."

"Oh, it's not easy, that's for sure, but not impossible. Moonshine usually does the trick."

I frowned. What was so special about moonshine? It packed a punch, but was also kind of awful. "Am I missing something? I've had moonshine, and uh…" I glanced at Lucas, who was making an absolute fool of himself.

"This is not your typical moonshine, my friend. When werewolves make that shit, it's not fit for us regular mortals."

"Damn." I whistled to myself and made a mental note to always turn down any drink offered by a werewolf. "How long has he been like this?"

Sam checked his watch. "Couple hours. Given his *were* metabolism, he should sober up pretty soon. Unless…" He gave me a mischievous look that I'd learned early on always came with a side of trouble.

"Unless?"

"Unless we keep his buzz going by plying him with shots."

Considering Lucas was now openly leering at anyone with breasts who came within four feet of him, that seemed like a bad idea. "Yeah, I don't know about that."

Sam sagged and gave a huff. "You're probably right. Shots wouldn't have the same impact and would eat up all my beer money." He glanced around, taking in the bustling room. "We were waiting for a pool table, but it doesn't look like that's gonna happen anytime soon."

"This place is packed tonight. Any idea why?" I asked, slowly pushing my way closer to the bar.

He shrugged. "The early semester crowd would be my guess. Students letting loose while they still can before the pressure of classes."

I pointed at Lucas who was doing an impressive impersonation of a whistling wolf. "Do you want to or should I?"

Sam barked a laugh. "Dude, if I couldn't have pried him off the bar by myself, I'd have done it ages ago."

I thinned my lips and stared at him with a flat expression.

"Okay, maybe not, but there's still no way I can manhandle a drunk *were*."

"I've got it. You grab that high-top that just opened up." Sam ventured off as the last few people gave way and I could finally reach Lucas. I placed a hand on his shoulder. "Hey, buddy. What do you say we move to a table?"

Lucas spun to face me. If Sam hadn't already told me he was drunk, I'd have known immediately by the shine of his eyes and the potent smell of alcohol on his breath. "Matt! What are you doing here?" Without warning, he threw his arms around my neck and I stumbled under his sudden weight.

"Figured I'd see if y'all were up for a game or two."

He pouted. "We would, but there's no tables! Can you believe that?"

"That really sucks, man, but good news. Sam got us a table." I pointed to where Sam had staked his claim on a high-top in the middle of getting bussed.

"Sweet!"

I took a step toward the table, only to have Lucas jerk me back.

"Wait! Have you met Gina? She's awesome. Super friendly and extra pretty. See, Matt! Isn't Gina pretty?" He gestured with a weaving arm toward the bartender, who thankfully wasn't paying his antics any attention.

"Yeah, buddy, she's real pretty," I said, then mouthed "Sorry," before more forcefully dragging him away.

"And nice too. Did I mention she was nice?"

"You sure did. Come on, Sam is waiting for us." By now I was practically carrying a staggering Lucas, who was still determined to return to the bar.

"I should introduce you." He stopped, and I nearly fell backward at the abrupt shift. "But then what if she likes you more?" He narrowed his eyes at me. "You're too pretty. You'd just steal her."

"I'm not interested in stealing her. Besides, I'm already taken."

Lucas smacked me on the back, and I wheezed. "That's great man! Who's the lucky person?" We stepped close enough to the table, and he spied Sam shooting death glares at a bar regular that was obviously trying to steal the table from him. "Sammy!" Lucas shouted, throwing his arms up in enthusiasm, leaving me to guide his stumbling ass to a chair.

Thank Nyx for demonic strength.

Finally, I got Lucas in a seat by Sam and heaved myself into one across from them.

Both Sam and Lucas shamelessly leered as a waitress in the usual short plaid skirt a crop-top walked up. "Hey, folks. What can I get you?"

"A round of waters. Better yet, make that a pitcher," I said before either of my companions could speak.

"I'll have those out in a jiff." She spun on her heel and melded into the crowd of bodies.

Sam scowled at me, and poor Lucas just looked confused. "What gives?" Sam asked.

I pointed at Lucas. "He at least needs to hydrate. If you don't want any water, that's fine. More for the rest of us."

"Rest of us? You not drinking?"

I shook my head. "More interested in hanging than drinking tonight."

"Suit yourself." Sam shrugged. The water arrived, and he ordered two beers, one presumably for Lucas.

By the time those arrived, I was seriously questioning why I'd come out. Playing pool was one thing, but sitting here while Sam teased a slowly sobering Lucas wasn't the distraction I'd been looking for.

"What's got you so down in the dumps?" Sam asked after taking a long drink.

Lucas leaned closer to him and not so subtly whispered, "Haven't you heard? He's *dating*." He straightened and thankfully reached for the water.

"Really now? Shouldn't that be a good thing?"

I hiked a shoulder and studied a swirl in the wood of the table. "I haven't done a lot of dating. Well, really any."

Sam snorted his beer, getting it all over himself and the table. "Like hell you haven't. You're like Mr. Charm around here. I won't believe it."

"Yeah, well, believe or don't believe, I don't think I'm very good at it. I have absolutely no clue what I'm doing most of the time."

Lucas leveled his hand at me along with a super serious expression. "What about making out? Have you at least done that?"

"A little," I answered honestly, my face heating.

He smacked the table, causing Sam and I to jump. "Well, there's your problem. Only a little," he scoffed. "Step that shit up. Face it, 'dates' are just a way to get to the fun stuff."

"I don't know if I should take dating advice from drunk Lucas," I responded dubiously.

Lucas gasped, clearly affronted. "Who says I'm drunk? I'm not drunk." He glanced at Sam, who unsurprisingly used his talent of illusion magic to transform himself into a sober Lucas.

"Dude, you're trashed," Sam deadpanned in Lucas's voice.

That Lucas didn't immediately start bitching Sam out for impersonating him—again—was more than enough to prove he was in fact trashed. He turned to face me. "Well, you definitely can't take advice from this asshole." He angled his thumb at Sam, who'd returned to normal.

"Please, I'm a wealth of good advice," Sam argued. They went on like that for a while, periodically dragging me into it until eventually I gave up.

I hopped down from my seat. "I'm gonna call it a night, guys."

Sam glanced wistfully at the queue of people waiting for a pool table. "Maybe next time we'll actually get to play."

"Yeah, drinking at a table-table isn't half as much fun," Lucas bemoaned, swirling his now warm beer.

Sam closed out their tab, and the three of us headed back toward the campus, where we parted ways.

I dragged my feet as I made my way to the dorm. So much for my efforts at a distraction. Thanks to Sam and Lucas bickering about what constituted good relationship advice, I'd spent the last three hours thinking about Alex, anyway. And I still wasn't any closer to figuring out what I was doing wrong. When I'd suggested this dating-thing, I'd warned Alex I'd stumble, that this was all new to me, but it felt more like I was flat on my face than feeling my way in the dark.

All too soon, I was standing in front of our door, the tarnished copper room number 2708 at eye level. I sighed and used my antique-looking key to open the door. No sooner did it swing open than I froze. What the hell was Alex doing here?

"Oh, hey, you're back. I was just about to turn in for the night." He closed the book he'd been reading after sliding in a bookmark and peeled himself off the couch. "You have a good night?" he asked as he stretched, highlighting his long, lean body.

I glimpsed his spectacular abs before his shirt slid back into place. "Uh, yeah. Guess so." My fingers twitched with the urge to walk up to him and feel those abs again, to feel all of him. Fall back on the couch and claim his mouth until neither of us could breathe, then kiss the rest of him.

"You guess so?"

I started at the teasing question and dragged my gaze away from where it was currently latched onto his abdomen. "What happened to your meeting? You're normally out later when you have one of those."

"Oh, it got canceled. Rubio had plans," he added with a chuckle. "Anyway, I'm glad you had a good night 'you guess'. I'll see you in the morning." He flashed me a smile and went to his room.

It wasn't until his door shut I realized I'd been holding the front door open this whole time. "Of course, the meeting got canceled," I grumbled to myself as I trudged to my bedroom, where fantasies of licking Alex's abs were probably going to keep me up half the night. "Stupid Rubio."

CHAPTER 7

A SIMPLE TOUCH

A

Maybe Rubio had a point. Perhaps our communication *was* lacking. But communication was a two-way street and Matt wasn't giving me anything to work with. I sighed inwardly, not really seeing the notes before me. Studying should have been easy with the dorm empty, but my head wasn't there. I *wanted* Matt so much it made my skin ache any time we kissed. But I also didn't want to push him. Except... maybe I needed to? What would it take to get him to initiate contact for a change? To touch me the way I longed to be touched and to touch him?

At least the friend part of our relationship had leveled out. But Matt wasn't supposed to just be my friend anymore, he was *supposed* to be my boyfriend. I blinked at my notes for Lit III and realized they were the same ones from half an hour ago. Frustrated with my lack of focus, I closed the notebook.

I'm totally going to bomb this class if I can't get my head on straight.

"You okay?" Matt asked right beside me. It was a measure of how stressed I was that I didn't even jump.

"Why do you ask?" I returned, neglecting to answer the question.

"You just seem distracted lately, like something is on your mind." He lifted his hand as if to comfort me. It hovered a moment, then fell back down.

I resisted the urge to roll my eyes. What was it about touching me that was so difficult? "I'm worried about this class. I'm not retaining anything, and my notes are a mess." It was some of the truth, at least.

He smiled. "I'm sure you'll be fine. You always are."

Normally, his unwavering confidence would have bolstered my spirits. Today it made me bitter. Why did I have to be perfect all the time? Why couldn't he take the lead for a change?

"Let me know if there's anything I can do to help," he offered.

I considered asking for a neck rub. If I was lucky, it could lead to more... which would inevitably stop well short of what I actually wanted. Except I wasn't that lucky.

"Do you mind if I sit on the couch and work on the research project? It looks like you've got the table covered." He smiled at the terrible pun and my cheek twitched in a half-hearted response that was more like a grimace. I knew he was just trying to cheer me up, but in my current mood, I wasn't interested.

I shrugged noncommittally, and he retrieved the gray tomb from the counter. He was practically obsessed with the thing, spending more time with it than me as often as not. I watched him walk over and plop down out of the corner of my eye. I should have asked for the massage. What was the worst that could happen? My mind immediately supplied several less-than-ideal outcomes, effectively killing any desire to do so now.

By the time the silence became oppressive, my nerves were a frayed mess. I pushed up from the table and made my way towards the door. Maybe a walk would clear my head. I grabbed my key, then turned to tell Matt I was stepping out for a bit and immediately lost my breath.

He sat with his legs stretched out to rest on the coffee table and had the book open on his lap. His dark hair fell across his eyes and round spectacles perched on his nose when he glanced up.

I couldn't help but sigh with longing. Matt was beautiful, a fallen angel among mortals. I wanted more than anything to push that damn book aside and straddle him. I'd take the glasses off, taste his delicious lips as I ran my fingers through his hair.

Wait, why is he wearing glasses?

"What?" he asked, shifting on the couch like he wanted to hide.

"You're wearing glasses." He'd never worn them before. I was certain of it. Nor had he ever mentioned needing them.

"Oh." He blushed lightly as he lifted them. "They're spelled so we don't have to go to the library every time we want to read this thing. Dorky, right?" He gave a self-depreciating laugh.

"No. It's sexy as hell."

His pink cheeks turned red. "Why would you say that?"

"Because it's true." I knew I should stop; I was clearly making him uncomfortable, but the words kept coming. "You're outrageously attractive, Matt," I added wistfully.

The red darkened. "But... But I look nothing like you."

I stared blankly back at him, completely blindsided.

"What?" He squirmed beneath my stunned gaze. "Why are you looking at me like that?"

A grin tugged at my mouth. "I think you just told me you find me attractive." I had no idea a blush could go to the tips of your ears.

He opened his mouth, but no words came out. Ultimately, he closed it again without saying anything.

I cleared my throat. "So, yeah, what I was going to say before. I'm going to go for a walk and get some fresh air. I'll be back later."

"Okay." That was it. Nothing about what had just happened. No "can I come?" or "how late is later?" Nothing at all. Did he even care?

Without another word, I left. Outside, the air was indeed fresh, but it was also misty and it felt like I was passing through ephemeral curtains of water. It didn't take long for my increasingly damp shirt to add to my irritation. Not ready to turn back, I opted to put up with it a little longer. I needed to figure my shit out or *all* of my studies would suffer, not just Lit II. That meant thinking about the one thing that was irritating me most of all: Matt.

Good grief, him and those glasses.

I shook my head. Perhaps it had been a mistake to ride the breaks. Maybe if I stopped forcing things to go so slowly, everything would work itself out and we could both get what we wanted. Of course, I had zero ideas about what that was for Matt. But then, I hadn't really been clear about my expectations either. Was it possible Matt was struggling as well?

It wasn't until I was back at our door that I even realized I'd been walking back to the dorm. Resigned to more awkward silence, I unlocked it and swung it open to see Matt still on the couch. He'd lost the glasses and the book and appeared to be sketching.

He looked up at my entrance, relief in his eyes. Why was he always so afraid that I wouldn't come back?

Might have something to do with the fact that I had threatened to do just that.

"Hey," I said, closing the door behind me.

"Feel any better?"

Irritation sparked through me. "Sure. I guess." "Better" wasn't the word I'd use. My shirt was sticking unpleasantly to me, and I just wanted it off.

"Be honest, Alex, what's going on with you?"

I stopped mid-stride and turned an incredulous look on him. "Me?" The nerve. All the thoughts that had been tumbling to no avail finally found an outlet... right out of my mouth. "Why won't you touch me?"

He blinked, mouth agape.

The lack of a response only fueled the anger I'd been ignoring for weeks. "I'm serious, not so much as a little touch. Are you afraid I'll bite? You don't initiate contact. Ever." I balled my hands at my side to prevent them from gesturing wildly. "This is feeling very one-sided. Oh wait, it pretty much always has been." I knew I was being unreasonable and taking my frustration out on him. I'd known what this would be when I agreed to it, but that knowledge did little to stop me. "You can't even admit you think I'm attractive," I said, pulling off the nasty shirt as I walked towards my room.

"And what? Your solution is to do a striptease?" he responded heatedly.

I stared down at the shirt in my hand, confused, then realized what I'd done. Rather than admit that hadn't been my intent, I let my temper get the better of me. "It's only a strip tease if you like what you see." I threw the shirt down and glared back at him. What right did he have to be angry? He wasn't the one being jerked around by a string. He stared rebelliously back, and I saw the glimmer of his fighter spirit. I wished to Nyx it wasn't so fucking hot, it was not helping the current situation at all. Now I was pissed *and* turned on.

When he said nothing, I spun to go into my room only to run into him. Damn, he was fast. Just as quickly, he reached up and pulled me down to mash my mouth against his. Stubbornly, I fought him for a second. I wasn't done being mad. Then his hands shifted to my bare back, and I lost my breath. That felt better than it had any right.

"Matt," I gasped the second he released it to work his way along my jaw to my neck.

His plush lips pressed firmly against the sensitive skin, followed by nips of teeth and light flicks of his tongue. It wouldn't take much of that before I had an impressive hickey. Too soon and not soon enough, he continued his deliberate path across my collar.

"Matt," I tried again, "What are you doing?"

"Exactly what you wanted," he replied between kisses. His lips on my skin felt like a brand. I lost my response in a moan I couldn't hold back. "You wanted me to start things. You've got it."

I groaned as his hands roved over every exposed inch of me—my shoulders, waist, back—as if he couldn't decide which part of me to touch. I was falling somewhere between ecstasy and torture. The exquisite sensations bordered on torture after so long. At the rate he was going, I'd have several hickeys. At some point, my hands had fisted in his shirt. I released it to tangle them in his hair.

"Matt." His fingers dug into my hips, forcing me against him. Another gasp escaped me at finding him every bit as hard as I was. I couldn't breathe. It was too much all at once. "Matt, stop." He ran his hands up my back and curled around my shoulders. "Please. It hurts," I groaned as he continued his aggressive trail across my chest. In exactly five seconds, I was going to come in my pants. Finally, I tightened my grip on his hair and forced his head back. Two midnight eyes stared back at me and I almost lost it, anyway. "Stop."

I shadowed out and rematerialized on the other side of my door, desperately needing space to catch my breath. The heat of his ardor still burned on my skin and the distance wasn't doing anything to lessen that. I wanted to go back, to finish falling madly into him.

I need to simmer down, is what I need.

I shadowed into the bathroom, turned the water on as cold as I could get it, finished stripping down, then plunged into the icy fall. Which did absolutely nothing. If anything, the contrast made it worse. I braced myself against the wall, letting the cold water pour over my back as desire roared unchecked in my veins. Safe in the confines of my space, my control slipped away to wash down the drain. I wrapped a hand around my shaft that was still hot to the touch despite the frigid water. One slow stroke turned into a frantic pump in search of release. Just the memory of his hands all over me was enough to drive me to the edge in record time.

Something tickled my senses, and I looked up to see Matt leaning against the door frame with his arms crossed. His eyes were still perfectly black, and he was watching me, raw hunger on his face. It was the final straw. I grunted and came all over my hand and the wall. He didn't look away. Didn't so much as blink.

The water continued to wash over me as the world swam back into focus, only now feeling even remotely cold. I dropped my hand and turned it off. Silence reigned as I grabbed a towel from the rack, practically snapping it free as a spike of anger stabbed through me. I didn't even bother to dry off, just wrapped it around my waist.

"It's rude to watch, you know. Especially when you haven't been invited. That's not fair." Despite feeling a little violated, I had to admit that some part of me had liked him watching.

He grabbed the hem of his shirt and pulled it over his head. To my amazement, he followed that by hooking his thumbs in his pants and dragging them to pool on the floor. His erection bounced at his movements and I swallowed hard.

"What are you doing?" I asked in disbelief. My imagination needed an upgrade. It wasn't doing Matt justice.

"You're right, it's not fair." He kicked aside his pants and stood there, his eyes once more their startling shade of blue. "Take whatever you want, Alex."

I took a step towards him and stopped. Even after finding release, I didn't trust myself. "Get in the shower." The glint in his eye was downright devilish and paired well with his crooked smile.

"Alright." He walked brazenly past me. "But it won't be as good of a show." He stepped into the tub and turned on the water. Still cold I noticed, then raised a questioning brow at me.

Now what?

"Go ahead, bathe."

He chuckled to himself, but complied by reaching for the soap.

This is wrong, I thought as I watched his hands glide over his slick skin. That should be me. I dropped the towel and stepped in behind him, my gaze riveted on the way his muscles rippled as he moved.

"Didn't you already have one of these?" he teased.

"Put your hands on the wall," I commanded, my voice thick.

He looked at me over his shoulder.

"You heard me."

He did so without further protest, having to lean forward ever so slightly to reach.

I started slow. Tracing the contours of his back with just one finger and then expanding to both hands. He let out a sigh that sounded more like a moan.

"Tell me what you don't like about your body." I brushed my lips across his shoulders, then wrapped my arms around him so I could explore his chest. He gasped as I explored his chest and trailed my hands down his torso. How long had I wanted to do this? "Tell me," I pressed.

"It's awful. Not like yours."

"Mmm, I love your body. I don't want it to be like mine," I said, sliding my hands down the front of his hips and coming back up the sides of his legs. He let out a groan and his hands fisted on the wall. "I didn't say you could move." He drew in a sharp intake of air, but dutifully flattened his hands. "Tell me when it hurts." His body shuddered, then quieted.

He held perfectly still while my hands roved over every inch of him. He was mine to touch and I damn well was going to. Eventually, I noticed he was struggling to keep his hands flat. Still, he didn't cry mercy. I pressed against him, enjoying the feel of our skin against each other, mindless that I was once again hard. His breath hitched as my shaft slid over his ass. For a moment, I feared I'd gone too far, but he held firm.

He really is going to let me do whatever I want.

The realization came with an unprecedented amount of trust. I took my time, dragging my hand across his abdomen, then lower to wrap around his throbbing erection. It pulsed against my hand at the same time his arms slipped on the wall and he released a deep groan.

"Say it, Matt." I squeezed the base and gave a firm stroke. "Say it."

"It hurts," he finally gasped, the words falling into another groan.

"Good." I released him and he sagged, leveraging his arms against the wall for support while his breath came in quick gasps. Before I could doubt myself, I shadowed, so that I was in front of him.

His eyes widened with surprise, and his mouth parted. Rather than give into the temptation of those delectable lips, I dropped to my knees in search of a different prize. I probably could have stared at Matt's beautiful cock, jutting out from a nest of dark curls, but I wasn't willing to test how long my luck would hold. Once more I took him in hand, reveling in the feel of velvet steel beneath my fingers. I placed my free hand on his quivering thigh, then brought his swollen head to my lips. Matt cried out with what sounded like a cross between ecstasy and pain. That's all it took for me to lose all sense of self. Most guys wouldn't say no to blowjob and would rather receive one than give. Some didn't mind either way or preferred mutual reciprocation. Me? I *loved* giving head. Loved being the one to give that pleasure, control it.

"Alex," he moaned. His whole body quivered beneath my touch, like a string pulled too tight, as he panted for air he couldn't hold. "Wait. I... you have to... *Alex*," he groaned again when I pulled him deeper. There was no way I was going to be the only one to lose it tonight. His entire body tensed and he let out a moan that sounded like it had been scraped from the bottom of his soul as his release shot down my throat.

To my amazement, his hands were still plastered against the wall, though his arms were noticeably shaking, probably from the effort of holding unbelievably still while I had my way with him. I leaned forward to place a trail of soft kisses along the curve of his hip and let out a dreamy sigh. "You can move your arms now."

Faster than seemed possible, his arms fell, and he yanked me to my feet. The moment I was upright, his mouth mashed down on mine in a punishing kiss. I moaned, arching into him and well on my way to be ready for another round. The fire of his kiss burned through us as he pulled me tighter against him. I hooked a leg over his hip, sacrificing balance to be closer.

His hands caressed my back as he continued to claim my mouth. When shifted his thigh between my legs, it was all the encouragement I needed to rub shamelessly against him. His grip moved to my waist, and he pressed me harder against him.

I broke the kiss with a gasp, tilting my head back as my second orgasm ripped through me without warning. His feather-light kisses along the column of my throat gradually brought me back to my senses. I lowered my leg, allowing the supposedly cold water to wash his torso clean.

Matt placed a tender kiss on my lips as he reached to turn off the water, his fingers trailing over my ass as he brought his hand back to my hip, where he traced lazy circles with his thumb. "You're insane," he said, his voice husky.

"So you've said," I replied, shadowing out of the shower. I grabbed my towel from where I'd abandoned it and tossed him a fresh one. "Tonight has been…" All sorts of words came to mind to describe how the evening had gone: eventful, amazing, mind-blowing. I settled for, "Exhausting. I feel like I could sleep for an entire day." At the very least, I could certainly stay in bed all day.

He looked at me like he could read my mind, but didn't add anything. He really didn't like to talk about things. For once, that was fine by me.

I walked into my room and ditched the wet towel yet again. Matt's gaze was every bit as potent as his hands on my body had been. I hid a shiver by diving under the covers. To my infinite surprise, Matt mirrored me. "What are you doing?"

"Going to bed," he said matter of fact.

I didn't really have a decent answer for that, so I lay my head back. His hand slid across my middle, and I let out an involuntary sigh. That was not conducive to going to sleep. I rolled my head to look at him. Naturally, his eyes were already closed. *You have to be the strangest creature, Matthew Duncan.*

The world was all soft darkness until mind-blowing sensation rocketed me back to wakefulness. My eyes flew open to find Matt had removed the covers and was returning the favor from the shower. I tried to hold back a cry, to no avail. Getting woken up by a blowjob was something that happened in fantasies and movies, not real life. And for someone who'd supposedly never done this before, he was doing exceptionally well.

I dug my fingers into his shoulder, desperate for something to hold on to. When that wasn't enough, I buried my fingers in his hair, moaning loud enough to wake the dead when he swirled his tongue around the head, then sucked me back into his mouth. He needed to stop. He needed to stop right now. "Matt, don't. Wait."

He listened about as well as I had and there was nothing I could do about it. The hand I hadn't noticed resting on my straining thigh shifted to caress my sac and I shattered.

"Night, holy crap, just..." The words tumbled out of me as he levered himself up beside me. I looked at him, still in a state of blissed out shock. Should have known his eyes would be crystal clear and calm as he watched me totally freak out after one of the best bjs I'd ever had. "Really dumb question, but are you sure you've never done that?"

"I think I'd remember," he said, trailing his fingers along my abdomen.

"Yeah. Right. Of course. It's just... how?" My mind refused to come to terms with his words and the reality of what had just happened.

"I paid attention."

"You paid attention," I echoed.

"I pay attention to everything you do, Alex. And people tend to do what they like." He shrugged, watching his finger trace swirls on my skin.

"So, you just... and didn't stop, because..." I just couldn't wrap my head around this.

"It seemed like a safe bet," he said, giving me a playful smile and returning his attention to the pattern he was creating.

I watched him a moment as he got lost in it. "What are you doing?" I asked softly.

"Hmm?"

"What are you doing?" I repeated, placing my hand on my stomach, just shy of his own.

Doubt flashed in his eyes, and he pulled his hand back. "Nothing."

"Why do you do that?" I asked, angling up to my elbow to be on his level.

"I don't know what you're talking about." He tried to turn away, but I caught his face with my free hand.

"Look at me." When he did, it felt like I'd been speared. There was so much hiding in those clear eyes, like a pool with no bottom. His eyes lidded when I leaned closer. "What do you want, Matt?" I whispered.

"I want you to kiss me," he replied softly.

I closed the distance a little more, savoring how our breath mingled. "No, you don't." I was close enough now that our lips practically touched, anyway.

"What?" he asked, leaning back slightly.

I smiled, my gaze still focused on his mouth. "I know what you really want." I leaned forward, passing his mouth. He gave a soft sigh, no doubt expecting me to kiss his neck. I didn't.

"If you know, then why are you asking?"

"Because I want to hear you say it," I whispered before sitting back to look at him. He searched my face, his accelerated breathing betraying his anxiety. I calmly waited, gently stroking his cheek while he struggled to find the words.

Why is it so hard for you to admit what you want?

"I..." he faltered. "I want to kiss you."

"You don't need to wait for permission, Matt."

He licked his lips, and I couldn't help but follow the path his tongue took. When he finally leaned forward, the kiss was slow and purpose-ful, lingering before going into another. Not at all the inferno I'd come to expect when he took what he actually wanted. The sweet press of lips had all the makings of a first kiss with none of the hesitation. He shifted so that I was lying on my back and slid his arm around to keep me pressed against him. The kiss deepened unexpectedly, searing me to the core and making me crave more. Then, just as abruptly, it dissipated back into small, lingering tastes. He shifted again and nuzzled into my side, resting his head on my chest. There, he could easily hear my heart beating way too fast.

I reflexively wrapped an arm around his waist, then kissed the top of his head. "I love you, Matt," I whispered into his hair.

"Alexi," he sighed, snuggling closer.

As surprised as I was to hear my actual name, I was really just pleased he wasn't running. I drifted back to sleep holding who I was pretty sure was the love of my life.

CHAPTER 8

SIEBEN HÜGEL

M

Something lightly brushed my face. My cheek twitched to make it stop, but it didn't work. With my eyes still closed, I ran through a list of possibilities. A bug? No, not crawly enough. Paper? Too consistent. A stick? Nah, too soft; too gentle. Maybe it wasn't a something at all, but a some*one*.

I cracked an eye and found deep emerald pools shining back.

Alex. Of course.

Now that I knew it was his slender fingers dancing across my face, the touch felt more like sparklers.

"Good morning," he said in a soft whisper that caressed my skin.

I hummed a reply and let my eyes drift shut again. For a moment, everything was perfect in the world. There was no constant anger, no pending deadline, just us. He gently stroked my cheek and I let out a contented sigh. A good night's sleep *and* Alex—the day was off to a great start.

As the fog of sleep lifted, the details of the night before rushed in to take its place. The argument. The hot make-out. The *shower*. What I did... My eyes flew open, and I saw my mounting panic reflected in Alex's eyes.

"Matt..."

I have to get out of here. What am I doing? This isn't me.

"Matt, don't."

I ignored the command and shadowed out of the bed, landing a few feet from the door.

Alex anticipated the move and launched out of the bed almost as fast as I had shadowed to cut off my escape. "Matt, stop."

"I have to... I can't... I don't..." I couldn't breathe let alone finish a thought. All I had was *run*. Suddenly, Alex grabbed my face and planted a single, firm kiss on my mouth that somehow expelled all of my anxiety, leaving me a hollow husk. I stood there frozen, not sure if I was breathing at all and not really caring. There was only Alex. Alex with his intense eyes that seemed to know all of my secrets no matter how I hid them.

"Stop, Matt. I have worked too hard for this to let you ruin everything because you're freaking out over nothing. Now, take a deep breath." He released my face and slid his hand down to my chest. I wasn't sure if it was to make sure I was doing as he said or to see if my heart was still beating. His brows wrinkled as he studied me for a few shaky breaths. "I wish you would tell me what you're so afraid of."

The passive request washed over me. I couldn't tell him I was absolutely terrified. That I didn't know what I was doing or even getting myself into. I couldn't admit that I knew if I got too invested and he left, it would utterly destroy me. Some part of me recognized it was already too late for that. I'd do anything for Alex. Anything at all. All he had to do was tell me. My breath started coming in pants again.

"Easy. I'm right here. I'm not going anywhere."

I wanted to make him promise that. Swear he would never abandon me like so many had before.

Determination flashed in his eyes, and his tone shifted from calm understanding to demanding. "Kiss me, Matt." My body jerked to obey, but his hand on my chest held me in place. "Kiss me like I know you want to," he added, his gaze sharp.

Something inside me snapped, and the rest of the world fell away. There was only Alex. I surged forward, removing his hand from between us, smashing my mouth against him so hard he stumbled into the wall and I was plastered against him. He gasped, and I used that as my opening to delve into his mouth with needy abandon while my hands explored every inch of him I could reach. Fuck, he felt incredible. I managed a gulp of air before I claimed him with another unforgiving kiss, fueled by the fire sweeping through me. That blaze absolutely terrified me, but I couldn't stop. I wanted more, *needed* more, and he was giving it to me. I kept waiting for him to pull back, to say enough that it was too much. Instead, I felt his fingers digging into my back as he arched into me. Felt his moan as I hungrily devoured kiss after kiss.

I would die for Alex. Knew it with a certainty that rang in my core. I couldn't breathe. Still, I kept kissing him and still he didn't stop me. He needed to stop me. Except he wasn't.

I braced my hands on the wall and straightened my arms. It wasn't much distance, but it was something. I had to stop touching him. He'd asked why I didn't touch him. *This* was why. Because I knew if I started, I wouldn't be able to stop. Mercifully, his hands fell away when I broke the kiss for longer than a microsecond. I closed my eyes, not wanting to see what he thought of me, and our ragged breathing filled my ears. Pain stabbed through my chest at the certainty that I'd just ruined everything because I couldn't control myself. And yet, it still wasn't enough, it would never be enough. I wasn't just addicted to kissing Alex, I was addicted *to* Alex and I had no idea how it had happened or when.

I tried to swallow, failed, and tried again. "I'm sorry," I finally managed.

"Don't be. That was... that was incredible," he said between pants.

I lifted my head to meet his gaze. A ridiculous smile dominated his face. But that didn't make sense. I was basically some possessed creature of darkness. Why was he grinning from ear to ear? Didn't he know how dangerous this was? How dangerous *I* was?

In an outrageously brave move, he leaned forward to rest his forehead against mine. I wanted to think he had a death wish, but the intimacy of the move rippled through me and I relaxed.

"I'm a demon too, Matt. I can handle the passion."

Passion, is that what this was? It felt more like some supernatural force of nature designed to incinerate the host and whatever they touched.

"It's okay. You don't have to be afraid." He wrapped his arms around me and pulled me close.

I completely melted into the embrace and him. My racing heart synced with the steady beat of his. I wasn't sure how long we stayed like that, only that I didn't want it to end. I needed Alex in a way I didn't know you could need another person. With him, I felt truly safe for the first time in my life. He finally pushed away a bit, and I looked back at him, finally feeling completely calm.

"I love you, Matt."

I searched his face. No matter how many times he said it, I didn't understand how he could.

"Does it bother you when I say that?"

"No," I said honestly.

"You look uncomfortable, though. Why?"

I thought about it for a moment. "No one has ever really told me that. I can count on one hand all the times." My face heated, and I resisted the urge to look away. "They're all you."

He looked surprised, but didn't say anything about it. Instead, he smiled and stole a quick kiss. "Then I guess I'm going to have to tell you more often. Unless you want me to stop?" I wasn't sure if that was a question or not, so I treated it like one.

"Please don't."

"Good, because I don't intend to. Now get dressed. I'm tired of being in the dorm."

"What happened to wanting to stay in bed all day?" I teased.

"There's always tomorrow," he said with a wicked smile. Then he smacked my ass and disappeared.

I shadowed to the other side of his door and walked the rest of the way to my room. Fall was already sneaking in, so I opted to grab one of the light jackets Jefferey had acquired for me. My stint under lockdown at the hotel already felt like a lifetime ago. Strange to think it was only four months. So much had changed.

Once I'd cleaned up, I wandered back to the living room. While I waited, I worked on the bookmark sketch some more. It was so close to being done that it was reaching that point of being overworked. Sooner rather than later, I'd have to let it go. I heard Alex's door open and put away the art.

"It's about time," I complained, turning to look at him and froze. Water beaded on the edges of his hair as if he'd just stepped out of the shower. I immediately flashed to last night and heat rushed through me. The look Alex gave me suggested he knew *exactly* what was going on in my head. I swallowed hard.

Out of the blue, he asked, "Why won't you tell me where you're really from?"

"Because I don't want you to look at me differently," I answered quickly, too frazzled to come up with a lie.

Surprise washed over his face. "But I wouldn't. It doesn't matter to me where you come from. I'd just like to know."

This is what I got for speaking without thinking. "You say that because you don't know," I said with a sigh. No way Alex would look at me like I was special if he learned I was really gutter trash.

"Wait, you're not a criminal, are you?" He smiled, and I recognized the question for the tease he meant it to be.

I shrugged. "Depends on who you ask. Several people have me branded at least as a juvenile delinquent." Only reason it wasn't something more was because I'd been a minor, but petty theft could still get your ass in jail.

He waved his hand flippantly as he grabbed his key and walked towards the door. "I already know about the deviant part."

"I didn't say deviant," I corrected him.

He glanced over his shoulder. "Didn't you?"

"Alex," I growled, shutting the door behind us.

"You need to learn to lighten up," he laughed. "It was just a joke." He hadn't gone as far into the hall as I'd expected and with the door shut, we were practically on top of each other. And *I* had issues with personal space.

"Didn't sound much like a joke," I said, pocketing my key and trying not to think about how close he was. Or how I wanted him to be closer.

"You're right, it wasn't." Heat curled around the words and danced in his eyes.

Desire burned beneath my skin. If I didn't get some distance between us soon, we were going to have a repeat of the shower out here where everyone could see. "So, what are we doing today?" I asked to reroute the topic. It might have worked better if my voice hadn't tipped.

He flashed a sinister smile. Alex knew exactly what he was doing to me and was enjoying it. The problem was, I was too. Before I could officially get myself in trouble, I started down the hall.

"Oh, I don't know," he mused aloud as he trailed after. "I just felt like we've had a pretty... eventful morning and could use some time outside of four walls."

"There's always the research project," I offered, except the book and all of our notes were back inside. Something told me if we went back in, though, we wouldn't come out.

He bumped me with his elbow and I nearly came out of my skin at the unexpected touch, despite how friendly it was. "What's with you and that project, anyway? You're obsessed."

"I'm surprised you're not more. It was your book that started this."

"I have something real to occupy my time." The same heat from before warmed the statement and had me wondering if I should have opted for silent study. "Seriously though, why are you so into it? I want to know."

I narrowly didn't let out a relieved breath. Academic Alex I could handle... mostly. "I have this feeling."

"What sort of feeling?

"I don't know. Like it's important. I keep hoping that eventually I'll read something and that feeling will make sense."

"Huh." He tapped his bottom lip like he usually did when he was deep in thought. "Is the feeling focused on the knight and our demon, or the wars?"

"Both?" I replied uncertainly. "I promise to let you know when I do."

"You better," he said so seriously I couldn't help but laugh.

Like that, we were back to normal. Just two friends out enjoying their Saturday. Except we weren't. We could pretend to be friends all we wanted, but we were something way past that. I now had a better idea of why Alex had said he couldn't just be my friend. After last night and this morning, I doubted I'd ever be able to be around him *without* wanting more. But was that a good thing or a bad?

"Matt."

I blinked, dragging my thoughts back to the present. "What?"

"You haven't heard a word I've said, have you?" Oops. He rolled his eyes and tried again. "I was suggesting we go down to Sieben Hügel and check it out. I've been meaning to explore, but haven't gotten around to it."

"Sieben Hügel. Is that something on campus?"

Alex looked at me like I'd grown a second head. "It means Seven Hills. It's the town right outside the university. Remember, we were going to check it out the other day?"

"Right! Sorry, I keep forgetting there's an actual town out there."

"I thought you said that ridiculous club wasn't on campus. If it wasn't in Sieben Hügel, then where was it?"

"How should I know?"

He gave me a look.

"I mean, it makes sense, but it's not like I was going down a bunch of back alleys. Plus, it was always dark, and it's in some kind of warehouse. I didn't exactly go wandering around. Class, the dorm, and there. That was it." I supposed there was the bar I went to with Lucas and Sam, but honestly, I had no clue if that was on campus or off.

Alex shook his head. "Well, now we're definitely going." He grabbed my arm and commenced dragging me outside.

Part of me said that he should be holding my hand, not my arm. I shied away from the thought. It was no one else's business what went on between us. When he let me, I took my arm back, surprising him. "I have two legs, Alex."

He raised his hands defensively. "Alright, point taken. No need to get snippy about it."

I deflated. What was wrong with me? I sighed and continued to follow him, albeit much more sedate.

Mercifully, our route didn't take us anywhere near the club. In fact, we went to a part of the campus I'd never seen. As I was looking around, I couldn't help but notice this part of campus was noticeably older than Mysterio College.

"You haven't been over here at all, have you?"

"What? No," I said, staring up at what I could only describe as a tower. I was dubious about calling it a castle, but that's what it looked like. "I had no idea this place was so big."

"And we still haven't left campus. Well, not yet. That's the exit." He pointed at a massive entryway with an arch that was easily two stories tall and at least fifty feet across.

"Whoa."

"You should see it from the other side." He walked forward and casually stepped across the invisible line that separated the town from the school. "Come on slow poke." He waved impatiently for me to join him. "What are you waiting for?"

I approached the entrance, my anxiety suddenly spiking, and tentatively stuck out my hand fully expecting to meet resistance.

Alex tilted his head as he watched me. "Uh, what are you doing?"

"I'm making sure I can actually walk through. The last time I tried to leave a place, there was a barrier spell on the door."

"What?" he asked in alarm.

I took a fateful step to join him and then let out the breath I was holding. Logically, I should have known that since I could go to other places off campus, it wouldn't be an issue. But I also didn't trust Vera as far as I could throw her. For a teacher, she had some real questionable methods for keeping her students in line... or maybe that was just me.

"Where was there a barrier spell?"

"At the hotel where Vera dropped me for two weeks before the start of last semester," I replied nonchalantly.

"She did what!"

I blinked, surprised by his outrage. "Yeah, she told Jefferey, the hotel manager, I was a flight risk and put a spell on the door so I couldn't leave. Everyone else could come and go as they pleased, but not me."

"Of all the... I can't believe she... The self-righteous..." he floundered, bordering on apoplectic.

"To be fair, she wasn't wrong. First time they left the door open, I made a break for it. At least when I ran into that one, it didn't hurt like hell. Not like the one at the club," I added with a shudder.

"What do you mean?"

"Well, the one at the hotel just didn't let me through. It was kind of like running into a wall—repeatedly, in my case. However, the one at the club felt like more like an electric fence."

"That's awful," He said, reaching out.

I shrugged and took a step back. "It happened." I looked around, eager for a way to change the topic and the fact that I'd just intentionally stepped away from his offered comfort. "So, do you know as much about this place as you do the university?"

He searched me for a moment before finally responding, "No, actually. I know a few interesting stories, though."

"Like what?" I asked, intrigued by his grin.

"Well, I can show you the cafe where Vera apparently met *her* teacher for the first time."

I frowned, worried I'd missed something. "Why would she meet him here? I thought she grew up in America?"

"She did, but she didn't actually meet her demon tutor until *after* they moved into the Manor their second year at Arminius."

"Manor...manor... Why does that sound familiar?"

"It's where the Shadows lived when everything went to pot. Actually, it's not that far from here, but they've added substantial protection spells over the years."

"So, not something we could just walk up and visit?" I asked, falling into step beside him.

He laughed. "Not really. I've heard they throw epic parties for elite guests. Though I can't really imagine Vera being the party type."

"I don't know. Maybe you just don't know her as well as you think."

"That sounds suspiciously as if you actually like her," Alex accused, giving me a sidelong look.

I shrugged. She really wasn't all that bad. I thought about how her tough-act facade had dropped outside of the orphanage and how, even as scary as she could be, Jefferey still called her Miss Scry despite her insistence to use her first name. "I think she might be a product of the situations she's been put in," I said as we continued walking aimlessly down the street.

Alex scoffed. "You *choose* to behave like a monster. That's not something you get to say people made you do."

I shook my head. I knew better. Not all monsters wanted to be that way. "You said the Shadows started younger than us, basically kids. How were they supposed to know better? They were told one thing and acted on it. When they found out the truth, they switched sides."

Alex's mouth twisted to the side. "You have a point. But look at the things she's done. None of the Shadows are blameless, yet she was the one who got the reputation of being the ruthless enforcer." He took a deep breath. "She slaughtered people, Matt. There were no trials, no juries, nothing. Just her will. No one could stop her, and now the rest of our kind will be feared forever. You asked me how I thought the Demon War started. If I had to guess, a lot like that. One rogue reminding the world to be afraid. The damage, irreparable."

"And yet, she's still trying to make amends. She knows what she did. She's not proud of it."

"How could you possibly know that?" he asked emphatically.

"When she took me to the hotel, I asked why everyone was afraid of her. She looked ashamed, Alex. *Ashamed*. She didn't want to tell me, and even said that when I found out, I probably wouldn't like her. Of course, I already didn't like her, but that's beside the point. At least she's trying. I've known plenty of real villains, Alex. They don't carry the weight of what they've done around with them, and they certainly don't make reparations," I finished hotly.

He studied me as if seeing me for the first time. "Eventually, you'll have to tell me where you come from."

"Not today, though."

He reached out like he could somehow soothe the anger that was boiling beneath the surface. I knew exactly what it felt like to be pigeon-holed. When everyone assumed they knew your motives. No one ever got my story straight, and I suspected it was no different for Vera.

I walked past him towards a quaint coffee shop. I didn't want his comfort. "Is this it?" It had to be. It was the only cafe I'd seen since we came into the town.

Sadness swept through his emerald eyes and he dropped his outstretched hand, shoving it forcefully into his back pocket before looking up at the sign. "Yeah, this should be it."

Without waiting, I went inside and up to the counter. I got him a coffee and me a hot chocolate. "Where should we sit?" I asked when he joined me.

He glanced around intently as he considered the assortment of occupied and unoccupied seats. "Here," he finally said, leading us over to a table that was a little out of the way. It was far enough off to have some privacy, without being so far as to be conspicuous.

"Interesting choice." I plopped into the wooden seat. Personally, I'd have preferred the cushy armchairs that had just opened up.

He took his time getting settled. Fussing with his drink and shifting his chair with far more excitement radiating off of him than a simple coffee shop warranted. At last, he looked at me. "*This is* where Vera and Gabriel sat the very first time they met."

I was about to ask what was so special about that when it hit me why that was such a big deal. For the first time in a couple of centuries, there had been two level two Shadow Demons sitting at a table together. One, almost an original, and the other, a miracle of happenstance. I took a nervous gulp and burned my tongue. When I looked back at Alex, he was grinning. It was hard to stay angry when he smiled at me like that. "I'm sorry," I said without preamble.

"For what?" he asked, sipping his drink far more carefully than I had.

"I shouldn't have gone at you like that about Vera. You grew up in this world and had an entirely different perspective about what was happening. This is all still new for me. I have no right to judge you for your views." I stared into my steaming mug of hot chocolate, feeling thoroughly ashamed of myself.

After a second, Alex let out a deep sigh. "No, you're right. I know nothing about her besides what I've heard or read in articles. How can I expect the world to look past the deeds of one Shadow Demon if *I* can't? I don't know what circumstances she was put in or what choices she was forced to make. She seemed to cultivate fear like it was a crop and exchange it like currency. But who knows the truth? The more people who feared her, the fewer people died. It'll take time for the wounds she made to heal, but I should be part of the solution, not the problem."

"I feel like you just signed up to be a goodwill ambassador," I said with a smile.

"Shut up." He laughed and chunked a sugar packet at me.

I caught it and promptly deposited the contents into my drink.

"I think you have a sweet problem," he poked.

"Simply supplementing the sweetness I don't naturally have."

"I think you're plenty sweet, Matt." His smile made my heart skip, and I finally understood what they meant in those romance books when they said "bedroom eyes". Then he added, "I mean, when you're not being a total pain in the neck." He winked, and we both returned to our drinks.

CHAPTER 9

CHECK UP

A

I gave Matt a little smirk as we squared off to spar. He winked back, and I mentally crossed my fingers that no one else was picking up the sex appeal practically oozing off of him. Three sparring practices in and we were definitely flirting more than we were fighting.

"That's it. Everyone stop."

Mat and I straightened and turned to face the front of the room where Vera was currently rubbing her forehead. She'd been more absent than not so far this semester. Whatever was keeping her distracted was also clearly giving her one hell of a migraine.

"I think it's time we mixed things up. George, you're with Yaren. Louise with Matt. Roland and Travis. Alexi and Ellie. Gilles and Kyle. She squinted at the room as if trying to figure out who she'd missed. Finally, she waved a dismissive hand. "The rest of you figure it out." She reached for a water bottle.

"Uh, Ms. Scry?" Kyle held up a tentative hand.

Vera released a heavy sigh that emphasized how exhausted she looked. "If you don't like your new partner, you can work it out amongst yourselves."

"It's not that."

Her eyes flashed as she rounded on him, and he shrank back. "Then what is it?"

Kyle's gaze darted to those closest to him, and he swallowed thickly. "G-Gilles isn't here."

Vera's eyes narrowed while her voice dropped dangerously. "And *where* is he? Miel!" she called for Gilles' roommate, but there was no answer.

"He's not here either. Hasn't been all week," Louise said, sounding almost timid.

The tension in the room increased until it felt like electricity should be crackling between our frozen forms. Matt shot me an anxious look, then gave a nearly imperceptible nod toward Vera.

"I could stop in on them, if you like," I volunteered.

Relief ghosted across Vera's face so fast, I almost missed it. "That would be appreciated. I'll have Anne send word to your next class."

I opened my mouth to protest—I'd meant I'd go *after* my classes for the day, not now—but Matt's elbow in my ribs silenced any protest. "Thank you."

Vera nodded, though her thoughts already seemed miles away. "Resume sparring," she said absently, as she tapped her lips and stared into the distance with a thoughtful expression.

I glanced at Matt, curious if he had any insight into her present behavior, but just shrugged before walking off to join Louise. Within seconds, Ellie popped up beside me.

"G'day, stranger," she said with a smile. Her thick Australian accent had softened somewhat over the summer, but it was still as unmistakable as the first time I'd heard her speak.

"Hey. Sorry, I was thinking about Gilles and Miel."

"Wild how they're both not here. Don't suppose you have any thoughts 'bout where they might be?" Her brown eyebrows lifted as she settled into a ready position.

I shook my head. "Hopefully at their dorm." Suddenly, I realized I didn't know which one that was. We hadn't all been in the same dorm for the summer semester and that hadn't changed for fall. "Blast. I forgot to ask Vera which dorm they're in."

She blocked my attack and danced back. "Easy. They're in Agate Hall." We traded a few more practice blows.

"How do you know that?" I asked, mildly surprised, before shadowing behind her. "You... close with one of them? Maybe I should let *you* go instead."

Ellie laughed and ducked out of the way, then spun to face me again. "Not likely. Louise, however, has been after Miel since last term. She may be low-key stalking them." She replicated the same move I had, appearing behind me. "Just between us, I don't think they've noticed... the stalking *or* the mooning."

I snorted and tested out a method I'd read about, but hadn't been confident enough to try on Matt. Typically, when we shadowed, we exerted control over the shadows within our immediate vicinity. Lacking those, we used extensions of our own essence. I extended my senses to where Ellie was still behind me and in mortal form. It didn't take much to detect the thin veneer of shadow substance emanating from her. Before she could shadow away, I seized control of the shadow surrounding her like a second skin. I felt the jerk as she attempted to pull herself into the shadow world and rebounded.

She gasped and walked around to face me instead. "You have to tell me how you did that."

I spent the remainder of class walking Ellie through how to hold a shadow in place. She'd nearly perfected it by the time Vera dismissed us, vowing to "test" it on her roommate, Louise, later. I was still laughing about her scheme when Matt joined me in the hall.

"What's so funny?" he asked.

"Nothing. How was sparring with Louise?"

Matt's eyes widened. "You'd never know it to look at her, but she's a freaking powerhouse. I could barely shadow fast enough to stay out of her way."

I snorted as we stepped out of Mysterio college. "You of all people should know better than to judge people by appearances."

"Yeah, yeah. Hey, you want me to go with you to check on Gilles? Pretty sure he's in Agate Hall."

I looked at him out of the corner of my eye. "Where'd you learn that?"

"Louise," he deadpanned.

Laughter burst out of me so unexpectedly, I stopped walking.

"Glad *you* think it's funny. I'm the one who had to spend half the class listening to 'Miel this' and 'Miel that'. I wanna know why *she* didn't already know where they are," Matt huffed.

"Maybe she's still working up to it, taking her time like someone else I know."

Matt ducked his head, but before I caught the hint of a rosy blush staining his cheeks. "I wasn't *that* bad."

"Agree to disagree. Anyway, you shouldn't have to miss class too. I know you're worried about that exam coming up."

He grimaced. "Good point. Okay, I'll see you back at the dorm this afternoon."

I watched him race off to his next class, marveling at the transformation. Just a few months ago, he'd have been more than willing to skip one or all of his classes, but now he actually seemed eager to go to them. I smiled into the morning sun as I angled toward the cluster of dormitories on the east side of campus.

Thankfully, the RA was in the front office and I didn't have to track them down to find out what room Gilles was in.

"How can I help you?" the noticeably green RA asked. His name tag read "Wilke," but that didn't give me any real clue what type of supernatural he might be.

"Uh, hi, Wilke? Vera—I mean, Ms. Scry—sent me to check up on Miel and Gilles…" I trailed off, not sure how to continue from there. Luckily, the name drop did all the work.

"Say no more." Wilkes buzzed me through to the main dorm. "They're on the third floor in room 3809. Let me know if you need anything else."

"Thanks." I intended to take the stairs to my right, but the elevator fortuitously opened right as I stepped up. A thin older man with goggle like glasses stepped off, sparing me a penetrative glance that made my skin crawl as I walked past him onto the lift. The doors shut, and I gave myself a good shake before pressing for the third floor.

When the doors reopened, it was onto a hall vastly different from the one in my dorm. Where Starling Hall had a plushy velvety green carpet, Agate Hall was all modern efficiency. The floors were an ashen wood while the walls were an unassuming cream decorated with thematically appropriate depictions of geodes and other natural stones.

I at last found the desired room at the end of the hall and knocked decisively on the door. A few moments ticked by without so much as a whisper of noise on the other side. Curious, if *anyone* was at home, I extended my shadow senses much as I had in class earlier with Ellie. An initial search turned up nothing, but wary of quitting prematurely, I pushed deeper. Then I found something.

Unlike the usual vitality that accompanied Shadow Demons, this essence felt more like a shimmer, a fading whisper of shadow. Significantly more concerned, I abandoned decorum and pounded on the door. The shimmer within moved, and I faintly made out the shuffling of feet inside.

"I'm coming, I'm coming. On se calme!" The door cracked open to reveal a rather grumpy Gilles in a robe. His eyes were puffy, and he had a tissue clutched in his other hand. "Alexi? What are you doing here?" he asked, his voice noticeably nasally.

"Uh, you've missed Battle Tactics all week. I opted to see what was up so Vera wouldn't."

Gilles winced. "Thanks. I owe you one."

"It's no problem. Is Miel here as well?"

"No. Bâtard went out to get decongestant and soup, but still hasn't come back. They—" Gilles broke off with a violent sneeze he barely contained in time with his worn tissue, then groaned. "That was three days ago. Blaireau gave me this damn cold, then left me to fend for myself. Probably back home being fed chicken soup by their mommy," Gilles sneered before succumbing to another sneezing fit.

"Why do you think Miel is at home?" I asked, taking a subtle step backward.

"Because they've been bitching about how they'd rather be there for *days*. Honestly, I'm glad they're gone. Though they could have had the decency to drop off the medicine *before* they bounced." Gilles sagged against the doorjamb.

"Why haven't you gone to the University healers? I'm sure they could clear up that cold, no problem."

He snorted, then groaned again. "Tried that. *Apparently*, colds don't warrant immediate attention. 'Better for the body to fight it off naturally,'" he said, adding air quotes.

"Wow, that really sucks. I didn't even know Shadow Demons *could* get sick like this," I commiserated.

"Tell me about it. Anyway, if it's alright with you, I'm going to crawl back into bed and sleep for the next decade." He was already reaching for the door before I could respond.

"Of course. I'll let Vera know what's up, so she doesn't come bother you and drop off some decongestant as well."

Gilles grunted what might have been a "Thanks," then shut the door with a heavy clunk. I ventured back the way I'd come, making a mental note to get extra soup for me and Matt just in case Gilles was still contagious.

CHAPTER 10

WITCH, PLEASE

M

My middle name was stealth. Well, not really. I didn't actually have a middle name. But it was today I crossed the open green, doing my best not to look conspicuous. I slipped around the edge of the ivy-covered stone of the Witch's College and ducked inside. A few people gave me strange looks, but most ignored me. Now for the hard part, finding the right classroom.

I wandered down the hall and tried not to look too lost as I glanced into various rooms. One was an impressive auditorium style. Another, everyone was floating, or I guess the right term was levitating. The most remarkable looked like a chem lab. No sooner did I poke my head into it than a student looked up. Whatever they were holding dripped into the beaker and an explosion of indigo smoke erupted along with the cawing of birds. The professor shouted something I didn't quite catch, and I quickly shut the door.

On the verge of admitting defeat and asking someone, the faint notes of music tickled my ears. I spun in place until I could determine from which direction the sound was coming from. Once oriented, I took off. A few turns later, I stumbled into my destination. Not that anyone noticed. They were all too busy staring at the same thing that had immediately caught my attention. Alex... dancing.

For once, I was actually glad I was on the shorter side as I slipped into the cluster of young women openly ogling my roommate. Not that I could blame them. There was something sensual about the way Alex moved, like he was made of music instead of flesh and blood like the rest of us. The walls of mirrors offered an impressive near three-sixty view of every turn, sway, and extension... and he was only following along with the instructor.

He continued to replicate the steps she was showing him until she clapped her hands. The music cut out, and I suddenly realized Alex wasn't the only student up there.

"Let's try it together." The instructor stepped back to give the six students room to move.

One woman raced across the floor and slid into position in front of Alex, narrowly heading off another. She tossed the other woman a smirk over her shoulder before returning her focus to Alex with a beaming smile. The other woman scowled at her back, then trudged over to the remaining young man on the floor.

The music resumed and once again, all eyes were on Alex as he gracefully executed the steps they'd been covering. Despite how much I enjoyed Advanced Spells, I couldn't be happier that it had gotten canceled today. I shrank into the crowd I'd infiltrated as Alex floated by on his sweep of the dance floor.

"Switch!" the instructor shouted. The couples seamlessly split apart and came together in new pairings. The woman that had lost out before boasted a triumphant smile as she fell in sync with Alex.

My heart sped up as I imagined it was me between his arms. Alex would smile and tease, his eyes glowing as he expertly guided us around the floor. We'd laugh when he spun me out, because it was silly. But when he pulled me back, we'd be pressed close together, chest to chest, hip to hip, our bodies perfectly aligned. He'd give me that seductive smile that never failed to steal my breath, then lean down to press our lips together. Right as I got lost in it, in him, he'd pull away and spin me, because he was secretly a terrible tease.

Shame I was an awful dancer and that would literally *never* happen.

One of the women near me let out a wistful sigh. "It's just not fair."

"You're telling me," another said, a noticeably dreamy look in her eyes.

"Think he's single?" a third asked.

The first gave a quiet snort. "We're not that lucky."

"Yeah," the other two swoon-sighed.

I stole another glance right as Alex dipped his current dance partner. Good thing he had demonic strength; poor thing looked she was going to faint. Feeling exceptionally smug, I extricated myself from the crowd and quietly left the room with none the wiser of my having been there. They could look and hope all they wanted. Alex *wasn't* single and, at the end of the day, I was the one he kissed.

Back in the hall, I moseyed through the halls, contemplating what sort of date I could surprise Alex with. Movies were great and all, but they were definitely more his thing than mine. The inevitable making out was nice, though. Okay, way more than nice. It was freaking fantastic, especially since we'd added blowjobs and handskies to the mix. I smirked to myself as I stepped into the bright afternoon sun, momentarily distracted from my quest to devise a date befitting Alex.

"Matt? Is that you?"

I spun around, glinting in the sunlight. "Gilles?" As my eyes focused, I saw it was him, his rich brown skin with burnt sienna highlights an impressive contrast to the faded stone at his back. "What are you doing here?"

He stepped closer, an amiable smile on his face. "I have a history of magic class here. Wasn't aware you had any classes in the witch's college, though."

"I don't." Gilles frowned, and I realized my response made no sense. "I was curious about Alex's dance class. Figured I'd see for myself what all the fuss was about. Still don't get why it's in the Witch's College."

He laughed. We hadn't quite become the good friends I'd hoped we would, but we got on all right. "You and, like, eighty percent of the university." He leaned closer and dropped his voice. "Just between us, it has more to do with the witch's desire to have everything in-house. Personally, I'd rather not have a generic course like History of Magic in this building."

"Why? Is it really far from your other classes?"

Gilles gave me a funny look. "Uh... no."

Now I was really confused. "Then why?"

His eyebrows furrowed. "Because it's full of witches."

"I feel like I'm missing something. Sorry, not sure if you knew, but I'm still kinda new to the whole supernatural." I spun my hand in the air to encompass the university "thing."

Gilles' eyes widened with understanding. "Oh wow. No, I didn't. In that case, you busy for lunch? I haven't eaten yet and I can fill you in on the drama they *don't* tell you in Demonic History."

Truthfully, I'd already had lunch, but he'd piqued my interest and I could always eat. "That sounds good. Student Center?"

"That was the plan."

We fell instep and made our way to the nearby commissary in the Student Center that hadn't been remodeled since the Renaissance. Probably an exaggeration, but given how old Arminius was, it wouldn't have surprised me. We each grabbed a prepackaged meal and made ourselves comfortable at a round wooden table, its surface the smooth you can only get after *decades* of use.

"Okay, fill me in on the witch dirt," I said as I removed my ham sandwich from its cellophane wrapper.

Gilles chuckled under his breath, opting to start with his potato chips. "You're really something else. We should hang out more. That's kind of on me. I got a little caught up in the uni-scene. Been going a little wild with all the sudden freedom, if you know what I mean."

If he wanted to take the blame for us not being better friends, I wasn't about to stop him, but I absolutely got where he was coming from. "Yeah, I get it. Did the same thing when I started last semester."

"Truly?" He leaned back in his chair with a relieved sound. "Thank goodness it's not just me. We'll have to swap stories some time."

Well, that wasn't happening. "Sure. Now, about the witches."

Gilles finished chewing his latest bite of chips and swallowed. "Right. So the books tell you—sort of—that witches and demons don't have the most stellar history."

"I've picked up on that. But that was like centuries ago, right?"

He snorted, then took a sizable chomp out of his sandwich. "As if," he said around a mouthful of food. He finished and took a drink. "The practice of 'summoning' demons only got banned in the last decade, give or take a few years. Not that witches care about laws that interfere with their priorities."

I spluttered, spraying half-chewed chips. "Shit. Sorry." I hurriedly cleaned the mess I'd made, though it didn't do shit for my head. "That can't be right."

"Oh, but it is. Funnily enough, it fell out of practice in smaller, rural towns before it did in the cities." He shrugged, crumpling up the empty chip bag and napkin. "Fewer places to hide, I guess. A little *too* suspect when your demon neighbor goes missing."

"Holy cow. That's wild. You, uh... ever see anything like that in Paris?"

Gilles' face fell, and he hunched over his trash, resting his forearms on the table. "Yeah. Ma tante. My aunt," he clarified when it was clear

I wasn't following. "She taught me everything I know about sailing." His features softened and a sad smile graced his lips.

We'd have to circle back to the sailing, because that was *cool*, but now wasn't the right time. "What happened?"

He took a deep breath and straightened. "She'd always been an explorer, a free spirit. The year I was twelve, she promised to take me on a summer-long adventure. Back then, we lived in the city's heart. Ma tante would come over every morning and we'd work all day to gather supplies and make plans. Then one day... she was gone."

"How do you know it was a witch?"

"We didn't, not at first."

The hair on the back of my neck stood up, promptly followed by the ones on my arms. I glanced at the table to find pieces of shadow worming across the smooth surface. It wasn't quite the pull Alex could exert, but that didn't make it any less disconcerting.

"Then someone started following us. My family was leaving a movie when I got snatched."

My heart lurched into my throat and I flashed to the memory of a rope burning as it cut into my neck in a dim alley. I'd gotten away by the skin of my teeth and got picked up shortly after by the people that would eventually take me to Superno House. Weird to think that had only been six months ago.

"Luckily, my family noticed pretty quickly that I wasn't with them and found me before the witch got too far with me. They confronted him in a narrow street a few blocks from the theatre. That's where we learned that the reason ma tante was nowhere to be found was because she'd let slip to her friend from work that she was a demon. Her *friend*," Gilles emphasized, his voice raw with hurt. "The witch that had caught me had heard about the power her friend had garnered and wanted a taste for himself."

"That's... that's awful." Had it been witches that had tried to capture me?

Gilles hung his head to study his hands as he picked at his fingers. "Dad said he was the one who pushed the man into the shadow world, but I think... I think it was me. I'd recently started manifesting—part of why my aunt wanted to spend the time together—and my control wasn't great. That's... that's a big reason I didn't enroll last semester. I didn't trust myself or the fact that there'd be witches here. But it's not exactly like there are demon-exclusive universities, let alone any that would take a Shadow Demon."

"It does take some getting used to. I can't tell you how freaked I was my first few weeks here," I confessed, earning an almost smile. "So, did you, uh, ever find your aunt?"

"Now that we knew where to look, it was easier. But by the time we got there, it was too late. All we found was the holding circle and two burn marks. One in the center of the circle and one outside."

"Fuck!" Several people turned at my exclamation. I offered an apologetic expression and dropped my voice to more of a whisper. "Shit, man. For real? What the hell happened?"

"We think the witch tried to pull too much power and literally burned them both out. That, or the witch didn't know how to control shadow magic. Either way, it was a foregone conclusion my aunt was never leaving that place with her will intact. I'm just glad the witch got what she deserved." He sank back in his chair as if the tragic retelling of his aunt's untimely demise had completely drained him.

I mirrored the move, overwhelmed with the fresh supernatural horror. Magic really wasn't all it was cracked up to be. Bad people were bad people anywhere. "Damn. That's just... Wow. I don't even have words."

"Yeah. Moral of the story? Don't trust witches."

I nodded. The only witch I'd ever really interacted with was Misty from the fight club, and I already didn't trust her. Now I had whole new reasons to give her a wide berth. We solemnly picked up our trash and ventured back outside.

"I've got to get to my next class," Gilles said. "See you around."

I tipped my chin at him. "Me too. See ya." We set off, thankfully, in opposite directions. Gilles was a decent guy, but as much as I wanted to know everything about Paris, I didn't foresee us becoming more than classmates. Man could get *dark* and I'd only recently discovered the light.

"Matt!"

At Alex's voice, I spun around.

"What are you doing here?" he asked, as he jogged to a stop in front of me.

The dark cloud Gilles had left hanging over me evaporated at the sight of Alex's broad grin. "Thought I might try to catch you for a late lunch. But I've got to get going or I'll be late for my next class."

"Yeah. We'll figure it out, eventually." He bumped my shoulder. "See you tonight?"

"Yep. What do you say we go for a walk around campus after dinner? Just me and you?"

His eyes twinkled, and I knew the low-key idea had been the right move. "You asking me out on a date?"

"If I am?"

"Then, yes. I'd love to" He leaned forward and my heart hammered in anticipation. The university clock chimed the hour. We both jumped and shared a chuckle. "Better get a move on. I'll see you tonight." He winked and turned on his heel.

I practically floated to my math class already looking forward to my kiss later, my conversation with Gilles all but forgotten.

PROFESSOR WARDEN

A

"Hey Matt," I called, walking into the living room, but there was no sign of him. If we didn't leave soon, we'd be late for the seminar.

He must still be in his room.

Then I'll just have to go get him.

As I crossed the room, I spied my book on the table and stopped dead. It was so rare for Matt to leave it unattended. After casting a quick glance at his door to confirm it was still closed, I swung over the back of the couch. The book sat there with a seemingly innocent piece of paper sticking out, though it no longer bore any resemblance to the pristine, white page I'd given him what felt like ages ago. As I pulled it free of the worn pages, I realized practically every inch was covered. I'd assumed each time I caught him sketching that he was working on something different, but the level of detail suggested it had only ever been this. And it was absolutely incredible.

At the heart of the drawing were two figures leaning towards each other. It actually reminded me a bit of the illustration from the book of the knight and the demon. One character was unquestionably Matt. He'd captured that lost look perfectly and there was something in his eyes... Not fear. Yearning? I dragged my gaze across the page. Where one figure was definitely a human version of himself, the other was absolutely a demonic representation. Shadow seemed to swirl around the figure almost seductively, drawing in the knight, or in this case, Matt.

And he said it wasn't a self-portrait.

Understandably, he'd colored the demon image much darker, and I had to tilt the paper beneath the light to catch the details. Despite recognizing what it was, something about the drawing seemed off. Where the human form was replete with details that screamed Matt, the demon was not. Almost like the demon was a completely different person. Someone powerful, reaching out to tempt the young knight with darkness. Maybe this was how Matt wished he could be? Then I noticed a detail that shattered my theory. The demon's eyes were not the black they should have been. They were a vibrant green.

I reassessed the demon. The set of the shoulders, the lean waist, how his hair fell in his face. Now that I was paying attention, I'd know those features anywhere, saw them every day.

The demon is me. I'm the darkness tempting Matt.

The revelation of how Matt saw me upended my world. He'd transformed a simple piece of plain paper into a masterpiece of artwork about me... about us. It hovered on the edge of perfection, missing the smallest detail. I plucked a colored pencil from the array abandoned on the coffee table and added light blue highlights to the eyes of Matt's figure. Now his image held the same life I saw whenever I looked into his eyes.

"What are you doing?"

I turned to face him. At some point, he must have emerged. "Matt, this is... this is..." There weren't words. I could barely comprehend what I was looking at. "Can I have this?" I doubted he'd be willing to give it up, especially after guarding it so closely, but it was worth a shot.

He shrugged, his typical response when he didn't want to get into anything as messy as feelings. "I suppose. If you really want it."

"I really want it," I said, a hair too quickly and his cheeks turned a light pink. "This is stunning, Matt. I knew you could draw, but this is a whole other level. Why didn't you want me to see it before?" I knew without question that he never would have left it out if he hadn't wanted me to find it.

"It wasn't done and..." he trailed off, shuffling his feet and looking abashed. He hadn't done that in weeks. I kind of missed it.

"And it's very personal," I finished for him.

He looked up at me from beneath his lashes.

I carefully laid the picture down and shadowed over to him. He started, but didn't have time for anything else before I snared him with a kiss. He returned it haltingly, betraying his nerves. I caressed the side of his face and didn't press for more. "I love you, Matthew Duncan."

"Please don't call me that," he whispered.

"Why not? It's your name."

"It doesn't feel like it."

I was in no state to start a philosophical debate about his name, so I let it go in favor of wrapping my arms around him. "Okay, Matt." This time, his response held more of the burn as he tilted his head back to kiss me. He was everything I'd ever dreamed of and so much more. I doubted there would ever come a day that I wasn't blindly in love with him. He slid his hands around my waist and I fell into a deeper kiss. I'd gladly drown in Matt if it meant he'd always kiss me like this. Finally, I pulled myself together enough to break away.

He stood there a moment, as if waiting to see if I would return.

"Thank you," I said, my voice rough from the emotion I was struggling to keep in check.

"It's just a picture," he said nonchalantly, his hands slipping from my sides. He didn't need me to make a big deal about it. He already knew, which was why he'd kept it hidden.

I thought about what to say next. That I now had a visual representation by Matt's own hand, showing how he felt about me, was mind-blowing. However, pointing that out was likely to make him shrink away. "Still, it's nice to have something you made. I'm sorry if I messed it up."

His eyebrows snapped together. "What do you mean?"

"I added a little color. See for yourself." I gestured at the table. He may have said it was nothing more than a picture, but he sure moved pretty quick to see what I'd done. It took him less than a second.

"My eyes aren't that color."

"That's a matter of perspective. And you're one to talk," I said, walking over and picking up the pencil I thought to be the likely culprit. "It's not like mine are—what does this say—Emerald Isle."

He scowled at me, then gathered several other pencils on the table. "Actually," he plucked the color out of my hand and held it up with three others, "they're Emerald Isle, Dusty Sage, Mountain Green, and New Spring." He replaced all the colors in their case before turning back to me. "Are we going to this seminar thing or what?"

"Yeah, we're going." I fought the urge to spirit the picture into my room before he could change his mind. I'd have to trust he was actually going to let me keep it. We grabbed our keys and made our way out of the dorm towards the College of History.

"What is this supposed to be about again, and why are we going?"

"For starters, going to the lecture counts as extra credit. I would have thought you, of all people, would appreciate that." Passing Demon History I, didn't automatically make him any better at Demon History II.

He rolled his eyes. "Voluntarily doing extra work is weird," he mumbled to himself.

I held the door for him and added what I hoped would be a sweetener, "The subject is about the Wars."

"We already know about the Wars of Power. That was *last* semester."

I lowered my voice so it wouldn't carry through the auditorium style room. "Not *those* wars. Professor Warden teaches the graduate classes. He's considered the premiere authority on Demon History despite not being a demon himself. If anyone knows about the War on Darkness, he would."

Matt considered me and I could all but hear the gears turning in his head.

I gave an exasperated huff. "What? That part doesn't appeal to you either? You agreed to come," I pointed out.

"I agreed because you asked me. But, Alex, I feel like we need to be careful. I still think someone was watching us at the library and asking questions about a war we shouldn't know about could lead to trouble."

"That's ridiculous. There's nothing to say we 'shouldn't' know about it, just because no one else seems to."

He shook his head, but didn't continue arguing. To keep the peace, I let him choose a couple seats at the very back, though I'd have much preferred to be towards the front where I wouldn't miss anything. As the room filled, I worried that Matt's paranoia wasn't about the wars at all, but about me... us.

I shouldn't have kissed him before we left. It's obviously messing with him.

While we waited in silence for the lecture to begin, his obvious desire not to be here grew until it infected me to the point of distraction.

I wanted to reach out to him, try to get him to relax, but I'd finally learned that would never fly. In the dorm, he would let me do whatever I wanted to him, but beyond those walls we followed strict rules of friendship. I tried not to let it bother me. I knew this was all different for him and that he was a very private person, but it would have been nice to at least hold his hand.

"Is that him?" Matt tilted his head toward the front of the room where a man with a clipped white beard stepped up to a dais. From the distance, he could have been anywhere between fifty and ninety.

I nodded, hoping that the acoustics in this place were enough to actually *hear* the lecture.

"And who's that?"

It took me a moment to figure out who Matt was referencing. "His TA maybe?"

A wiry man, wearing glasses so thick I could see the lenses back here, scurried to help Professor Warden set up his notes. His thin brown hair was both dull and made him look even paler than he already was. The assistant said something in the professor's ear, then shuffled off to the side.

Matt's lip curled with obvious distaste. "He looks like a rat."

"Don't be rude," I snapped under my breath. It may have been true, but the man was still in a position of authority and deserved respect.

He rolled his eyes and slouched in his chair.

Oh, he was going to be difficult tonight. I barely stopped myself from rolling my eyes in response and returned my attention to the front.

"The Demon Wars came centuries after the Wars of Power," Professor Warden said with a voice that easily filled the room and bellied his soldier-like posture. "They were a direct reflection of the pervasive fear and chaos of the time." He paused, scanning his audience, then with the hint of a smile, stepped away from the podium. "Now, what is often forgotten here is that while we call these wars, they were really no more than minor skirmishes scattered throughout history. Let's face it, supernaturals don't exactly play well with others."

I hissed through my teeth, and Matt cast me a quick glance.

Below, the professor continued, gesturing with his hands to encompass the room, which was, in fact, predominantly demonic. "At any given time, one race or another was constantly at odds. The witches tampered with the elementals, creating both the incident at Pompeii and the Great Flood. Werewolves fought against encroaching settlements by terrorizing the countryside. And let's not forget the demons of the sea—krakens, sirens, the ever-dreaded leviathans—that effectively stalled the exploration of the planet. Many supernatural species inspired fear and awe in their human counterparts, but none so much as the demon. With so many different kinds and no way to understand them, it's no wonder demons found their way into every religion." His smile widened, and he held his hands out by his side. "In short, Demons became the bogeymen in every story."

The room gave a collective chuckle, and I had to bite my tongue. I didn't find always being the villain remotely humorous.

"Most, over time, came to uneasy truces with mankind," Professor Warden continued when the laughter died down, resuming his circuit of the stage. "Fire demons retread to lands inhospitable to mortals. Sea demons retreated to the depths where man could not reach. In fact, the majority of the demon classes found some way to avoid the spread of humanity." He held up a finger. "Except for one. The Chaos sect. This collection of unclassifiable dark powers refused to be cowed so easily. Remember, by this point, mankind has already learned to fear the unknown, not to mention the witches summoning demons for their own misdeeds. But all of this paled compared to the sheer terror the Chaos sect instilled in man."

Several demons from the Chaos sect snickered around the room. How they'd gotten their name was no secret—trouble was all they brought. But that didn't make what the professor was saying right. Just like humans, not all demons were the same, even in the Chaos sect.

"It was this sect that was primarily responsible for what we collectively refer to as the Demon Wars."

I seethed in my seat, my fists clenching on the armrests. Lies. All lies. He made it sound like humanity was simply defending itself. That the Chaos sect had started it and other demon classes tried to avoid the fallout. That wasn't true, or at least, not all of it. We had proof that there was an actual war being waged that no one knew about and *all* the classes had taken part. My hand flew into the air.

Matt looked at me with horror and sank even deeper into his chair.

"Yes. Young man at the back. You have a question?"

"And the Shadow Demons? Where do they fit in?"

Something dark flashed across the professor's face, gone before I could place it. Behind him, the TA flipped vigorously through a notebook. Professor Warden stared at me for a long second, then let out a hearty laugh. "I'm glad to see we have some Shades in the house."

Laughter rolled through the room, and I bristled. Meanwhile, Matt looked like he was going to die of mortification. "You haven't answered my question. What about the War on Darkness?" I insisted.

"I see someone has been reading one too many fairy tales," he said with a noticeable edge that didn't prevent another burst of laughter.

I clenched my jaw so hard my teeth cracked. Suddenly, Matt grabbed my arm, and I glanced at him, fully prepared to unleash the rage bubbling beneath my skin.

He met my furious gaze with a warning glare. I tried to shake him off, but he held firm. "Look around," he hissed under his breath.

Pools of shadow swam around my feet, with more tendrils from all over the room joining it by the second. I took a deep breath and focused on regaining control over the wayward shadows. With my anger in check, I returned my attention to the professor I'd exalted less than an hour ago.

"Case in point," he said, hand extended in my direction. "If the stories around the supposed War on Darkness are to be believed, that would mean that Shadow Demons of the highest levels worked together in concert. Coordinated assaults. Lead armies." He barked a laugh and I nearly bit my tongue clean off from the effort of holding it. "As you no doubt can see for yourself, *that* is extremely unlikely. As the Shadow Demons are a fairly recent addition to our fine establishment, many of may be unaware that they are traditionally a solitary class with a reputation of not getting along with their own race, let alone others. Not to mention, their grasp on their own powers tends to be questionable at best. That lack of control is largely believed to be what almost wiped them out," Professor Warden finished, looking directly at me. I was hard pressed to determine if that last was intended to be academic speculation or some kind of threat, and I wasn't planning on sticking around to find out.

"To hell with this." Without another word, I walked out, feeling like everyone was watching me. I was still breathing hard when I ran into Matt in the outer hall. For a brief second, I couldn't understand how he'd gotten there, then I realized he must have shadowed, which is exactly what I should have done.

His blue eyes were intense as he asked, "Are you alright?"

My fists clenched and unclenched by my side. "No, I'm not." I was not a naturally violent person, but I wanted to hit that man. To be so humiliated and by someone who should have been above that.

He gave a sharp nod, as if he understood the rage flowing through me. "Come on, we're going back to the dorm," he said and immediately started walking off.

I stayed rooted to the spot, still trying to fight the urge to march back in there and give that so-called professor a piece of mind and maybe my powers, too.

"Alex," Matt said sharply, and my feet started moving. In hardly any time at all, we were back in our room and I was still fuming. "He was lying," Matt said, tossing me a carton of ice cream. I didn't wait for him to give me a spoon, instead forming one out of shadow. He gave me a face and set the spoon he'd grabbed on the table.

I chomped into a bite of the frozen treat, numbing my teeth. "Why do you say that? He certainly seemed to believe the bullshit he was spewing."

"Did you see the way he looked at us? That man *hates* Shadow Demons."

"That's absurd. He simply ridiculed us in front of everyone," I said angrily, waving my ephemeral spoon. "He clearly doesn't know shit about real Shadow Demons. I ought to report him."

Matt shook his head. "I've seen hatred before. He loathes our kind. He did a good job of keeping it in check, though. And he wasn't just ridiculing us, he was creating a distraction. Did you see what the TA started doing the second you spoke up?"

I shrugged, vaguely recalling the TA frantically flipping through papers. "He was going through notes."

"No, he was looking for something. I'd bet you anything it was our names and power levels."

"But you don't even know what you are."

"I'm a level seven."

My spoon winked out of existence, causing the scoop it had been holding to fall onto the floor. "Wha—? How did you figure that out?" A *seven*? I knew he was stronger than me. I just had no idea about how *much* stronger.

"I found a testing spell in an old grimoire. It measures potential, not just active strength."

How was he so calm about this? He couldn't possibly understand what that meant. A seven. When was the last time the world had seen one of those?

He sighed as if blowing my mind was taxing. "Try not to get too worked up. You'll always be stronger than me, Alex." With that, he got up and put away his ice cream, then disappeared into his room, leaving me to figure out what the hell had just happened.

CHAPTER 12

DANCE LESSONS

M

I never should have told Alex my power level. On the one hand, it certainly seemed to distract him from the horrible fiasco at the seminar. On the other, he was probably going to expect me to start actually applying myself more in class. Far as I was concerned, it was an arbitrary number. Like Scylla had told Oliver back at *Superno House Orphanage,* all the power in the world meant nothing if you didn't know how to use it. Which I didn't, not consistently anyway.

Of course, I'd done the same test on him. Being a level nine was still nothing to snub at, but it rankled that he'd *technically* been right about my being stronger. Alex was just better at everything: school, shadowing, relationships... Something soft slammed into my face, breaking my line of thought.

"Earth to Matt."

I snatched the pillow from Alex before he could smack me again. "What gives?"

"You haven't been paying attention for a while now. I'm beginning to wonder if you want to study at all."

The honest answer was no. I could think of several other things I'd rather do with Alex besides study, most of which didn't require clothes. We'd had a few make-out sessions since our *eventful* shower, but nothing as outrageously hot. Thinking about conquering Alex's mouth while we ground against each other had me chubbing up instantly. I squashed the thoughts before I ended sporting a full-on tent. If I couldn't get a handle on this, it was going to get me into trouble. As it was, keeping any measure of distance outside of the dorm was damn near impossible.

Through sheer stubborn determination, I dragged my mind out of the gutter and focused on the last thing he'd said. "Want to study and need to study are very different things." I stuffed the pillow between us with maybe a little too much force. My horniness was definitely giving me an attitude.

Alex snorted and set his textbook aside. "I seriously doubt you actually *need* to study. I don't know why you don't give yourself more credit, Matt. You act like you're some sort of dunce, but you're far from it. Then there's the whole Battle Tactics issue. I swear it's like you're intentionally trying not to get it."

"Can we not talk about that?" I groaned, flopping back. As if wanting to jump his bones wasn't distracting enough, I did *not* need a reminder about how I'd gotten my ass handed to me in the last few classes.

"Fine. What do you think of Vera shifting Ballroom from an elective to a core?"

I lurched forward to stare at him. "You mean that ridiculous dance class you have on Wednesdays?"

"Yep."

I'd stopped by once out of curiosity when one of my classes had gotten canceled. Unsurprisingly, Alex had been smooth as silk and graceful to boot. I groaned and hung my head in my hands. "You've got to be kidding me." I'd never be able to move like that.

He shook his head, his smug smile growing.

"You'll probably have to tutor me in that too," I bemoaned.

"So, at this rate, am I basically tutoring you in everything?"

"It looks that way." Which I was a hundred percent fine with. *I wonder if I could convince him to study naked… Dancing might not be so bad then.*

"You don't need my help, Matt."

I rolled my eyes and pushed away the sexy thoughts. "You've never seen my try to dance."

"We could fix that," he teased.

"Not until I absolutely have to, and not a moment before."

"Come on, it'll be fun." He leaned forward and grabbed my arm, presumably to pull me to my feet.

I resisted, pulling back, and he took the opening to tickle me. No one had ever been brave enough to try anything like that before, and it came as a complete surprise to me I was ticklish at all. "Stop it," I gasped, laughing and trying to fight him off.

"Concede," he persisted.

"No, cut it out. It's not funny," I managed through fits of laughter. No wonder tickling was a form of torture.

"*I* think it's hilarious."

Finally, I got enough leverage to push him off. He sat back, chuckling to himself and looking a bit flushed. I imagined I looked much the same. How easy it would be to close the distance between us and—

A ringing cut through the air. I looked down at the coffee table to see Alex's phone. In perfect blocky letters, it proclaimed the caller to be 'MOM'. We looked at each other, then simultaneously dove for the phone. Alex was fast, but I was faster.

I snagged the device and hopped out of reach, answering it before it could stop. "Hi, Ms. Roman," I said, out of breath. Alex stared daggers at me, and my resulting smile stretched from ear to ear.

"Hello?" The woman's voice sounded pleasant, with the same touch of British accent Alex had.

"This is Matt. I'm sorry, Alex can't come to the phone right now."

"Give it back," Alex hissed. I stuck my tongue out and moved further out of his reach.

"Matt? Matt-Matt?" his mom said in my ear. "Well, *hello*. It's a pleasure to finally speak to you. Alexi has told me so much about you."

"Oh he has, has he?" I raised a questioning eyebrow at Alex. His eyes widened and he lunged a hair too slow to catch me.

"Of course. So how are things? I hear classes are going well. Keeping your grades up, I hope."

I kept Alex in my line of sight as he stalked me around the couch. "Funny you should mention that. I was just trying to convince your son to tutor me in ballroom. He's a natural on the dance floor. You should see how the women drool."

She might have giggled, but it was too faint to tell. "I'm sure Alexi would love to teach you how to dance, Matt."

"Maybe you should tell him that." I dodged another desperate grab. "He doesn't seem too interested." My foot caught on the end table and I went flying over the side of the couch to land with a resounding thud that knocked the wind out of me.

"Everything alright dear? Sounds like quite a ruckus over there. I haven't called at a bad time, have I?"

"Of course not, Ms. Roman," I said as I stood tried to regain my bearings. Mid dusting my ass, I realized with alarm that I was standing *in* the couch. I went to take a step, but my leg wouldn't budge. Everything from my thighs down was stuck. Desperate to get free, I tried harder, each failed attempt to move adding to my panic.

Alex snatched the phone from my hand. "I'll have to call you back, mom. Now I have to tutor Matt in how to shadow properly. He appears to have gotten himself stuck." He hung up and tossed the phone on the kitchen table before swinging around a chair. He took his time primly sitting down, then stared at me.

"What do I do?" I asked, my voice bordering on a shriek.

"How should I know?"

"Come on, Alex, don't be like that. I'm sorry, okay? Just, please just help me get unstuck. I can't stay like this forever. Can I?" When he wasn't quick to answer, my panic tripled. "Oh god, can I!"

Alex fought to keep his laughter to himself... and failed. "First, you need to calm down. Freaking out is only going to make it worse."

"Worse! Worse like how?" I swiveled as much as my captive state would allow.

"Easy. Calm down, Matt. Give me a minute to think."

My mouth snapped shut to give him the quiet to come up with a solution. Inside, however, I was frantic. I'd heard plenty of horror stories about people getting stuck, but no one ever mentioned how to get *un*stuck. Alex pensively tapped his lip while the quiet drove me insane. Just when I thought things couldn't possibly get worse, black spots swam lazily across my vision.

Oh no, not this too.

"You know what?"

I looked at him, hopeful for a solution. Preferably before the darkness swallowed me whole.

"I think I'm a better kisser than you."

The black spots vanished in my surprise. "What?"

He gave a decisive nod. "Yep, I'm sure of it."

"You want to debate this *now*?" I gestured wildly at the couch.

"What? It's not like you can defend yourself. And it's hardly a debate so much as a statement of fact."

My mouth fell open in shock. *He's mad. Absolutely bonkers.* "How about you come over here and we'll see how well I can defend myself," I growled.

He surprised me yet again by flowing effortlessly out of the chair, then swayed closer with a look in his eye that had my pulse fluttering nervously, but like he'd already said—it wasn't like I could go anywhere. He stopped right at the back of the couch, leaving only a few inches between us.

"Alright, defend yourself. Prove you're better."

I opened and closed my mouth a few times before I pushed words out. "You can't be serious."

He shrugged. "It's not like you're doing anything else."

I searched Alex's face like it could give me a clue what was really going on, but he was a blank canvas. "You're absolutely insane."

"So you keep telling me. Now, are you going to prove me wrong or do you admit defeat?"

I narrowed my eyes. *Of all the hair-brained things to want to do. Fine. You want a kiss? You've got it.*

I twisted my fingers in his shirt and yanked him closer. Distantly, I heard a squeak of surprise, then it was drowned out by the pure taste that was Alex. That, plus the overwhelming smell of lavender, was enough to make me lightheaded. Kissing him really was like a drug. My heart raced as I lost myself to it. I tugged on his bottom lip with my teeth and kissed him deeper. Maybe he'd be down for no-clothes studying after all.

Alex slid an arm around my waist, and I gasped at suddenly being pressed against him. I gave up my hold on his shirt to caress his face, urging the kiss deeper. This was so much more than he'd given me in ages. I needed this, ached for it. It still wasn't enough. I wanted more. It didn't matter that I was already struggling for air.

Finally, my lungs refused to take the abuse anymore. I broke the kiss, panting for air. Even after several steadying breaths, I still felt in danger of passing out. Gradually, my wits returned, and I glanced down to see Alex's arm between me and the back of the couch. I looked back up at him with his smoky smile. "You crafty bastard," I said, snaring him with another kiss.

"For the record," he chuckled between kisses, "you are definitely the better kisser."

"I suspect that's a matter of perspective."

"Why do you have to fight me on everything?"

"Is that a real question?" The heat in his gaze was almost hot enough to melt me all over again. "Good call, by the way." I trailed my hand down the arm he was using to separate me and the couch.

"I couldn't very well have you falling back through, now, could I?"

"Well, thanks," I replied, clearing my throat. If he didn't stop looking at me like that, the couch was going to be the least of our problems. As it was, there was no hiding my erection, seeing as how it was digging into his thigh. I was tempted to create some much-needed friction and wondered if maybe now was a good time to mention that I was interested in more. A lot more.

As if reading my thoughts, he released me and stepped back.

"Um, so what do you want to do now?" I asked, suddenly awkward. Was I doing something wrong? Did he not think I could handle it? To cover the rising heat in my cheeks, I ducked my head and suggested, "Back to studying?"

"Actually, I thought we could see who really marshaled the forces in the War on Darkness. Was it really Shadow Demons? Our book hasn't been all that clear. Why don't we hit up the library? See what we can find? Who knows, maybe we'll get lucky." The idea of getting lucky sounded better than the library.

"Are you sure? I thought you weren't really into the research project, especially after the seminar and the assignment basically getting scrapped."

"It sucks that they've decided not to go forward with the original project. But we've already put in so much work and I'd like to know how it all ends. Plus, we still have to get to the bottom of that weird feeling of yours." He turned to gather his things from the table.

"Hey, wait." I grabbed his hand. Automatically, our fingers laced. He looked down, clearly surprised, and I tugged him back for one last kiss. As it lingered, I fought the urge to keep it going. "Thank you," I said sincerely, then let him go.

"I didn't really do anything." He swung his pack onto his shoulder. "You just needed to be distracted long enough to do it yourself." His smile was reassuring, but it didn't change the fact that I'd been really scared and he'd casually come to my rescue. My own personal knight in shining armor. "As for the library, I promise we can leave if you feel like anything is off. I don't want you to be uncomfortable, but that really is the only place we're going to find the missing links to this puzzle."

"You realize that there's a very good chance that those pieces are hiding in the restricted section. Right?" I pointed out, closing the door behind us.

"That is a distinct possibility. But it's not like you haven't gone in there before."

"Are you volunteering me?" I asked incredulously.

"Okay, okay, we'll exhaust other avenues first. We still need to finish that enormous history. Who knows, maybe the answers are already in there and you won't have to go searching."

"You better hope they are or that the librarian decides to be helpful again. I'd never be able to check different books before succumbing to the aversion spell."

"I meant to ask, what was it like?" He glanced at me as we walked side by side down the hall.

"Nice try. I'm not about to pour out all my worst fears for you to catalog."

He shrugged. "Worth a shot. Perhaps if I knew some of them, I could help you with whatever is blocking you from using your powers properly."

"What do you mean, blocking me? I thought you said the only thing in my way was me."

"I did, and I still think that. It stands to reason that if you have some weird fear, it could be what's holding you back." We stepped aside to let a student with balancing a precarious display pass on the sidewalk, then resumed our way. "At least consider them yourself if you won't tell me. I want to help. You could always start by telling me where you're really from," he prodded with a grin as he opened the library door.

"Are you ever going to let that go?"

"Not likely," he replied, his smile widening.

I rolled my eyes and made my way to the usual table. We could save the lamps for another time. Right now, I wanted the comfort of being surrounded by other students. "Where should we start?" I asked as he unloaded our notes.

He straightened with his hands on his hips and surveyed the stacks of books lining the library. "Honestly? I haven't the faintest idea. We could try to find more information about any Shadow Demons that were around at the time. See if there's a reference to some kind of coalition. Or we could look for the identity of the mysterious child. Then there's the matter of finishing this monstrosity." He rested a hand on the giant gray tomb that made the worn table beneath it look new. "Maybe we should split up?"

"No." I didn't want to leave that book unattended in case it magically found its way back to the shelf. Nor did I want one of us holding it while we were on our own in the stacks. "How about someone stays here to hold the table while the other checks the shelves?"

His eyebrow lifted. "And who's getting stuck with babysitting duty?"

"We'll take turns. You can choose first. Do you want to stay or do you want to go?"

His gaze softened and for a moment, it was like we were the only two people there. "I'll always want to stay, Matt."

"Okay." I was three steps towards the shelves when what he'd said registered. I stumbled and glanced back, but he was already absorbed in sorting the notes we'd accumulated so far. It was strange to think about what we'd become. Even despite all my efforts to keep our private lives private, I still wanted to go back over there and kiss him for his simple statement. He couldn't possibly know how much such a small thing would mean to me. I watched him a little longer, then resumed our quest for answers.

CHAPTER 13

WHAT'S IN A NAME?

A

The door to the dorm clicked softly as it opened and I smiled to myself. Finally, four o'clock. I pushed my homework aside to greet Matt, who'd crossed the room in the scant few seconds it took me to stand. I didn't even say "hello" before he captured me with a toe-curling kiss. Most people could look forward to a noncommittal peck on the cheek or the barest brush of lips when their partner got home, but not with Matt. Every day when he returned from his classes, it was like he hadn't seen me in weeks. You'd never know it had only been a few hours, not even a whole day.

Instinctively, I wrapped my arms around him and he pulled me tighter. Some days the fire burned hotter than others and today was feeling like a scorcher. It felt good to be so wanted. I let myself fall into the feel of his lips against mine. The now familiar ache grew. I wanted more from him, had wanted it for weeks. Barely controlled desire beat relentlessly against the walls I maintained. Eventually, those needs would have to be met, but that was not something we'd ever talked about. Of course, knowing Matt, it wasn't something that *would* ever be talked about either.

Reluctantly, I pulled away, appreciating the tender feel of my lips. "Hi Matt," I said with a wistful sigh.

"Why do you always say it like that?" he asked, tempting me with another kiss.

I forcibly shook off the fog that always seemed to cloud my mind when he was around. "Why do you always kiss me like that?"

"Do you want me to stop?"

"Absolutely not," I said, leaning in with a grin.

He snared me with another kiss that I barely escaped with my senses still intact. Well, mostly intact. My heart gave a happy skip when he trailed his hands down my arms to lace our fingers together. I loved this latest development and even more that he'd been the one to initiate it. He gave my hands a light squeeze and smiled. "Why don't we watch a movie tonight?"

I extricated myself and walked back towards my discarded chair before my desire got the better of me. "Except you don't really like movies. You're only saying that because you're hoping we'll make out."

He pulled up a chair and took out his homework. "I'd be lying if I said it hadn't crossed my mind." I laughed, and he smiled, his eyebrows lifting as he waited for an answer.

"Alright, we can watch a movie tonight." His grin broadened, and I held up a finger. "*If* we finish all of our work."

His face immediately fell into a frown. "You're incorrigible."

"I see we are using our big words today," I teased.

He gave me a playful push. "Shut up and do your homework."

"What does it look like I'm doing?"

"Stalling. Talking. *Not* doing homework. Focus, Alex. We have plans."

I thought about correcting him. *He* had plans. I was just getting dragged into them. Already, he was bent over his notes, intently scratching out what looked to be spell equations. I itched to brush his hair back so I could see his startlingly blue eyes, but restrained myself and set to work.

Literature blurred into Ethics, which morphed into Lit II. I wasn't sure how much time had gone by when I felt something rubbing up and down my leg. Startled, I glanced at Matt. He at least appeared to be absorbed in his latest assignment. I subtly leaned back to peek under the table. Sure enough, he was mindlessly stroking my leg with his foot. What was even more interesting was that at some point, I must have shifted and my foot was doing the same to his ankle.

"So, what do you want to watch?" he asked without looking up, his foot continuing its ceaseless motion.

"Um..." I cleared my throat and quickly shifted my focus.

He looked up. His pen stopped, but not his foot. He blinked innocently. "What?" When I stared blankly at him, he shifted gears. "How about the one where they discover a new layer in the earth? That one looked pretty interesting."

"Sure, that sounds great. I'll order the Chinese."

He gave me one of those smiles that stole my breath and made my heart skip. "No, let me." He pushed his chair back, taking his foot with him. After so much attention, my leg immediately noted the absence. "It doesn't look like you're finished yet," he added, trailing his fingers leisurely across my shoulders as he walked behind me to grab the menu from the usual drawer.

I gave an involuntary shudder that he thankfully didn't seem to notice. I know he thought I played games with him—which, in fairness, I did—but he had no idea what he did to me daily.

"Do you want the chicken and broccoli this time or the lo mien?" he asked, his face scrunched in concentration as he considered the menu.

"What are you having?"

"I think I just want the soup," he said after a moment.

"You always say that and then you eat mine, anyway."

"So, do you want a soup?"

"I'll do the lo mien." I listened to him place the order. Sounded like I'd be sharing again, not that it really bothered me. I laughed to myself and returned to my endless mountain of homework that I'd said we needed to finish first. It was only Thursday, I still had plenty of time. But fair was fair. Yet, try as I might, there was no focusing while Matt was unoccupied. I diligently persisted until the food arrived and then gave up.

Once the table was clear, I grabbed my carton of lo mien and joined him on the couch. He's already set up the movie and was sitting with his legs crossed under him, steadily decimating his soup. "You're adorable, you know that?" I said, taking a seat. He finished slurping a spoonful and hit the lights, but not before I caught the barest makings of a blush.

We continued to eat in silence, then about twenty minutes into the movie, we switched entrees. I finished his soup, and he polished off my lo mien. When we were done, I put the dishes in the sink, then returned to the couch. He'd finally uncrossed his legs, so I took the opportunity to lie down, using his lap as a pillow. The moment I settled, he began absently tracing around my ear and gliding his fingers through my hair.

The movie played on, but I wasn't really paying attention. I shifted so I could look up at him. His fingers simply adjusted their path to trace the features of my face. He wasn't watching the movie either; he was watching me.

I wish I could freeze this moment, capture it in a picture, or a painting, or something.

His finger slid around the curve of my face to follow the outline of my mouth. My heart couldn't seem to decide if it wanted to beat fast or slow or not at all.

I pushed myself up to my elbows, and he met me halfway. The kiss was slow and languid, as if he was trying to draw out every feeling I had. Matt was very good at that. He curled a hand around my head both to support it and so he could kiss me deeper. He tasted like ecstasy, and I wanted more. I shadowed out and rematerialized, kneeling beside him. Surprise replaced his alarm at my sudden disappearance when I captured him in a kiss of my own. He pressed back eagerly, but it still wasn't cutting it. He angled his body towards me, having to move his leg onto the couch to do so. I grabbed his ankle and pulled so that he lay beneath me.

He chuckled as he reached up to pull me down. "You can be really pushy sometimes."

"It's never bothered you before." I caught his arms and moved them over his head.

"Did I sound like I was complaining?" It was likely meant to be teasing, but heat laced the words.

"A little," I said and leaned down to claim his mouth. His return was instant. That ache was growing again. I let it, devouring the kisses he so willingly gave. It still wasn't enough. I pulled back. "Take off your shirt," I commanded breathlessly.

Without a word, he complied, leaning forward and pulling the offending garment off. It barely had time to drop to the floor with a muffled thud before I kissed him hard enough to force his head into the cushions while my hands explored his newly freed torso. Then my mouth followed in their wake, tasting and teasing as I went. This is what I wanted. He let out a moan arching into me. I gave him a light bite, which earned me another delicious groan. I worked my way lower until his hand tangled in my hair. My journey slowed, and I took my time teasing his already quivering stomach with kisses while I palmed his erection through his jeans. How hot would he look with his release painted on his chest?

"Alexi," he moaned.

I snapped up. "What?"

In answer, he grabbed the back of my neck and forced my mouth down to his. The resulting kiss rocked me to my core, and I completely forgot what had distracted me. I slid my arm around his waist, and his body molded to mine. He rocked his hips up, grinding our straining erections against each other. I gasped, and he stole a kiss that snatched the rest of my breath.

There was no way I could keep on like this. We were quickly getting out of hand and my control didn't have near enough concerns about that. Clearly, I wasn't the only one aching for more. But we weren't ready for that, not yet, and I wasn't about to give in without him explicitly saying anything. Nor did I have any intention of coming in my pants, though avoiding that was becoming more impossible with each roll of his hips.

Reluctantly, I retreated from the inferno that was threatening to burn us both. I did what I could to dial it back, adjusting my angle to a slightly less precarious position and focusing on lighter touches. Finally, I got the blaze down to a low simmer.

"You're missing the movie," I whispered between kisses.

"To hell with the movie." He slid his hands beneath my shirt, then glided them along my back and sides. It was almost enough to make me toss what I'd gathered of my control right back into the wind.

I stole my resolve and pulled the cushion off the back of the couch. "Roll on your side." He made to turn, and I stopped him. "Not towards me. Face the screen."

His mouth fell open, and it took him a moment to respond. "You're really going to make me finish watching this?" He gave an exasperated huff, but did it anyway.

Without the cushion, there was just enough space for us to lie side by side. It was a tight fit, but as long as he was okay with that, then so was I. Once we were situated, I snuggled into his back and pressed his ass against my persistent erection. I fought the urge to grind against him, to reach over, unzip his jeans, and finish what we'd started. He shimmied his hips again, getting comfortable, and I smothered a pained moan. I considered telling him to stop moving around, but suspected such an order would have exactly the opposite effect and I wasn't sure how much more of this torture I could take before I completely embarrassed myself. Mercifully, he let out a sigh and stopped moving. I wrapped an arm around him, fanning my fingers across his tight abdomen, and nuzzled into his neck.

"Why did you pick this one?" I asked quietly.

"The ocean is interesting. Also, it has mythical monsters. So that's cool."

I nipped lightly at his neck. "Monster is a misnomer."

"Mythical creatures then."

"You know, *you're* a mythical creature." I blew gently on the tiny hairs at the nape of his neck. He gave a full body shiver, and I immediately regretted it. *I can do this. I can touch Matt without getting totally consumed and losing control.* He relaxed after I laid a trail of kisses on his shoulder.

"I'm nothing special."

"You're very special, Matt. You're smart and funny, sweet, thoughtful, kind of a pain in the ass, but sexy as hell," I said, nibbling his neck some more in direct contrast to my determination to keep the situation and my libido under control.

"You're biased."

"Your point?"

He turned to look at me. His eyes searched my face and for one tiny moment, I thought he was actually going to say he loved me.

When he said nothing at all, I said it for him. "I love you, Matt."

He continued to study my face, then quietly turned back to face the screen. He mercifully settled down without any more squirming, and we finished watching the movie.

When it was done, he followed me into my room, where he ditched his jeans. I tried not to stare at his toned legs or his wonderfully sculpted back as he slid beneath the sheets in nothing more than skin-tight briefs. Apparently, we weren't done spending time together.

I followed suit and joined him, dubious about how this was going to go. Heavy make outs usually accompanied our joint sleeping ventures, and I wasn't sure I'd survive another round tonight. To my surprise, he immediately curled into my side, laying his arm across my chest so that his hand rested over my heart. My hormones certainly didn't appreciate the test of their already strained control, but I also couldn't bear the thought of him moving away.

This was the side of Matt I lived for—even more than the searing kisses and heated looks—moments like this, where he was all mine without reservation. I placed a kiss on his forehead and drifted off, feeling content, albeit wanting.

CHAPTER 14

EXPERIMENTATION

M

I let out a deep breath as I pushed open the door to our dorm room. This was the night. Alex had his weekly tutoring meeting followed by some get together after. He'd be gone for hours or was supposed to be. I wasn't sure how much I trusted that after that other meeting had gotten canceled. Typically, I'd be all for more time with Alex, but tonight I needed him to be out until late-late.

A quick glance around the room didn't reveal any sign of him. No backpack by the door. No neat stack of textbooks on the dining table. Not that I really trusted any of that. I let my shadow senses expand as I dropped my bag and double checked the room, even going so far as to search Alex's room. While I was in there, I couldn't help but dally.

The smell of lavender permeated the air, subtle yet undeniable. I inhaled deeply, letting the soft scent ease the tension in my shoulders. I'd been planning tonight for a while, had gone through painstaking efforts to get everything together. But that didn't magically erase my nerves. A poster of Arminius University caught my eye, and I smirked. Alex really was a bit of a dork. It was one of the things that made him so special.

I trailed my fingers along the comforter Alex had thrown across the bed in a messy semblance of made. It struck me as funny that he was so put together in most things—school, appearance, life—and yet, things like making his bed, putting away his clothes, even cooking eluded him. With a sigh, I left the temptation of the rumpled bed to double-check the bathroom.

Once I was positive Alex was nowhere to be found in the dorm, I headed to my room. In contrast, mine was barren. I didn't have posters or knick-knacks. My bed was made like it was going to be in one of those house magazines. Even my laundry was sparse. Access to a washing machine whenever I needed one wasn't a luxury I'd had before and constantly having clean clothes—without holes—was a treasure I cherished. The only thing even mildly out of place was my set of colored pencils and sketchbooks on the otherwise clear dresser.

I walked to my nightstand and pulled open the drawer. My persistent nerves had me clenching my fists and taking another steadying breath. Putting off this little experiment I had planned wouldn't be hard; I'd already put it off twice. But then I doubted I'd get a better opportunity than this. With a sharp nod, I tossed the bottle of lube onto the bed and grabbed the anal douche, grateful I'd thought to read the directions for the strange bulb before tossing them, then made my way to the bathroom.

After scrubbing every inch of my body within an inch of life and *finally* gathering the courage to use the douche, I was as ready as I was ever going to get. But first, I wanted to do another sweep of the dorm. The last thing I needed was Alex showing up in the middle of everything. I wrapped a towel around my waist and repeated the same sweep I had earlier. Still no Alex. I let out a relieved breath and returned to my room, where the bottle of lube seemed to stare at me from the bed. I turned off the overhead light, then laid down.

This didn't have to be weird. People did this all the time. *Guys* did this. Liked it. Maybe I would too. I grabbed the bottle from beside me, removed the safety seal, then put a liberal amount on my fingers. Start slow, that's all I needed to do. One baby step at a time. Despite the pep talk, I continued to lie there frozen.

"Maybe smaller steps," I mumbled to myself. I swallowed thickly and closed my eyes. It didn't take long for my thoughts to wander to Alex, specifically our last date. The way he'd pressed me into the couch and teased my torso with hot kisses. Within seconds of reliving the memory, I was hard and aching. I trailed my fingers down my chest until they tickled my happy trail. I bit my bottom lip as I took hold of myself like I'd wanted Alex to do that night.

The familiar fantasy that it was his hand instead of mine came to life. I'd wanted Alex to touch me before, but once he had, I craved it. Needed it. No matter how I looked at it, I couldn't understand why he kept backing off. I'd thought for sure we'd go farther the other night, but just like all the other times I encouraged him, he pulled away.

What am I doing wrong?

The doubt crept in, killing my erection. I blew out a hard breath. Whatever it was, I could fix it and this was the first step to proving to Alex that I was ready for more. I brought the fantasy back up, focusing on what *had* happened instead of what hadn't. When it felt like I could blow at any second, I reached for the lube again and switched hands. My left hand now on my shaft, I let my right drift lower, spreading my legs wider and pulling my knees up to reach better.

Anxiety fluttered in my chest and I paused right as I reached the tense muscle of my hole. Maybe I was wrong and I *couldn't* do this. Just because I wanted to try, was curious even, didn't mean I could actually go through with it. I squeezed my eyes tighter and continued to slowly stroke my dick in an effort to calm myself down. Finally, I convinced my hand to move again. I got as far as circling twice, then stalled out at pressing deeper.

I flopped my head back against the pillow. I felt like a fucking contortionist and a coward. How did I know I didn't like a thing if I'd never tried it? "Ugh. This would be so much easier with Alex."

I took a second to imagine what that would be like. If it was Alex hovering over me, melting me with kisses, and guiding me. He could be one bossy fucker, but I'd be lying if I said I didn't eat that shit up. Everything was easier when he told me what to do. I trusted him more than I'd ever trusted anyone in my life. He made me feel safe, cared for...loved. He'd tell me exactly what to do and I wouldn't have to over think this, I could simply experience. I let out a deep breath and forced myself to relax as I fell deeper into the conjured image.

Alex placed kisses along my neck, working his way with agonizing slowness to my mouth. Meanwhile, my hand slid up and down my shaft with the same measured strokes he'd used before. "*That's it,*" he purred in my ear. "*Nice and easy.*" He hummed appreciatively. Or maybe that was me. "*Good. Now circle that tight hole.*"

I bit back a whimper and did as he said.

"*Slowly, my love. We're not in any hurry. There, just like that.*" He placed an open-mouthed kiss on my chest, and I moaned. The finger on my rim was slick and not bad. I had no idea the muscle could be so sensitive. Before I realized it, I'd already pushed the first knuckle of my middle finger inside.

Panic seized my lungs, but I quickly squashed it down, imagining Alex on top of me, conquering my mouth while he slid his finger inside.

"Oh." Surprise briefly took me out of the fantasy. Damn, it was hot in there.

"*Deeper,*" Alex ordered, his emerald eyes intense. I complied, and he captured my mouth. "*Do you want more?*"

"Yes," I gasped, the fantasy twisting into a weird combination of imagining it was his long fingers and him telling me what to do.

"Slide in and out. Slowly."

It took a few tries and more lube, but eventually I managed a smooth glide that definitely wasn't all bad. I might even go so far as to say it was nice. My poor dick ached for more friction than I was giving it, but I was too focused on my ass to give it the attention it deserved. I let out a moan as I picked up the pace. This wasn't a terrible start, but Alex was bigger than one finger.

"Get on your knees with a pillow below you."

I didn't question it, my brain too fogged with fantasy and my body too keyed up. Once I was situated, I released a loud groan at the friction the pillow provided. It wasn't much, but it was better than I'd been managing. This time, when I pressed my finger against my hole, it slipped inside with almost no resistance.

I was on the verge of release when Alex whispered, *"Now another."*

Considering how close I was and how good this already felt, that sounded like a fantastic idea. Shame my body had other ideas. I added yet more lube and slowly worked in the extra digit. The stretch was more than I expected and took me a little off guard, as did the slight burn that accompanied it.

"Almost there," Alex crooned, and I imagined his hands caressing my back while he traced my shoulder with kisses.

Finally, I had both inside. I resumed the steady glide, letting the natural rock of my hips set the pace. In a surprising amount of time, I was back at the edge and panting into the pillow beneath me that I'd never be able to look at the same way again.

"Alex," I groaned as my movements got jerkier. "Oh fuck. Alex. Alexi." I cried his name as my ass clenched and I came all over the pillow. With a shudder, I removed my fingers and collapsed into the mess. Once the haze of orgasm thinned, I let out a breath of air that might have been a laugh. I'd done it. I'd actually done it. And I could absolutely do it again. I also needed another shower.

CHAPTER 15

SAGE WISDOM

A

Mariah clapped her hands together. "I'm calling it. Meeting adjourned. Time to par-tay!" Her tight red curls swished around her dark mahogany face as she did a little dance on the table.

"Hey!" Rubio shouted as he walked back into the room, not sounding the least bit upset. "I step out for one minute and come back to pure anarchy." He threw his hands out in an exaggerated pose, then gestured at me. "Come on, Lexi, you've got my back."

"Pft. I'm with Mariah on this one." I could certainly use a night out. Much as I loved spending time with Matt, I needed time with other friends. Maybe it would help clear my head.

"Damn right you are." She did another little dance, this one decidedly more victorious. "Lina! Give me a hand!" The exuberant sphinx held out her hands, still doing some happy shimmying.

Lina, our newest member and a jinn, laughed and stepped close to the table to help Mariah down. Her bright turquoise hijab offset her golden skin, which seemed to glow as she reached up. Once more, I was tempted to ask where she'd gotten the fabric. It would look incredible on Matt.

I mentally shook my head. Tonight was about hanging with my tutoring group, *not* thinking about Matt. I finished packing my things in time to catch the soft look that passed between Mariah and Lina. We were all pretty sure something was going on there, but no one wanted to be the first to say something. Not that fellow tutors dating would be an issue. The two were just so adorably sweet around each other, it was almost too much.

A spike of envy stabbed through me. Why couldn't Matt and I have that? Was it me? Had I somehow pushed him too far despite all my efforts not to? Was I just... not enough?

You never were.

I hadn't heard my ex's voice in my head in months. Daniel's derisive intrusion put my teeth on edge and I growled as I savagely pushed it back into the dark where it belonged.

"Yo, I didn't think you disliked bars like that."

I looked up to find Rubio watching me with a startled expression and realized I'd made that angry sound out loud. "Uh, no. I don't mind bars. I was just..." I scrambled for a believable excuse that didn't involve baring yet more of my insecurities to the infinitely confident incubus. "Frustrated with my notes not going into my bag properly."

His gaze narrowed as it flicked between my seamlessly aligned books and me. "Uh-huh. Come on, first beer is on me." He glanced at me as I shouldered the evidence of my blatant lie. "You drink beer, right? If not, I'll grab you a *cock*tail."

I snorted at the horrific pun.

"Maybe a Sex on the Beach? Or a Juicy Screw? Ooh, I know! How about a Dick Sucker?"

"Enough, enough," I squeezed out through side-splitting laughter. "A beer is fine. But I wouldn't mind it being a little... fruity." I wiggled my eyebrows to show I could play this silly game, too.

"Ha!" Semyon barked as he walked past us. "I knew I liked you, Alexei," he said, pronouncing my name more like its Russian counterpart. "You don't let Rubio get away with nothing." He shook his head, freeing bits of straw to float to the ground. Even after working with the man for months, I still couldn't get my head around his hair literally being made of straw, but apparently that was common for Polevoi.

Rubio waved away Semyon's snark, and we fell in with the rest of the team. While I might have grown up exposed to supernaturals—thanks again, Mom—nothing could have prepared me for the sheer variety I'd encountered at Arminius. Half the ones I'd believed were children's stories and legends were actually real. While ones I'd been whole-heartedly convinced must exist *somewhere* were not, or at least, no one could find proof of existence.

Shadow Demons were like that, I mused as we meandered our way off campus. We didn't exist for the longest time. Then, suddenly, we did, and we always had. Hell, our Battle Tactics class had fifteen people in it. Well, ten now. Didn't change that it was hard to prove something when you couldn't find it. I sincerely hoped that those that had left the class and the university eventually returned. I didn't want our kind to disappear into obscurity again.

That line of thought brought me back to Matt and what we were still referring to as "the research project". How were we supposed to prove there'd been a war, an attempted genocide, if we couldn't find verifiable evidence?

"Someone's lost in their thoughts." Rubio clapped a hand on my shoulder.

I offered him a weak smile. "Sorry. Were you saying something?"

"Just that if you didn't already know, you should definitely avoid Le Breuvage Sorcière." He pointed out a hole in the wall joint that blended effortlessly with the surrounding shops.

"Why?"

"Because it's a witch hangout."

I frowned, not following the logic at all. "Why would that matter?"

"Because you're a demon—a rare one—and some reputations have been *earned*." Rubio's normally jovial eyes took on a steely glint. "Summoning might be banned and while the Shadows have made their stance very clear, not much impedes an enterprising witch."

I swallowed hard. I'd never had any experience with being summoned by a witch before, but I'd heard the stories. Judging by Rubio's demeanor, the uglier bits of those stories held more truth than I'd given credence.

Like someone had flipped a switch, Rubio was back to his bright, charismatic self. "Anyway, here we are!" He threw out his arm with a grand flourish.

I took in the neon sign, blinking in intermittent flashes of red, orange, and yellow, as well as the hodgepodge of guests flowing casually in and out. Judging by the crowd, the Topaz Lounge wasn't purely supernatural and equally patronized by the locals. "Have you been here before?"

"A few times. Place is an absolute gem," Rubio said, raising his voice to be heard as we made our way inside with the rest of our group. "It's got a pretty relaxed vibe, but the best part is that they only play vinyl and they have a dance floor."

"Woo!" Semyon and Rikka shouted as they made a beeline for the modest dance floor already cluttered with dancers.

I laughed at their exuberance and followed the others to a set of couches and tables. Before I could sit, Rubio touched my arm and leaned in.

"Come with me to the bar. I promised you a drink."

"You really don't have to."

Rubio hooked my arm. "Sure I do."

We wove our way to the bar and took a seat at the counter. Rubio flagged the bartender who signaled he'd be a few minutes in getting to us. I'd just settled onto the bar stool when Rubio turned to me.

"Alright, spill."

"I don't know what you mean." I fiddled with a coaster a previous occupant had left behind.

He placed a hand on my arm, and I glanced at him. "Hey, we're friends, right?"

"Of course."

His gaze sharpened. "Good, then I don't need to sugarcoat that you still smell like frustration."

"Rubio," I hissed, my gaze flitting between the various people around us that were definitely human locals.

"Don't 'Rubio' me. What's really the issue? I take it things have not really improved with Matt."

I shifted beneath his unwavering gaze. "They have... And they haven't." My shoulders slumped, and I rested my elbows on the counter. "He's definitely more willing to engage—only in the dorm, mind you—but he still hesitates. I don't know what to do. Is it me? Maybe Matt's just not that into me. My ex was right." I groaned and massaged my temple. "I'll never be enough for someone. You've seen Matt. Why the hell would he choose me?"

"Whoa!"

Rubio's abrupt response snapped me out of my spiral. "What?"

"First off, you can stop that negative self-talk shit right there. As your friend, I won't hear it. And as someone who would be more than willing to date the fuck out of you, it's not even remotely true. Second, did your shitty ex really say that to you?"

My cheeks burned with embarrassment. Normally, I was better about not vomiting my insecurities all over my friends. "Not in exactly those words."

"Well, whatever words he used, they're utter bullshit." Rubio's indignation seemed to roll off of him in waves. "As for your roommate, I've seen the way he looks at you. I've also seen the way he looks at me when I'm with you. Your boy is battling some major jealousy."

I snorted. "Not likely. Why would he?"

"Maybe because you're not the only one dealing with insecurities." He lifted a golden brow. "You may not see it, Alexi, but you are hot as sin. If he's not as enthusiastic as you would like, try asking yourself if there's a reason he's not sharing. You know, kind of like someone else."

The heat on my face seeped beneath my collar. "Easy for you to say. Getting laid for you is as easy as thinking about it." Rubio's face darkened, and I immediately regretted lashing out. "Shit. I'm sorry. That was way out of line."

He held up a hand. "No, I get it. You think I don't know how people see me? Sex is my nature, not something I chose. Hell, half the time it doesn't even feel optional or within my control. But just because I *can* get laid whenever I want, doesn't mean it offers me any kind of fulfillment. I envy you and Matt in a lot of ways."

"Why?"

Rubio's features finally softened. "Because at least you can trust that what you have is real. You may not see it, but Matt is completely wrapped around your little finger. That man would move heaven and earth if it would make you happy."

"You really think so?"

"I *know* so. I wish I could have that kind of certainty with my own partners. Being an incubus isn't all it's cracked up to be. Sure, the sex is phenomenal, but I never know when a connection is to me or what I am."

"Wow, I never thought about it that way."

He shrugged. "Most don't."

The bartender finally got around to us, giving me a few minutes to sift through my thoughts. Rubio seemed so certain about Matt's attraction, his feelings. If it was so obvious, why couldn't I see it? What was really holding him back? A beer dripping with condensation slid in front of me. I couldn't help but smile as I noticed the label on the bottle.

"What's got you grinning?" Rubio bumped my shoulder and my smile widened.

I brought the beer to my lips, savoring the first sip as it filled my mouth with flavor, a distinct undercurrent of fruity notes. "Matt got me this beer when he asked me to tutor him. It was the first drink we ever shared."

"Sounds like someone knows you."

I plucked at the label, working hard to hang onto that optimism. "Yeah, I guess so. While you're dishing out all this wisdom, mind if I ask for a little more?"

"Lay it on me." He took a swallow from his bottle and gave me his full attention.

"If Matt really is that into me, then why... Why won't he be with me outside of our dorm?" I finished, voice soft. "He doesn't... doesn't *act* like he's ashamed or anything, but he also doesn't act like he does when we're alone."

Rubio set his beer down. "That's tough, man. It's possible he's uncomfortable with PDA."

"Yeah, but it feels like more than that. He doesn't have a problem acting like we're friends. He still has zero concept of personal space. I guess you could say the vibe is off. He... shies away?" I looked askance at Rubio, really hoping he had some insight to share.

He considered his drink for a long moment, rolling the bottle between his palms. "I hesitate to say this, because I don't really know the guy, but is it possible he's dealing with past trauma? Like you have your issues because of your shitty ass ex. He could have something similar. Or entirely different." He shrugged and took a drink. "All I know is that in my experience, when people's behavior is inconsistent with what they say or feel, trauma is usually involved."

I stared ahead, catching my reflection in the mirror placed behind the bottles of liquor on display. Matt was such a private person, and I knew for a fact there were at least a couple of things about his past that he hadn't shared with me. I figured he'd get around to it when he was ready, but I'd never considered it could be trauma related. Finally, I took another drink to clear the unexpected thickness in my throat. "Thanks. That, uh, that really helps."

"Anytime." He clinked his bottle against mine. "Now what do you say we rejoin the others?" It was only then that I noticed he'd already gotten us fresh beers.

"You said only one beer."

"Eh," he hiked a shoulder, "you can get the next round."

I finished my current bottle with a chuckle, then grabbed the new cold one and followed him to where the others had started some kind of party game that looked like more laughing than any actual game I recognized.

Hours later, my body was exhausted from laughing and dancing, but my mind was still ruminating over everything Rubio had said. Talking to Matt was always a tricky endeavor, especially since he wasn't overly keen on volunteering information about himself. I was torn between taking the persistence approach where I kept asking or encouraging him to open up.

I opened the door to our dorm room and closed it as quietly as I could, not wanting to wake Matt so late in the evening. Of course, it was for naught. I turned from setting my things down to find Matt standing in his doorway, pajamas askew and a glorious case of bed head.

"Hey," he said sleepily. "Have a good time?"

"Yeah," I replied just as softly. "What did you get up to?"

His face flushed, but that also could have been a trick of the light considering the entire room was only lit by the undermount light from the kitchen. "Nothing. Stayed in."

I wanted to run my fingers through his hair and give him a sweet goodnight kiss, but also knew my breath would smell like beer and didn't want to come across as a hypocrite. Instead, I opted for a sincere smile. "Go back to sleep. I'll tell you all about it in the morning."

He rolled his shoulders and seemed like he wanted to say something, but all that came out was, "Okay." He turned to go back inside, but paused and looked over his shoulder. "Goodnight, Alex."

I smiled again. "Sweet dreams, Matt." There was definitely no mistaking his blush this time or the way he scurried into his room. Chuckling to myself, I fixed a glass of water and did the same.

CHAPTER 16

ORPHAN MATT

M

"There's nothing here," I said, closing the current dead end. We'd exhausted every demon history that even vaguely mentioned Shadow Demons and nothing. Forget finding snippets about the Wardes or the War on Darkness, we couldn't even find general sightings of our kind. Back in the day, Shadow Demons weren't considered rare, so where the hell were we? "You'd think we were made up. There aren't even allusions to our abilities, understated or otherwise."

"There has to be something," he said, echoing my frustration as he turned another page in the massive anthology. The pool of magical light instantly began transforming the words and reviving a faded picture to what was likely its original, rich color. "Look at this."

I leaned in to get a better view of the illustration. The yellow light made a tiny circle, so being able to see meant getting close enough that Alex's lavender scent wafted around me. Heat curled in my chest. It was getting harder not to touch him in public. It was getting harder not to touch him, period. As it was, I wanted to slide my hand along his thigh and feel him lean into me. It certainly would have been more comfortable considering our cramped seating at the tiny table. I let out a steadying breath. There was hardly a soul up here. No one would know if I placed a small kiss on the curve of his neck.

"Look familiar?" At the sound of his voice, I snapped out of it. He was going to be the end of me.

"What am I looking at?" I asked, trying to focus. There was a grizzled older man with a small boy standing next to him. Unrealistically, the pint-sized child was holding a broad sword easily twice his size.

"Don't you see the resemblance? Matt, that kid looks just like you."

I frowned at the image. "No, he doesn't."

"Come on, you can't tell me that isn't exactly what you looked like as a toddler. Just look at those eyes."

With a resigned sigh, I did as he asked. Sure enough, they painted the eyes a bright blue, but that didn't mean anything. Lots of people had blue eyes and painters exaggerated. "Maybe, but I don't actually know what I looked like when I was that little," I admitted, leaning back in my seat. The nearness of him was wreaking havoc on my concentration and I needed to be alert in case I felt those eyes watching us again.

"What do you mean? I'm sure if we compared it to a picture of you—"

"There aren't any pictures," I cut him off.

Alex floundered for a second, but didn't relent. "That sounds like an exaggeration. Surely there are a couple out there. I bet you were an adorable baby," he teased, poking me in the ribs.

I shifted away from him and glared straight ahead. "Trust me, there aren't. Just drop it, okay?"

"How could you possibly be so sure?" he scoffed. "Was there a fire or something?" His concern was the final straw.

"Because no one wants to take pictures of an orphan," I snapped.

"What?" The single word was barely a whisper, but it still sounded like a gong to my ears.

"You want to know where I come from?" I growled, turning on him. "Nowhere. I don't know who my parents were or why they didn't want me." The second the words left my mouth, I squeezed my eyes shut, if only to hide Alex's expression of shock. I willed time to go backwards, so I could hold my temper better and keep the traitorous confession from ever spilling out.

"Oh, Matt," Alex said, his voice soft with sympathy... and pity. I'd never wanted that from him. The contents of my stomach rolled, threatening to crawl their way up my throat.

"Told you you'd look at me differently if you knew the truth." I slid my chair back hard enough to make it screech and stood, not even bothering to gather my notes. The half-empty bag bounced on my back as I slung it over my shoulder and turned to leave.

Alex reached out lightning fast to stop me. "Matt, wait."

I looked down at where he had hold of my hand. Even with anger roaring through me, I had to consciously stop myself from squeezing it. My gaze rose to meet his. There was so much sadness in his eyes, I couldn't stand it. Whatever he saw in mine, he let go. His fingers slid from mine like the last drop of rain to splash into nothing on dry ground. That hurt almost as much as the way he was looking at me.

I shadowed across the room and walked out of the library. It was done. Alex officially knew everything about me. Nothing would ever be the same. All the things that I loved about our friendship and...and everything else was over. It wouldn't matter how he tried, he'd never be able to look past the pitiful orphan that no one loved. The pain in my chest welled up, threatening to drown me. He knew, and it was all my fault. I'd ruined everything.

I wandered around the campus until my feet were too tired to keep getting lost. Not that it helped. My head didn't clear, the hurt didn't ease, and I still didn't know what to say to Alex after blurting the truth I'd worked so hard to keep hidden. What *could* I say? I'd been so worried about the *world* taking him from me it had never occurred to *me I'd* be the one to take him from myself. If I'd had it my way, he never would have known that I'd literally been abandoned since birth.

Even after hours of wracking my brain about what to do, I was no closer to an answer. Was it even possible to undo the damage I'd done? Or was this it? Alex would lose interest in the loveless boy and move on. The semester would be over before we knew it. He or I could easily switch dorms at that point. It wasn't anything he hadn't suggested doing before.

I fought for breath as my chest constricted, each more painful than the one before. My steps slowed, and I stared up at Starling Hall, a sharp sting in my eyes. Walking into the restricted section was easier than voluntarily walking away from Alex. I teetered closer to completely falling apart. Deep down, I'd always known this was inevitable and that it had been stupid to expect anything else. People like me didn't get to have nice things. There was no way I could ever actually keep Alex. One way or another, he'd be gone. If years of being bounced around had taught me anything, it was that no one ever stayed. All that was left was to face the music.

Maybe it would be easier if I left before he had the chance. I could talk to Vera, see about transferring before the end of term. As much as it pained me to give up any extra time I might have with him, I didn't think I could take months of that pitying look. With a determination I didn't feel, I made my way to our dorm. A tiny voice inside said that Alex would be worried by now. A much louder one said it didn't matter; he'd be over me soon enough.

Alex immediately looked up from the breakfast table as I walked in. Notes and several other books lay scattered around him. He could have been doing homework for all I knew. That's what I got for thinking he might be worried.

I shrugged off my pack, letting it slide to the floor with a thump I felt in my stomach, and closed the door. When I looked back up, he was standing.

Here goes nothing. Just need to stay focused. Say what I have to say and get to my room.

I pushed past the lump in my throat and stepped deeper into the room. "Don't worry about trying to pretend like everything is fine. We both know it's not. I've got Vera's information somewhere. I'm... I'm going to see what I can do about getting transferred to another room."

"What? Why?"

I closed my eyes like it could block out the questions. "Because I... I can't take you looking at me like that until the term is over." The ache in my chest intensified, causing the words to come out tighter than I would have liked.

This is already so much harder than I expected. I'm never going to make it to my room.

"How am I looking at you, Matt?"

Against my better judgment, I met his gaze. He was looking at me like he always did. That wouldn't last though, not now that he knew how worthless I really was. I dropped my attention to the floor, not trusting myself to speak.

"I told you before, it doesn't matter to me where you come from. I just wish you'd trusted me enough to tell me sooner," he added, walking forward. My feet refused to obey my silent commands for them to move, so I was still standing in the same spot when he stopped in front of me. "You're still you. You're still Matt. That hasn't changed. *You* haven't changed."

I shook my head, still keeping my gaze locked on the carpet. "You're just saying that because you feel bad. No one has wanted me since the day I drew breath. Why should now be any different?"

"Ma—"

I cut him off, snapping my head up to meet his startled expression and slicing my hand through the air. "Don't. You can say whatever you want now, but I. Know. Better. *Everything* will change. You may not mean it too, but it will. It always does. You'll realize what everyone else realized, that I'm no one."

"I have *never* thought you were no one."

"Alex, just don't." The pain was so much worse than anything I'd endured in the ring. Cutting off a limb would hurt less. "I... I... can't..."

"Matt."

"You don't understand." The stinging in my eyes returned.

"Matt," he said again with more force.

"You'll never understand," I hiccupped.

"Matt, shut up and just let me love you," he demanded, and dragged me into the cocoon of his arms.

I tried to resist, but the more I fought, the harder he held me, until I finally sagged against him in defeat. I didn't want to fight Alex. I'd give anything for his words to be true, to believe that my past didn't matter, didn't define me. But history said otherwise. Too many times I'd let my hopes build, only to have them smashed.

"We don't have to talk about it if you don't want to," he said softly as the kiss he placed on my neck.

I wrapped my arms tentatively around him, fear holding me back from griping him just as tightly.

"It's okay to hurt," he whispered.

That's exactly what the pain in my chest felt like, a big ball of hurt. I finally squeezed him back and let the damn break. Soul-crushing sobs tore through me with the mercy of a tidal wave while I held onto him, the only stable thing I'd ever had in my life.

He rubbed my back in a steady motion until the flood subsided. "There's nothing you could do or be that would ever make me stop loving you." He didn't complain about the fact that I was probably close to cracking his ribs or that his shirt was now wet. He let me stay just as I was until I was ready to let go.

I buried my face in his shoulder and clung tighter. I needed those words to be true. I didn't want a life without Alex in it. "I'm sorry," I mumbled when I finally released my death hold on him.

"There's nothing to be sorry for," he replied, calmly wiping the remaining tears from my face.

I blinked at him with heavy lashes and chose to believe the sincerity in his emerald eyes. How was it possible to care about one person so much? Before Alex, I wasn't sure if I'd ever truly cared about anyone before. I took a step back and awkwardly wiped my snotty face with my t-shirt. He remained quiet while I took my time pulling myself back together. When I no longer felt like I'd burst into tears again, I took a deep breath and glimpsed the table behind Alex.

"What's all that?"

He didn't need to turn to know what I was asking about. "I found something." That got my attention. "Come here, I'll show you." He grabbed my hand without waiting for a response and led me to the table.

When we sat down, I shifted so that I was still touching him and laced our fingers to keep his hand captive. He didn't comment beyond giving my fingers a light squeeze.

"Here, you'll need these." He passed me the spectacles I'd acquired from the witch in my Advanced Spells class.

I struggled to put them on with my left hand, but refused to release my hold on his hand in order to use my right. "What?" I asked when I realized he was staring at me.

"You really do look hot in those." The heat of his words shone in his eyes and a matching heat burned on my cheeks.

"Shut up. What am I supposed to be reading?"

He gave an exaggerated eye roll and slid over *Volume Six,* which was already opened to a section. "Start here and tell me what you think."

While I took my time reading, he rested his head on my shoulder. The familiar move helped dispel the last of the tension hanging on to me. Halfway through the selection he'd indicated, I looked over at him in disbelief.

He smiled knowingly. "It gets better."

I returned to the page and kept reading. Eventually, the information was too much, and I had to stop. I sat back, which also had the unfortunate side effect that he stopped laying on me.

"I know." His smile was definitely more smirk-like now.

"That's... That's a detailed description of the opposing forces. It's... it's everyone." Try as I might, I couldn't wrap my head around the sheer enormity of it. "All the different classes. I had no idea there were so many. I've never even heard of some of those. And the generals... the commanders...."

"They're all Shadow Demons of the highest ranking. No one is below a level ten."

"How does no one know about this? There should be records everywhere. This wasn't some skirmish fought repeatedly over a century. It's an all-out war between humans and demonkind."

"Told you it got better."

"The commander, the one in charge of scouts—Sop- Soap- Sop-ti-something."

"Sopteală?"

"That's the one. I've seen that name before." I released his hand and practically fell across the table to reach a notebook. The cover fell open to reveal the name of its owner. Once it had read Alexi Roman, now it proudly proclaimed to belong to *Alexi & Matt Roman*. For a moment, I forgot what I was doing. I hadn't realized what that would look like when I'd so brazenly added my name to Alex's notebook. An unexpected warmth along with a light fluttering filled my chest. I shook it off and flipped through to the page I needed. "There," I said, pointing to my notes about Matthias. "That was the name of his demon lover. If she was in charge of scouting parties, then that would explain his first entry."

Alex's eyes went round as the ramifications sank in. "That would mean she literally knew him his entire life."

I peered at the ancient history that had already provided so many clues. "You don't suppose there's any mention of that in there, do you?"

"I don't see how there couldn't be. Matthias Warde was literally sleeping with the enemy. Someone was bound to notice eventually."

"I wonder who caught them," I said at the same time Alex said, "I wonder how it started." We shared a look, then burst into laughter, bringing a reprieve from the earlier seriousness.

As the laughter subsided, I shifted my hand to caress his thigh and glanced up to see his stunning eyes staring back, completely absent the pity I'd expected.

"I love you, Matt."

My heart felt like it might burst. I wanted to tell him the same, but didn't know how. For lack of words, I leaned forward and kissed him. What I couldn't express in words, I could this way. I was Alex's for as long as he'd have me.

CHAPTER 17

ADVANCED SPELLS

A

It broke my heart to learn that Matt was an orphan, and it made me even sadder to realize he'd never intended for me to know. His issues with authority, the anger, his quiet nature, why he didn't like to talk about his past certainly made a lot more sense now. But knowing the truth didn't change how I felt about him. If anything, it helped me understand him better. Matt wasn't a private person by choice; it was by necessity.

How many times over the years had he had his heart broken? Demons did not do well in foster systems unless someone specially placed them. To think, he'd only known about being a demon two weeks before arriving at Arminius University. I couldn't even begin to imagine the pain he must have gone through as family after family rejected this strange child they could never hope to understand.

More than anything, I felt like a total jerk for threatening to leave all those months ago. I had a pretty good idea what he'd likely faced when he ventured into the restricted section. Matt could take anything, and had proved it more than once. What he was most afraid of, was being alone, being abandoned yet again. That was why he always looked at me like he was surprised I'd returned and why he kissed me like he might never see me again. It would take time, repeatedly showing up, to convince him I wasn't going anywhere.

I loved Matt with every fiber of my being and could feel that love growing every day. Every instinct in me wanted to take away the hurt he kept bottled inside, but to do that, I needed to understand him, how he grew up. Not prying into his childhood would be difficult. Either way, pushing him to share would likely only result in pushing him away.

"He'll open up in time," I told my reflection in the bathroom mirror. Until then, I refused to behave any differently than I had before I knew the truth. I squared my shoulders, strengthened my resolve, then left to join him.

When I walked into the living space, he was sitting on the couch studying something with intense concentration, hair still wet from his own shower and looking sinfully attractive as he worried at his bottom lip. Had I ever been so attracted to someone in my entire life? Anytime I saw him, I had to remind my heart to beat. Even him sitting there innocently reading was enough to make it stutter.

On an impulse, I moved behind to stand behind him and massaged the back of his neck. He immediately let out an appreciative sigh that bordered on a moan. I bit back a chuckle. It amazed me how he responded to things and I was positive half the time he literally had no idea how those reactions came across—it was part of his charm. I peered over his shoulder to see what held his focus. To my surprise, it wasn't *Volume Six*.

"What are you working on?" I asked, digging a little deeper and making him groan.

"A shadow spell."

"Oh? What's it supposed to do?" I worked my way out to his shoulders, kneading the knots of muscles, and was rewarded with another inaudible sigh.

"It's *supposed* to cloak a portal from other Shadow Demons—since we're the only ones who could see it anyway—but so far, all I'm getting is a faint shimmer."

"Portal. That sounds like third year studies. And since when is your class book in calligraphy?"

He shifted beneath my hands, which had gone still. "This isn't the class book. The grad student sitting-in lent it to me."

"Why would a TA loan you a vintage grimoire?" I asked, because what else could it be? "You must have made quite the impression on him." First spelled glasses, now a book easily worth both our weights in gold? No one was *that* generous without an ulterior motive.

Matt reached back and squeezed my hand as if he could sense my thoughts. "She's a fifth-year witch who's studying under Professor Hallow. I think Vera was involved somehow."

I pulled my hand free and stepped away. "Why would the Dean of Witch Studies have anything to do with Vera?"

He tilted his head back to look at me, a wrinkle between his furrowed brows. "Because the dean is Kyra Hallow, as in Kyra Hallow of the Shadows. Pretty sure Vera knows she's still not my favorite person after the ordeal with the hotel. Makes sense she'd get someone else to do her dirty work."

"Vera taking a personal interest in you isn't surprising, though how she's going about it is questionable. "

"Still don't see why," he scoffed, closing the frustrating book and tossing it on the coffee table.

"Because, Matt," I walked around the couch to face him, "you're a level seven. Aside from her, you're probably the strongest Shadow Demon to manifest in ages."

"Fat lot of good it does me. I can't even get this stupid spell to work."

I crossed my arms and raised an eyebrow. "You mean a highly advanced spell that most third years probably wouldn't be able to do? That one?"

He gave me a crooked smile. "Yeah, that one."

"Walk me through it." I plopped down beside him, causing the cushion to bounce.

"Do I have to?"

I bumped his shoulder. "It's obviously bothering you. I promise to make it worth your while."

He raised an intrigued eyebrow. "When you put it like that... Okay, but we'll have to start with a portal."

I shook my head, unable to suppress my smile.

"What?"

"You're incredible. You're sitting here bemoaning that you can't do a cloaking spell and, in the same breath, you just casually mention you have to make a portal first. Like it's no big deal. I've been practicing with manipulating shadow for years and *I* still don't know how to make a portal. I'm not even sure I can."

His frown bordered on a pout. "Of course you can. I'll show you. Give me your hand."

More than a little dubious of how he planned to "show me", I offered my hand.

Matt stroked down the length of my arm before grabbing my wrist. My heart did its usual putter at the touch. I expected to see a mischievous smile, but found focused sincerity.

"Feel for the shadow world. You're looking for where this world meets that one. Got it?"

I nodded. Sensing the shadow world was easy, I'd been doing for as long as I could remember.

"Now, you're going to reach into it just enough to break the barrier without actually crossing over. Don't worry about not having an anchor on the other side. You don't need one for this."

"Where's your anchor?" I asked absently while I did as he said. I had little doubt that he would have been playing with portals without creating both sides.

He turned to look at me. For a moment his eyes searched mine, then he returned his attention to where rippling shadow surrounded my hand. "The anchor is in the freezer."

"The freezer?"

He shrugged. "How else do you think I get your ice cream so fast when you're in one of your moods?"

"I don't have moods."

He snorted, sparing me a derisive look before returning his attention to the ripple of shadow. "Focus, or you're going to lose it. Now, exert your will into the circle so that it'll sustain itself and stay open."

"Uh... That sounds hard." We'd already sailed way past the things I knew how to do. Matt may believe I was better at all things shadow, but he was the real savant.

He smiled at me enthusiastically. "Not for a nine." He stared intently at the pool of shadow, then declared, "You've got it."

I wasn't a hundred percent what I'd done, but I definitely felt the breach solidify. Curious, I stuck my hand in and it didn't reappear on the other side. "Huh."

"Okay, now for the spell to hide it." He retrieved the book and held it open for me on the same page he'd been agonizing over. "Go slow. The spell doesn't need speed, but it requires pronunciation. It may take a few tries before you're comfortable with all the words. Place your hand over the portal you've made, but don't touch it. If you do, then the cloak will be on the other side. Then we definitely won't know if it worked."

I nodded, still not convinced I could do any of what he said. Before attempting to pronounce anything, I read the lines several times. When I felt confident enough to try it, the words sounded like shadows slipping past my lips and tasted of smoke. The air shimmered faintly beneath my palm, then... Nothing. I let out a disappointed breath. "So much for thinking I could do it when you couldn't."

"Did you drop the portal?" He squinted, then scowled. "I could have sworn you had it stable. We'll just have to start over." He shifted the book out of the way to retake my hand.

I looked from him to the portal, floating exactly where I'd left it. "What are you talking about? It's right there."

Now he looked really confused. "No, it's not. One second it was, then it wasn't. It must have collapsed. That's fine. It was your first go."

"Give me your hand." He begrudgingly placed his hand in mine, then I slowly pushed his hand through the portal.

Understanding illuminated his face. "You did it!"

"I suspect you did, too. The spell doesn't hide it from the *creator*, it hides it from everyone else."

He quickly summoned his own portal and repeated the spell. Some of his inflection could use work, but the moment he was done, the portal winked out of existence. He looked at me for confirmation.

"I don't sense anything." Matt's smile could have conquered the world. It had certainly already conquered my heart. I extended my essence and collapsed my cloaked portal. Without waiting to see if he'd do the same, I leaned forward and kissed him on the cheek.

He blindly swiped at the air and turned to me. His lips met mine and the rest of the world disappeared. I cradled his neck and urged him deeper. He certainly didn't feel tense now. He slid an arm around me and pulled me closer until I was practically on top of him.

Unbelievably, the kisses stayed slow and purposeful, a steady burn versus the blinding inferno. The smell of sage enveloped me as I kissed and nipped along his neck, adding flicks of my tongue to soothe any pain. He let out a groan, which only encouraged me. His breathing turned ragged and I could feel his heart racing beneath his shirt.

"Alex."

"Hmm?" I inquired noncommittally while I continued to taste his skin. His sigh certainly sounded like he was enjoying it.

"I need more. I… want more."

I pulled back to look at him. Where I expected to find his gaze darkened to midnight with lust, I found the blue crystal without so much as a stray cloud of doubt. Was he really saying what I thought he was saying?

He cupped my face, then gave me a kiss that had my heart stuttering. "I want you, Alex."

I was too shocked to breathe. I stood and pulled him up after me, catching him with a bruising kiss. "Are you sure?" I didn't want to jinx it, but I needed to know. Needed him to say it.

"Hell, yes," he said, wrapping me in a kiss that burned away any lingering doubts.

He's going to incinerate me right here.

I pulled away after giving him a slightly more chaste kiss, then grabbed his hand and led him to my room. My heart pounded so hard, I couldn't think straight. I released him by the bed and yanked open the nightstand drawer. After a few moments of digging, I only came up with lube, which I tossed it on the bed. "Um, give me a minute?"

He seemed a little confused, but nodded. "Of course."

I scrambled into the bathroom, where I promptly fell against the closed door. Sweet mother of midnight, we were actually going to have sex. *Finally.* The thought alone had me tenting my pants. Now all I had to do was find some fucking condoms. I nearly let out a triumphant shout when I found a pack under the sink along with another essential. Trusting Matt to be patient, I freshened up. Then, after a deep breath that did nothing to calm my errant pulse, exited the bathroom.

"You're going to want these." I placed the string of foil wrapped condoms in his hand and gestured at the thankfully full bottle of lubricant. "And a lot of that. No such thing as too much lube."

His mouth twitched like he was fighting a laugh. "This isn't exactly my first time."

"Have you done this exactly?"

The almost smile vanished. "No."

"Then forgive me if I care about my body."

"Your—" He cut himself off, though it took a moment for the confusion on his face to fade. He stared at the condoms in his hand, then placed them on the bed. "I understand."

Before I could press my point, he captured me with a slow kiss that sent tendrils of desire curling through me. I was way past wanting Matt. I needed him on a level I couldn't begin to comprehend. He slipped his fingers beneath my shirt, trailing them up my torso until my shirt was so bunched, he had to pull it over my head. I reached for my pants' button, but Matt gently waved my hand to the side and guided me to lie on the bed. The cool sheets against my back had me gasping while he decorated my chest and quivering stomach like he was trying to map my body with his lips. By the time he released my erection, I was floating in a sea of ecstasy.

"Don't forget the—" The reminder about the lube died as he licked my dick from base to tip with the flat of his tongue. I dropped my head back with a moan, getting lost in the incredible heat of his mouth. Then his hands were back, gently caressing my calves and tickling the fine hairs on my legs. When he straightened to remove his clothes, I felt like I'd had a full pitcher of that sweet concoction he'd made last semester.

Finally, he crawled on the bed to join me, repositioning us in the middle. I cradled his face while he bestowed sensual kisses that threatened my grasp of reality. Then a slick finger brushed my entrance, and I released a pained moan that bordered on a whine. I'd expected to have to walk him through prepping me, but he didn't need any guidance as he slowly stretched me with deliberate movements. By the time he slid inside, there wasn't even a hint of a burn, only pleasure tingling in every cell of my body. Even then, he continued to move like we had all the time in the world, combining tender kisses with soft caresses and long thrusts. One thing was for certain: I'd never had a lover as thoughtful or sweet as Matt.

I hummed contentedly, tracing the contours of Matt's back while he peppered my chest and shoulders with light kisses. His lips drifted lower, and I laughed, feeling lighter than I had in months, maybe years. There was no chance of going back now, though I doubted there ever had been. My heart and soul belonged to Matt, without a doubt.

"What are you doing?" I asked playfully, tilting his head up to taste his lips.

"I told you. I want you."

I laughed again and ran my fingers through his hair. "You have me. Though I wouldn't be opposed to another tumble," I added with a wicked smile.

He licked his lips and swallowed. "That's not... I mean..."

I sat up fully and held the side of his face, worry killing the last of my afterglow. The sex had been incredible for me, but maybe it hadn't been for him. "What?"

"I want... I want you to top me," he finished in a rush, his cheeks burning a dark pink. "Is that the right term?"

Swallowing suddenly became impossible. "Yeah," I croaked. "But, Matt, this isn't... You don't have to bottom if you don't want to."

"I know." His blush darkened until it reached the tips of his ears. Despite his embarrassment, his voice gained strength as he continued. "I'm... curious. I want to know what it's like. With you."

Oh.

"If you're sure..."

"I'm sure," he said at the same time he tackled me back to the mattress and captured my mouth in a searing kiss I felt to my toes.

It took an effort, but I pushed him back. "Would you like a few minutes to... um..." How did I ask this delicately? "Freshen up?"

He shook his head, already leaning down for another kiss. "No need."

I dodged his lips, and he made a noise of frustration when they landed on my cheek. "Matt, I really think—"

"I already did." He laid a trail of kisses down my neck. "Grabbed those too." He gestured at a new box of condoms sitting on the night-stand. "Since you're bigger than me."

"When did you..." I trailed off as I recalled that he'd taken an exor-bitant amount of time retrieving water earlier. "You're really serious about this."

"Why wouldn't I be?" He stared at me without blinking, then doubt crumpled his face and he retreated. "Unless you don't... If you're not interested..."

I quickly reached for him before he could decide to shadow away. "I'm interested. Very interested."

A tentative smile lit his face. "Yeah?"

"Oh yeah. It's just... been awhile since I wasn't expected to bottom."

His face darkened again, this time with malevolence. "Your ex better pray we never meet."

I laughed, taking him off guard, and cupped his face with both hands. "You, my love, are an absolute treasure. We can try this, but you have to promise me, if you decide at any point, you don't like it, you'll tell me." He nodded, and I shifted my hands to grip his chin. "I mean it, Matt. Promise me."

"I promise," he whispered.

I brushed my lips over his and gave him a gentle push. "Lay back and try to relax. I want to make you feel good."

"I know you will."

The trust in Matt's eyes nearly undid me. Fortifying my nerves, I grabbed the supplies, noting with surprise that he'd sprung for the high-end barely-there condoms, and placed them close by. Then I layered his body with kisses until he was writhing with impatience.

"Alex," he moaned, as I slowly stroked his erection.

"I just want to make sure you're relaxed."

"I'm relaxed," he gasped, hands and feet digging into the mattress.

Not entirely convinced, I put a liberal amount of lube on my fingers and situated myself between his legs. I couldn't even remember the last time I'd topped, but it didn't diminish how keyed-up I was to be doing it now. "You're sure?"

"Sure. Very sure."

I spread his cheeks and placed a slick finger on his rim. He released a hiss that turned into a little moan as I circled the sensitive muscle. I took my time working in a finger. When I could slide with no resistance, I pushed deeper, getting lost in the tight heat.

"Fuck."

I went stiller than if I'd just come face to face with a gorgon. "What? Is something wrong?"

He arched his back, causing my buried finger to glide again, and released a deep groan. "Why does that feel so much better when you do it?"

I blinked a couple times, not sure if I'd heard him right. "Wait. You've... On yourself?"

He lifted his head, revealing pupils blown wide. "Of course. I wanted to make sure you knew I was serious."

All other thought fled as I imagined Matt fingering himself and thinking of me. "How many?" I asked, voice suddenly raw.

"Huh?"

"How many fingers?"

"Two," he confessed, just shy of sheepish.

I nearly choked on my surprise. He was going to be the death of me. Banishing the filthy images that had sprung to mind in favor of the one in front of me, I pulled myself together. "We'll need a little more than two." I resumed moving my hand and his eyelids fluttered. "You'll tell me if it's too much?"

"Yeah. Yes," he repeated clearer.

By the time I had him sufficiently stretched, Matt was clawing at the sheets and I wasn't sure if I'd even make it inside of him before I blew. Doing my best to avoid his hungry gaze, I rolled on the condom, added more lube, and lined up with his clenching hole. I pressed his knees closer to his chest and worked my way in with shallow thrusts, then had to stop or risk exploding. He felt so good. His body was a tight vice of the most delectable heat.

Matt made a noise that sounded suspiciously like a whine. "Move already," he groaned so hard I felt the vibrations.

I slid nearly all the way out and slammed back in. Once. Twice.

He bowed off the bed. "Yes. More."

All the control I worked so hard to maintain shattered. I recaptured his mouth with a ferocity that surprised me. There was only his body and mine. There was nothing gentle about the way I rode him to a chorus of panting moans. Any hope of regaining some semblance of restraint vanished when he wrapped his legs around me, his heels urging me deeper. Then he tightened around me to the point of pain. I struggled to remain coherent as I came hard enough to see stars.

I collapsed on top of him, devouring his mouth, though I had zero air to spare. Not that he seemed to mind, given how his hands roved over my body like he could pull me inside forever. Then round two became round three, and I stopped counting.

I disintegrated into exhaustion, rolling away to stare at the ceiling. When my breathing and heart rate returned to normal, guilt sprouted. I'd behaved like some kind of depraved animal. I wasn't sure when I'd stopped checking in or when I'd started manhandling him into different positions, each one somehow better than the last. Anxious, I glanced over at him. He was the picture of sedation, his head pillowed on his arms with a dreamy smile.

I rolled onto my side and kissed his shoulder. Decency evaded before, but I could try to make up for it now. "Come on."

"Pretty sure I did. A few times," he added with a chuckle.

"Very funny."

He smirked and burrowed deeper into the mattress with a contented sigh. "I thought so."

"Get up. We're taking a bath." I stood and stretched.

He let out a groan of put upon despair. When I looked back to encourage him, hunger once more shone in his eyes. It was almost enough to get my blood going again. I mentally shook myself.

Care first, more later.

"You heard me."

He continued to bellyache, but got up. "I don't want to take a bath. I don't even like baths."

I snared him with a kiss, and he melted into me. With a force of will, I checked the heat I could feel building. The word insatiable came to mind, but I wasn't sure which one of us it applied to. "You'll thank me later."

He gave me a look. Explaining to him that this had nothing to do with believing that he couldn't handle this and everything to do with taking care of him was pointless. He would do it, because I told him to, even if he whined about it the whole time. Just in case, I grabbed his hand and led him to the bathroom. I filled the tub with steaming water and got in.

"Now you."

He eyed the steaming water. "Maybe I'll get the next one. It's a small tub."

"Matt."

"Alright, alright," he said, then carefully stepped in. He leaned back into me and the hot water immediately did its work, every muscle relaxed.

"See, not so bad," I said after a while. When no quippy comeback was forthcoming, I shifted to look at his face.

Of course, he's completely passed out.

Ever so slowly, I shadowed, careful not to let him slide further into the water. Once I was dry, I leaned down to scoop him out, for once grateful for demonic strength. With the help of some manipulated shadow, I got him back into the bed, then returned to drain the tub.

When I was done, I slid in beside him and brushed back the hair that had dried on his face. As if by reflex, he reached out to wrap his arm around my waist. I relaxed into the possessive embrace and drifted off, watching my perfect angel sleep.

CHAPTER 18

UNEVEN GROUND

M

When I woke, Alex filled my vision. Warmth filled my chest, along with happy flutters. Damn, he was beautiful. With those pronounced cheekbones, slender nose, and complexion most people would kill for, he was more art than mortal. I resisted the urge to trace his features, kiss him awake. It was rare for him not to be up first, buzzing around teasing me for wanting to sleep the day away. I ached to touch him, but he'd earned the right to catch a few extra Zs.

My stomach growled, and I checked to make sure the sound hadn't disturbed him. Reluctantly, I shadowed out of bed. I grabbed some sweats, not really sure who they belonged to. They fit well enough and that's all that mattered. Rather than risk the door creaking, I shadowed directly to the kitchen, where I searched for something more substantial than cereal. When it turned out we had everything to make egg sandwiches, I felt like I'd struck gold.

Humming to myself, I pulled out a mixing bowl and set a pan on the small stove. The eggs gave a satisfying sizzle when they touched the heated surface, and my stomach growled again.

"What are you doing?"

I chuckled to myself—so much for worrying about the door—and turned to look at Alex. Like myself, he hadn't bothered with a shirt. My heart stuttered as I took in his lean frame and ridiculous waist. Nyx, he was stunning. He must not have seen a mirror yet, though, because his hair was everywhere. I tried not to laugh. No matter how much he messed with it, it never seemed to do any good. Suddenly, I realized he was still waiting for an answer.

"I'm making breakfast. I don't know about you, but I'm hungry."

"I didn't know you could cook." He rubbed his arm, then joined me in the kitchen, his usual air of confidence notably absent.

Anxiety shot through me. Had I done something wrong? He'd called me out last night. He was right. I'd never done anything like that before. What if I'd messed up somehow or didn't do something right? I tried to squash the insecurity, but it lingered like a gnat buzzing in my ear.

"They're just eggs. Not too complicated." I gave a casual shrug to hide the fear now ricocheting inside.

"How are you feeling?" he asked, his voice betraying a note of anxiety.

I shifted the eggs so they wouldn't burn. "I'm fine."

"Are sure? I just wanted... You might be..."

I removed the eggs from the burner and killed the heat. I could finish the toast in a moment. This clearly needed to be handled first. "Would you stop asking me if I'm okay?"

He looked like he was about to ask again, anyway. What was he so nervous about? I'd *asked* for this.

"I'm good. I promise. No tenderness or anything."

"But I—"

I stepped in close, rubbing my hands along his arms. "If anything, I should ask how *you* are feeling." His eyebrows scrunched together, and I ran my fingers through his messy hair. "Seemed like you needed that more than I did."

He swallowed and looked away. "I'm sorry."

"Why? I'm not." I offered him a crooked smile. I was about as far from sorry as you could get. "So, how *do* you feel?"

Finally, he cracked a smile of his own. "I feel great, Matt."

"Good." I stretched to give him a sweet kiss, but my small kiss good morning got lost in the sweeping command of his own.

There's my confident Alex.

"I've wanted that for so long," he said between kisses that were already stoking the fire inside.

I leaned into him, enjoying the way his arms wrapped possessively around me. "I could tell."

"Shut up." He laughed and kissed me hard enough that I stumbled backward and nearly sat on the table. The resulting twinge had me second guessing my optimism of not being sore. Maybe a marathon of killer sex was not the *best* way to see if I liked bottoming.

"I can't believe I'm saying this, but probably best to wait at least a short while," I said with another kiss.

He smiled, lighting my world more than the sun ever had. "Of course." He pulled me tight and the feel of the table disappeared.

I molded against him, melting into the embrace and getting lost in the way his tongue swept along mine. It'd be so easy to suggest going back to bed, which was not at all conducive to waiting. I pulled away, though it was possibly the last thing I wanted to do. "The eggs are getting cold."

"How can I help?"

"Start the toast? I'll warm up the eggs and get the plates." I hated giving him the instructions, because it meant he let me go. I wanted to stay lost in those kisses, to feel his touch everywhere. After last night, I'd have thought the inferno that burned inside would have diminished at least slightly but, it felt closer to the surface than ever. I reigned in the fire and tried to focus. Once we finished eating, we sat in companionable silence while Alex finished his coffee.

He peered at me over the rim as he took a sip. "What would you like to do today?"

"Honestly? I'd be happy just spending it with you."

His eyes widened, and his cup hovered at his lips. I wasn't sure why that surprised him. I always wanted to spend time with him. That wasn't new.

"We could go into town," I suggested.

He gave me a smile that made me feel tingly all over. "In that case, we should probably clean up."

"That reminds me." I couldn't believe I was actually about to ask this. "Did I fall asleep in the tub?"

His smile got bigger. "Yes, and it was *not* easy getting you out."

"In fairness, I told you I didn't need a bath."

He walked around the table to grab my plate. As he reached forward, he placed a small kiss on the curve of my neck and I gave an involuntary sigh. "Thought you said you weren't sore," he whispered in my ear.

"Oh," I squeaked, grateful he was behind me and couldn't see my face burning. "Right, so, getting ready."

"I said get cleaned up."

I turned to face him and prayed my face wasn't scarlet. "What do you mean?"

"I'm going to take a shower. You're welcome to join me," he said with a perfectly straight face. Alex could give people lessons in maintaining a poker face.

His casual invitation effectively obliterated all of my efforts to rein in my blush. "But we already took a bath."

"Sitting in scalding water hardly counts as getting clean." He waved a dismissive hand as he walked toward his room.

I continued to sit there at a total loss. A shower together was about as far from waiting as we could get.

He stopped in the doorway and turned back to me. "Are you coming?" His eyebrow lifted, giving the question a more commanding tone.

All the moisture in my mouth vanished and my heart started doing double time while my ass remained glued to the chair.

"It is possible to just take a shower, Matt."

I seriously doubted that, especially where he was concerned. Still, his words finally got my feet moving. I drifted after him, feeling like he'd caught me in some kind of spell. When I arrived in the bathroom, he'd already stripped down and was adjusting the water. He turned around and caught me blatantly staring.

His emerald eyes flashed. "I thought we talked about watching."

Yep, we did and you pointing that out is not helping. There is no way I can do this.

He tested the water temperature, but didn't get in.

"Just a shower, right?"

"Sure." He stepped under the cascade. That sounded dubious at best and the polar opposite of convincing. He gave me a look that fell somewhere between curious and commanding.

I swallowed thickly. If I didn't hurry, he was bound to make another crack about watching. Quickly, I ditched the sweats and stepped in, keeping my back to him. Maybe if I couldn't see him, I'd survive this.

Get a grip. It's not like this is the first time you've ever taken a shower with Alex. Except not much cleaning had happened then either.

My pep talk was not helping. If anything, it was making matters worse. Then Alex's hand slide around my waist and I about near jumped out of my skin.

"You know, for someone who says they're fine, you're awful jumpy." He chuckled and removed his hand. "I told you, just a shower."

I turned to fuss at him for messing with me, but the words never stood a chance. Before I could open my mouth, Alex captured me with a kiss. Barely suppressed desire roared to life. I kissed him back and groaned when his fingers dug into my hips.

Just as suddenly as he'd caught me, he released me, giving me probably the sexiest smile ever seen by demonkind. "Just a shower, right?"

"Damn you, Alex," I said breathlessly. We both knew I was his to do with as he pleased. Apparently, I was his personal plaything this morning.

"Turn around," he ordered.

I immediately obeyed.

"Pass me the soap."

My heart hammered loud enough that it eclipsed the spray hitting the tub and probably could be heard in the dorm next door. "What are you going to do?" His laugh tickled my ear, reaffirming my belief that he was definitely toying with me.

"I'm going to wash your back. You asked for just a shower, so that's exactly what I'm going to give you."

"For the record, I never asked for this shower," I said over my shoulder.

"Didn't you? At any rate, you made it very clear that is all it would be," he said as he worked the soap into a lather.

I barely didn't gasp when his hands glided across my shoulders. I squeezed my eyes shut as if it could somehow dull the ecstasy of sensation.

Sweet merciful Night, he won't need to do anything else. The feel of his hands alone is threatening to undo me.

Right when I thought I wouldn't be able to take a second more without turning into a puddle, the touch vanished to be replaced by a waterfall of hot water.

"Your turn."

I turned to face him in disbelief, and the growing suspicion that this was some kind of payback. I flashed to daring Alex to do a body shot.

He held up the soap like a challenge. "You don't have to if you don't want to."

I glared at him before snatching the soap, and he turned around to reveal the perfect canvas of his back. A whimper caught in my throat. Alex knew I had problems touching him, namely that I couldn't seem to stop once I started.

Unsurprisingly, the second I touched his skin, I got totally lost in the feel of him beneath my hands. The soap became a medium in which to paint the contours of his body. He sighed, though it sounded more like a moan.

What is it about being touched that feels so special? Is it because, as Shadow Demons, a good part of our essence is technically intangible and touch creates a connection to the physical plane?

Abruptly, I realized I wasn't washing his back anymore. In my musings, my hands had wandered around to his chest and now he was leaning against me. My senses clearly already having fled, I bent to kiss his neck, earning another sigh. "You are absolutely impossible," I whispered, my lips brushing against his smooth skin.

"What else?"

"Far too attractive for your own good."

He snickered. "That so?"

"Yeah, that's so." Thanks to entirely too much soap, he easily spun within my arms and I found myself looking into an emerald that seemed to define the color.

"I love you, Matt." The following kiss seemed to devour everything I still couldn't find the words to tell him. I got lost in the world that was Alex. He could have whatever he wanted from me; I'd never stop him. "I think we're clean enough. Don't you?" he asked, nipping at my swollen lips.

"You're a regular comedian," I said, stealing another kiss for good measure.

"I'm glad you think so."

"Does this mean we are or aren't going to town?"

"Definitely going," he replied a little too quickly.

I gave him a cheeky smile, finally feeling like I was getting the upper hand for a change. "Alex, are you afraid to be alone in the dorm with me?"

"I don't know if afraid is quite what I would say."

"And what *would* you say?"

"That you're right, and we should wait. If we stay here, that won't happen." He cleared his throat, no doubt realizing that his words were having the opposite effect of getting us to leave. "Go get dressed, Matt."

"Are you sure that's what you really want?" I purred.

"Matt, please, just go." His breathing had turned into pants and I could see my desire reflected in his eyes.

Rather than argue, I shadowed to my room, creating a sizable puddle where I landed. There wasn't a doubt in my mind that he was still standing in the shower, trying to pull himself back together. I was tempted to shadow back and see for myself, but if I did that, we wouldn't leave at all.

See, Alex, you're not the only one who can play games.

CHAPTER 19

MORBID CURIOSITY

A

I never could have imagined how easy being in love with my best friend would be... Or how difficult. Making love to Matt was a life-defining experience. The way we fit together made me realize how incompatible I'd been with previous boyfriends. We'd all but perfected the art of silent communication in the bedroom, easily reading the other's needs. If only that same understanding extended beyond the physical... and beyond the dorm.

A series of giggles caught my attention, and I glanced over to find the latest couple to have entered the coffee shop. Envy that I struggled to keep in check blossomed in my chest at seeing the way the couple leaned into each other, doting smiles, and laced fingers. They probably took for granted that they could hold their partner's hand in public and be obnoxiously cute. Of course, I doubted their bedroom passions could hold a candle to mine. I smiled to myself as I drank my fresh cup. Night Matt's hands. Half the time I felt like an instrument and he knew all the right notes. Like last night. The way he'd...

"What are you thinking about?" Matt's hallmark angelic expression accompanied the unexpected question, making me wonder for the thousandth time if he could secretly read my mind.

My sip went down the wrong way and ended coming partially up my nose. Man that burned. He casually passed me a napkin, his face still deceptively neutral. "What do you think I'm thinking about?" I asked, stalling for time.

"Obviously not about swallowing."

My choking fit returned with a vengeance, while the barest hint of a smile played at the corner of his mouth. How anyone could buy that affected look of innocence was beyond me. Matt could be an evil imp whenever the fancy struck him.

I need to get a handle on this before it turns into one long series of innuendos that ends with me needing a healer.

"Tell me about your childhood." Matt's smile vanished and I could have kicked myself. Much as I wanted to know about his past, bluntly asking wasn't the way to go about it. Already his jaw had tensed and his shoulders might as well have been carved from stone. Before I could utter an apology, though, he started talking.

"I was literally a baby—maybe a couple months old—when they found me on the steps of a Catholic church in Norfolk, Nebraska. No note, no explanation. I don't remember the name of the place, just that I wasn't there very long. Makes sense now that it didn't last." I could definitely see how a demon baby in a Catholic church might not go over very well. "Anyway, after a brief stint there, I got sent to my first orphanage."

"First?"

"I've been in eight." He spared me a quick glance, then returned his attention to his almost empty cup and forgotten muffin.

I schooled my shock. Eight was downright obscene.

"I was five when they placed me with my first foster family. They were really nice until I started having fits. I don't know what started them, but no family wants to put up with a toddler that goes off the rails at regular intervals and has fainting spells. At least not one they can send back. So they did." Matt let out a long breath, his shoulders pulling closer together as he hunched in on himself. "The next family wasn't so nice. They thought they could beat it out of me. That didn't go over so well. I was stronger than they expected for a child and I broke his arm. That was the first time I ran away," he added, his muffin turning to crumbs beneath his fingers. My heart broke into pieces, much like Matt's dry muffin. Rejected, passed around, beaten—no wonder he was so reserved.

"When did the fighting start?" I asked.

He looked up at the ceiling. "Let's see, after I broke Mr. Jefferson's arm, I got branded as violent. They like to keep those kinds of kids together. Which doesn't make a damn bit of sense. That's like asking for trouble, which is exactly what they got. Lewis was the first kid I ever hit... on purpose. I was seven and in Lincoln by then."

"I thought you said Omaha."

"When I exhausted the orphanages with room, I got shipped to a neighboring city. Anyway, Lewis had been on my case for months. I don't know what about me bothered him so much, but I was definitely his personal punching bag. I did everything I could think of to avoid him. Even told an adult. That was an epic mistake." Matt rolled his eyes and his lip curled in a silent snarl. "Not only did they not help, but Lewis beat me to a pulp for being a snitch. As much as I didn't want to get moved again—it got worse every time—I finally couldn't take it anymore. One day when he went to hit me, I got out of the way in time. He didn't even realize I'd moved until my fist slammed into his face. That's when I figured out how fast I could be. I didn't have to get hit if I didn't want to."

"Sounds like your true nature was trying to manifest."

"Wish I'd known that then. Certainly would have made some of those fights easier. After Lewis, they became a blur of faces. My repu-tation seemed to precede me, and at each new place, the self-appointed top dogs sought me out. I did what I could not to provoke them, not that it ever did any good. As I got older, the kids got meaner... and bigger while I stayed on the small side."

Understanding from our initial meeting dawned. "That's why you started weight training."

He nodded. "Figured if I could hit them hard enough they never thought to retaliate, I'd be golden. But even when I won, it didn't end. There was always a fresh set to take their place. I was the only thing that ever stayed." His voice hitched, a veil of anguish casting a shadow over his face. "I ran away at least a dozen more times... or tried to. They always caught me. Longest I stayed on the street was a month before I got picked up in an alley in Omaha. They took me to a halfway house and then almost immediately turned around and shipped me to Superno House. I wasn't even there twelve hours before I got dragged outside by four of the strangest things I'd ever seen." He paused, and I wondered if I should say something. Did I ask what Superno House was? From the Latin I knew, it was obviously a home for supernaturals. "Sometimes, I wonder what would have happened to Oliver—a fire demon—if Vera hadn't shown up when she did. I wonder what would have happened to me," he added, playing with the empty cup again.

The defeat in his voice wounded my soul. This was the world that my beautiful Matthew had come from. My Matthew, who loved to smile and laugh, who was wicked smart and funny, who didn't think he was attractive, and believed in fairness to a fault. I ached to kiss him, hold him, tell him that all of that was in the past. He didn't have to fight for the right to be alive anymore; he deserved to be happy. I placed my hand on the table near where he was still holding the empty cup. I knew the unspoken rule. Much as I longed to touch him, to reassure him I'd never leave, never abandon him, I couldn't. Not here.

"All that matters is that you're here now. Vera did come, and she brought you to—" I wanted to say "me", that she brought you to me, instead I said, "The school where you could learn what made you unique."

Matt didn't respond, just sat there staring at my hand, my fingers less than an inch from his own. He released his cup, causing it to slide a short distance and leaving his hand on the table beside mine. Electricity arced between the hair's breadth of distance. The battle of whether to accept the comfort I'd extended or not warred on his face. A few heartbeats went by in silence, then he curled his fingers inward.

My heart sank. Forget envying other couple's ability to display affection publicly, I just wanted to comfort my boyfriend. He deserved to have that comfort, to be told constantly how much he was loved. A sudden shock rippled through my finger and I glanced down to discover Matt had reopened his hand and closed the fraction of the distance. The touch was nothing more than our fingertips grazing, but it was touch. I'd take the win. In a stroke of inspiration, I shadowed his hair back from his face. The move was light enough that it could have easily been a breeze from the door. Yet he looked up, snaring me with indescribably sad eyes.

"Anyway, enough about me." He withdrew his hand to resume picking at the crumbling mass that used to be a muffin. "What about you? Tell me about growing up in the UK. I know you at least grew up with your mom." He gave a half smile, no doubt recalling having spoken to her briefly himself.

"Okay," I began and leaned back, painfully aware of the distance between us. "I never knew my dad, and that's fine with me. I'm not sure I want to know anyone who could do what he did to my mom. She was completely devoted to him and he still left her all alone and pregnant. So, it was just me and her. But I couldn't ask for a better mother. You'll have to meet her sometime."

"I'd like that," he said quietly, staring into his empty cup again.

"Things weren't always easy, though. I know people think I've had a charmed childhood, but she worked really hard to give us a good life. It's difficult being a single mom in this world, especially with me as a son."

He snorted. "I refuse to believe you were some sort of terror growing up."

"I was a terror in other ways," I said with a playful grin. Something flashed in his eyes, but he said nothing. "What else? I've never been in a fight aside from the time I tried to get Kyle Stanton to stop pulling on Karla Lott's hair."

"What happened? Did the teacher yell at you?" he teased, clearly not believing I'd ever been in trouble a day in my life.

"No, she did."

He laughed. "You sure you're not a knight? You seem to have a habit of coming to the rescue."

"I do not ride around rescuing people," I huffed.

"Sure you do," he said warmly as the last of the ice thawed from his eyes.

"Are you telling the stories, or am I?"

He held up his hands in surrender and gestured for me to go on.

"It wasn't until I was nine that my mom told me about my dad."

"Why did she wait so long?"

"I think it was really hard for her. She loved him. What's worse, she started by telling me I looked just like him." My sigh ruffled the napkin beneath my cup. "It can't be easy looking at someone every day that reminds you of the person you loved most. Honestly, if I hadn't been in the picture, I wonder if she'd have continued on at all. She talks about him like he was the greatest love of her life."

"Do you believe in that?"

"I believe in forever." I traced the pattern on my mug while I wrestled with the resentment that typically sprouted when I spoke about my father. "He must have loved her back at least a little, because he told her what he was. Good thing too. I started manifesting early. Not as early as you apparently, but enough that she needed to take measures to keep us safe. We moved a few times until she found a place with a near enough supernatural community that I could get exposure to both worlds. Before that, I'd never met another supernatural. I might have been a little too eager."

Matt's lips twisted like he was fighting back a grin.

"Shut up."

"I didn't say anything." His suppressed grin broke free, and he laughed.

"You were thinking it."

"What was I thinking, Alex?" That was a double-edged question, and I was not about to dignify it with an answer.

"At any rate, it was awesome meeting all of those people, or it was until they found out I was a Shadow Demon. Then they started avoiding me like I caused the war, not some faceless demon none of them had ever met."

"How long have you known?"

"I mean, I guess forever. But my mom really helped with that because she knew what to look for."

"Not that."

I frowned, not following. Then I realized he was staring at the spot our hands had touched. "Also, pretty much forever." I was about to launch into how there were so many other sexualities besides gay or straight when he cut off my train of thought.

"Tell me about what's his face."

"Daniel?" I instantly regretted saying the name out loud.

A darkness passed behind Matt's eyes and his jaw tightened.

"I'd rather not talk about him. There are some betrayals you don't forgive." Matt knew very well that Daniel had cheated on me. "If you really must know, he's a narcissistic jerk and a bully," I finished hotly.

Matt's eyes widened before his gaze dropped to the massacred remains of his muffin and his shoulders caved inward.

Guilt itched beneath my skin. Of course, Matt would be curious about my ex. "I'm sorry. I shouldn't have snapped. It's just, he was never much of a friend and he made me feel weak. Ironic, considering he's only human."

Matt looked up sharply. "You're not weak. You're one of the strongest people I've ever met." The force of his words took me aback. I didn't realize Matt thought so highly of me.

"Let's get out of here before you break that muffin down to the molecular level." I indicated the pathetic remains of his half-eaten breakfast.

He chuckled and dusted his hands. "You're right, we should head back."

We both disposed of our trash before making our way back to the dorm. As we walked, we talked about the town and classes. Despite pointedly veering away from anything too heavy, I couldn't shake the feeling that our conversation at the coffeehouse was still bothering him. To be fair, it was still bothering me. I didn't like the idea of Matt comparing himself to my ex.

My thoughts must have been showing, because as we walked up to our door Matt asked, "Are you alright? You seem upset."

I glanced down the hall to make sure no one was around, then grabbed his wrist and shadowed both of us through the door. He was still holding his key ready when we appeared on the other side.

"Whoa, that was different," he said before I pressed him against the door, claiming his mouth with a hunger that had turned acute when I'd shadowed us. His key clattered heavily on the floor. Then his hands were on me, sliding beneath my shirt, clawing at my back, pulling me closer.

"You are nothing like Daniel. You're warm and tender and caring," I said between kisses. "I didn't know it was possible to love someone as much as I love you." He may not be willing to say it back, but his body responded with an alarming passion at the confession. There was a need in Matt that I'd happily spend the rest of my life trying to fulfill.

I yanked him away from the door and dragged him toward my room, shedding our clothes along the way. We slammed into the closed door, panting for breath, while I fumbled for the knob. Then we were stumbling to the bed, mindlessly bumping into anything and everything. The nightstand shook when we landed on the bed, bringing me out of my stupor long enough to grab supplies. Matt pulled me back for more devouring kisses, his tongue sweeping boldly into my mouth while his hands branded my skin.

I tangled my fingers in his hair and pulled his head back, not remotely surprised to find his eyes solid black with lust. Mine likely looked the same. "Top or bottom," I asked, my voice so husky it was nearly a growl.

"Bottom," he panted, without an ounce of hesitation.

I mashed our mouths back together, nipping at his lips before venturing across his jaw and down his neck. His resulting groan spurred me on and in seconds, I had lubed fingers pressing against his hole. He released a strangled whine that turned into a deep moan when I slipped inside and intentionally rubbed his prostate. "Damn, you're tight," I said through gritted teeth, adding another finger.

Matt clawed at my shoulders, bringing me closer until we met in another bruising kiss. He attacked my lips with a ferocity I echoed in my core while I continued to stretch him. Then he was gasping for air and shoving a condom at me.

I rocked back on my heels and held his gaze as I rolled it on. "Touch yourself," I ordered as I positioned myself at his entrance.

Gazes still locked, he wrapped a hand around his erection and stroked firmly. His back bowed off the bed as I thrust in one long drive, but he didn't release his hold. He managed a few faltering strokes before I removed his hand to lace our fingers and laid over him. Completely in sync, Matt wrapped his legs tightly around me while I relentlessly drove into him. Sweat glistened on both our chests, our breaths came in ragged gulps, and we still kept snatching at each other's lips.

Matt convulsed, and the warmth of his release surged between us. His ass clenched in time with his orgasm, and my ungodly pace faltered. I rammed into him a final time, then went still as my own ecstasy crested. I gave a couple half-hearted thrusts as I rode out the wave, then sagged on top of him. Rather than complain at the undoubtedly uncomfortable position, he peppered my sweat coated shoulders with kisses.

Once I'd caught my breath, I retrieved an abandoned shirt from the floor to clean us up. No longer sticky, we curled up, facing each other. "I think we might have a problem," I said jokingly as I brushed his gloriously mussed hair from his face.

His smile twinkled in his eyes. "Who says it's a problem?"

I chuckled and dropped my hand to the mattress between us. "Touche."

His hand joined mine, fingers intertwining. He lifted our joined hands to place a kiss on the back of mine. "Thank you."

"For what?"

"For being you."

I caressed his face with my free hand, heart melting. "Matt, I am more myself with you than I have ever been in my entire life." I leaned in to kiss him and to add weight to the words. He met me halfway, kissing me back, slow and deep. "I love you," I whispered against his lips. His only response was to hold me tighter and kiss me deeper.

CHAPTER 20

MYSTERY IN THE STACKS

M

One of these days I was going to have to figure out how to tell Alex how I felt. Eventually he'd ask, and I had no clue what I was going to say. Unsurprisingly, that led me to the library. Much as I worried about being watched, it didn't change that I needed room to think and I seemed to do that best here. Maybe it was the quiet. Or perhaps it was the soft light. Could be that books didn't judge, didn't care who I was or where I came from.

My mind wandered as I trailed my fingers over spotless and dusty spines alike. For all that I hadn't wanted Alex to know about my past, I should have known better than to assume he'd reject me over it. But then, a lifetime of being told you were worthless, of having anything you held dear taken from you, didn't vanish overnight. I reached the end of the current stack and sighed before aimlessly wandering to the next.

It *was* nice to learn a little more about him. I was never sure how to ask people about themselves when I wasn't interested in reciprocating. Luckily, Alex didn't have that problem. I wondered if he was serious about me eventually meeting his mom. If I was being honest with myself, I didn't exactly have an outstanding track record with moms, but for the first time in years, I was actually... optimistic? Maybe I *would* get to meet her and maybe she'd like me. Alex seemed pretty positive she would.

I smiled to myself as I recalled the way his face lit up anytime he talked about his mom. Anyone that could inspire that kind of reaction from him, I wanted to meet. Not like Daniel. My nails scratched the wooden shelf. I had zero desire to ever meet him. He sounded like a total dick. Asking Alex about him had been a mistake.

My shelf hit its end, and I glanced around to see where my musings had taken me. The sign on the stack across the way read *History - Demons 1300-1800*. I thought again about the wild idea I'd shared with Alex before, about him being part of the Warde line. It wasn't wholly impossible, considering the only thing Alex knew about his father was that he was a Shadow Demon. If his dad *had* been a Warde, then maybe he'd left to protect Alex's mom. Fanatics were always bad news, *especially* when people thought they were gone.

I chewed on my lip while I considered the stack across from me. Maybe I could find more information on what became of Matthias Warde and his demon lover today. Thus far, I'd only uncovered the demon's name, nothing else. Even the demonology where I'd first found her was vague about her origins and there was nothing after. That part made me a little anxious. Typically, when people disappeared like that from history, they were dead. Of course, demons were a little different. It wasn't uncommon for demons to fall off the grid for whole swatches of time, only to reappear somewhere else.

Finally, I veered away from the stacks toward the rows of study tables. A few were occupied, though not as many as I would have expected. Fortunately, my usual one was vacant. I slid into the chair, my mind still whirling with potential places to search for answers, or at least clues. I wasn't even sure why it mattered so much, except I had this burning *need* to know. Maybe Alex was right, and I *was* obsessed. I'd already searched through several demon histories and come up empty. I could always return to the dorm where both the ancient history and Matthias Warde's journal were... and Alex.

I groaned inwardly and dropped my head in my hands. This couldn't possibly be as hard as I was making it. *Normal* people didn't have a problem telling their partners how they felt. Why was it so hard for me? Alex made it look easy, like it was the most natural thing in the world. But how could I admit to him I was absolutely terrified about how strongly I felt without sounding like a total basket case?

Frustrated with myself and the whole situation, I surged out of my chair and stalked back toward the *Demon History* shelves. I was nearly there when I had a better idea than combing back through books I'd already searched—I'd search the records for the Wars of Power. It wasn't until I was standing before the truly massive collection of history that I realized I'd never been over here. Where the hell did I even start?

With an agitated growl, I snagged a couple of volumes from the start of the war and some from the end. Maybe I'd get lucky and find a decent thread to follow. It wasn't like I needed detailed accounts of the various factions or how they tore each other apart. I needed a list of the key players, starting with the originals, which had been noticeably absent from my other research.

Rather than heft my stack all the way to my table only to have to come back when they didn't work out, I plopped on the floor. I cracked open one book at random, then almost gave up right there when I spied the heading of the first section—*Primordial Power*. How could I have forgotten that demons didn't even have a set race until *after* the Chaos Wars? Before that, they were basically masses of energy wreaking havoc, mostly with each other. And why the hell were there so many "wars" in the Wars of Power? Wasn't one enough?

My irritation growing, I swapped the volume for one that covered a later period. If I could just find a reference point that made *sense*, I might actually get somewhere. But with each ancient volume I scanned, that task felt more impossible. One thing was evident—the original demons got *around*. Five useless books later, I shifted my focus to volumes that covered the conclusion of the wars. Maybe I could find a list of surviving demons instead.

Fairly confident in my new tactic, I resumed scanning with renewed gusto. I'd finally found a promising thread when nearby voices broke my concentration. I picked myself up, body sore from sitting on the floor for so long. For once it seemed like I was going to be doing the shushing instead of the other way around. Holding my place in the book with a dusty finger, I abandoned my nest of books and made my way toward the noise with a scowl. As I approached, the voices got clearer until I realized they were in the next aisle over parallel to where I was standing.

"Are you sure he said Warde?"

I froze and stared at the shelves separating us.

"For fuck's sake, I don't know what the old coot called him. He said someone was snooping around the library, so we're in the library."

Curiosity and vindicated paranoia thawed my limbs. Careful not to make noise, I kept pace with them.

"Be quiet," a familiar voice hissed. "We don't want anyone knowing we're here."

"Why not?"

"Because, you idiot, they might be the one we're looking for."

I struggled to place the two voices, but wasn't having much luck while they were whispering.

"Is it true he's in our class?"

"That's a really dumb question." Recognition tickled at my senses so close I could touch it.

"Oh, right." They were silent a minute, then asked, "Can you believe there's been someone hiding who they really are?"

"Would you keep it down? You want everyone to know?"

"I was just asking. To think, we've been training next to someone playing for the other team this whole time." *Alex.*

"Don't get me started. I still haven't decided whether to take them to Thomas or take care of the abomination myself." The distinct sound of knuckles cracking had fear spiking through my chest.

Barely controlling my panic, I carefully shifted books to get a look at the owner of the hateful statement. *George.* Why was I not surprised?

"You don't suppose it's Ellie, do you?"

I shifted my gaze. *And Kyle. Of course.*

"You better hope not. There aren't enough female Shadow Demons as it is, and they'll kill whoever it is when we find them."

They don't know who they are looking for. I was almost too scared to breathe as I put the books back. One at a time, they slowly resumed their rightful places.

"But why?"

"Something about purifying the bloodline. It doesn't matter what Thomas' reasons are, we can't stand for something like that either. It's not natural. Honestly, I'm glad that he'll kill whoever it is rather than try to convert them. We can't tolerate someone like that in our ranks."

I nearly swallowed my tongue. In my mounting anxiety, I misjudged the angle of my current book and an adjacent book landed on another with a muffled thud. I grimaced and held perfectly still.

"Did you hear that?" George hissed, barely loud enough to be heard.

"You're letting Thomas get to you. He's a conspiracy nut if you ask me," Kyle sneered.

"Watch it. That conspiracy nut can—"

I was too busy making a dash for the exit to catch the rest. The campus whizzed past me in a blur of color, making me regret not practicing shadow walking more. I wasn't sure why I was in such a hurry. I knew for a fact that Alex was in the dorm. At least, that was where I'd left him. But I needed to see it for myself. Needed to know he was safe. George had more than one lackey and any number of them could be on the hunt. My stomach churned, and I ran faster.

By the time I shadowed through our door, I'd forgotten about why I'd gone to the library in the first place and nearly pitched face first when I came to an abrupt halt in the living room. Relief flooded through me at seeing Alex standing safely in the kitchen. Thoughts raced through my mind faster than I could grab them. *We needed to be more careful. I needed to tell him how I felt. We should run. I couldn't lose him. I lost everyone I cared about.*

"Matt?" Alex finished drying his hands and set the dish towel on the counter. "Are you alright?" He stepped toward me.

"I…" The words died. My heart felt like someone was trying to tear it apart. Why couldn't I tell him he meant everything to me?

His eyebrows pinched together. "Hey, what's wrong?"

"I…" Why couldn't I say it? It was three damn words.

He took another step, worry now clear on his face.

"I'm happy," I blurted. A smile teased his lips and the knife in my heart twisted. My world would be so dark without him.

"O-kay, I'm glad to hear it," he said, laughter teasing the edges as he reached for me.

I grabbed his hand. "*You* make me happy." My heart was going to beat itself out. His eyes softened and his concern melted away into a smile determined to steal what little breath I had left.

"You make me happy too, Matt," he said softly, continuing his reach with the captured hand to cup my face.

I closed my eyes and leaned into the caress. When his lips brushed against mine, I returned the gentle kiss while a renegade tear ran down my cheek. He couldn't know. If he did... I broke the kiss and wrapped him in my arms, holding him close.

"Are you sure you are alright?" He tried to pull back, but I tightened my hold, using the movement to wipe away the traitorous tear, and buried my face in his neck. "O-Okay."

The scent of lavender flowed around me as he squeezed back. I'd do anything to keep him safe. Literally anything. If Alex knew there was danger—real trouble—he'd want to do something about it. He wouldn't lie low. Wouldn't wait for things to blow over. He'd want to confront them or, heaven forbid, *tell* someone. I knew George's type. He'd absolutely kill Alex if he found him and it sounded like this mysterious Thomas would do the same. I couldn't let that happen, wouldn't let that happen.

"I'm fine. It's just been a weird day." I swiped another kiss, then made my way to the couch.

He sat beside me, worry once again in his eyes. "Do you want to talk about it?"

"Um..." I floundered for something believable. As it was, I was dubious about my ability to lie to him. He seemed to have a gift for ferreting out my secrets. "I went to the library."

"Need to think about something?" He gave me a knowing look.

Shit. I'm already failing miserably.

"I... found something about our demon."

"Soptealǎ?"

"Yeah, her." I took out the last book I'd been holding before I heard George and Kyle talking. "Turns out she's a direct descendant of an original. At first, I thought she might actually *be* an original because I couldn't find anything at all. Then I found this." I passed him the book.

"What made you think to check in these old things?" he asked, scanning the page.

I shrugged and slid my hand onto his lap beneath the book. I didn't even realize I'd done it until he laced our fingers together and gave mine a gentle squeeze. "The only wars anyone seems willing to talk about are the Wars of Power. We know the Demon Wars took place after that. I just back-tracked. Starting with a survivor list from the last great war just made sense. All the commanders and generals were substantial levels. Those would definitely be mentioned if they'd been around," I added, leaning into him. Here, at least, we were safe.

He snaked an arm around me as he leaned back, the book still in his other hand. "You would tell me if something was bothering you, right?"

"Of course." The lies kept coming. I needed Alex to be safe, and I was willing to do whatever it took to make that happen. The real question was how. I needed to find out what those jerks knew. Figure out who the hell the Thomas was and what his beef was. I couldn't protect Alex from an enemy I didn't know.

The thought of intentionally spending time with George brought the taste of bile to my mouth. I shoved it down and tried to determine the best way to go about it. Worming my way into their group after Battle Tactics was probably my best bet. But it would have to be after Alex left. Which would make me late for my next class. Others would likely suffer as well. While I was enjoying my classes and might actually be *good* at some of them, keeping Alex safe far outweighed my desire to stay enrolled.

It felt wrong to be thinking about how to deceive Alex while curled up next to him. Logically, I should work on putting more distance between us. Already, we were slipping up whenever we went into town for the day. I'd been stupid to think no one would be watching us there. Even the casual touches would need to stop. I couldn't risk me doing something stupid, because I couldn't keep my hands off of him. Not when it could get him killed. As for at the dorm... I couldn't, not yet. There was no way I could quit Alex outright; it would break me.

"Huh, I never realized Vera's husband was a Xiander. That makes more sense," he mused while he steadily stroked my arm.

"I think I'm over all of this." I scooted closer, though there wasn't anywhere else to really go. "We found what we were looking for. We don't need to keep searching."

"You don't want to so see what happened to their child?" He tried to look at me, but I refused to cooperate. If he saw my face, there wasn't a doubt in my mind he'd know I was lying.

"I'd rather..." I started, then changed what I was going to say. "I just don't want to go to the library anymore. You were right. I was obsessed. But all these people are long gone. It was silly to get so wrapped up." I tightened my fingers around his hand.

I couldn't do this. Of course, I wanted to know what happened. We'd discovered a massive cover-up, and the child was proof. Plus, being part demon, the kid could even still be alive or have children of their own. But if giving up this ridiculous quest meant Alex would stay here where it was safe, then it was a no-brainer.

He chuckled. "So *that's* what all of this is about." I fought his attempts to make me look at him, but per usual, he won. "You know you're allowed to have hobbies, Matt. Our relationship doesn't have to be all or nothing."

The merriment in his eyes made me want to scream. I wanted to shout at him to stop being so damn understanding. It wasn't like that at all. Maybe it *would* be easier to tell him. He'd just keep pressing til I caved.

"I love you, Matt," he said unexpectedly.

The knife in my heart drove home.

CHAPTER 21

AWKWARD ANSWERS

A

The main entrance to Mysterio College shut behind me with a clang. I groaned as I realized I'd forgotten all about the question I'd been dying to ask Vera. If I thought it could wait any longer, I'd have risked asking her during our next Battle Tactics class, but there was no guarantee she'd be there. As it was, she'd missed all of last week. It was now or never. Resigned to being late for my next class, I turned to go back inside.

Mere yards from her office, I heard voices coming from the classroom we'd been using this term. Worried someone had snagged Vera's attention before I could, I peered through the open door. To my surprise, Matt was still there, though I could have sworn he'd hightailed it out first thing and more alarming, he was talking with George and company. Concern blossomed in my chest and I took a step towards the room, fully prepared to intervene before talking could turn into fighting. Then Matt laughed. I froze, not entirely sure what to do.

"Roman?"

I jumped and spun around. "H-hi, Ms. Scry."

She rolled her eyes. "For the love of Nyx, call me Vera, or I'm telling Matt you were spying on him."

I blanched. I wasn't spying. Was I? Matt was free to do as he liked. My gaze slid toward the voices still emanating from the room behind me. But since when did that include spending time with George?

"Can I help you with something?"

"Um... yeah." I wanted nothing more than to march into that room and demand to know why Matt looked downright chummy with the trio of bullies. But at Vera's implication that I was spying, that didn't strike me as the wisest course of action.

"And that would be..." Vera prompted.

I cleared my throat and returned my attention to her. "I had a question about shadowing."

"You're going to need to be a little more specific. Why don't we talk in my office?" She lead the way down the hall and stopped a few doors down at her office.

I looked back into the room one last time and followed, closing the office door behind me.

"So, what's this question?" She plopped into a leather chair that looked rarely sat in behind a heavy desk riddled with papers. Despite her name on it, she didn't really look like she belonged there. Vera was a warrior, not a scholar or diplomat, a *warrior*. She'd done equally incredible and horrific things. But seeing her now, with her red hair in a frizzy ponytail and her casual attire the furthest thing from professional, it was difficult to reconcile the horror stories she'd inspired.

How could someone who looked barely older than *me* be responsible for such heinous acts? Perhaps Matt was right, and she really was only a product of her situation. It was also entirely possible that the stories had intentionally been exaggerated to cultivate an aura of fear and mystery. My mind strayed back to Matt laughing with George.

What's he doing?

It wasn't until Vera spoke again that I realized I'd been standing there, lost in my thoughts. "It hasn't been long." She leaned back in her chair, causing the leather to squeak, and steepled her fingers. "Frankly,

I'm just glad they aren't at each other's throats anymore. I believe I have you to thank for that."

"What? Oh, sure."

"Now, what did you actually want to know?" she asked again.

I'd considered a thousand different ways to ask, but the most logical was also the most direct. "What's it like shadowing someone else?"

"Considering how adept you are and the fact that you are well ahead of the rest of the class, I'm going to assume you're not asking for the theory of how. You've already done it and want to know why it's not always the same."

I nodded. While I hadn't exactly shadowed as many people as she believed, shadowing Matt that day definitely qualified as different.

"Gabriel would tell me I need to let you come to the answer on your own, but I always found that trying and a tad tedious when he did it, so I'll spare you." She leaned forward to rest her arms on the desk, mindless of the papers beneath. "The experience is unique depending on how intimately you know the person being shadowed. For example, if you shadowed a family member, it might feel like a reassuring hug, whereas a stranger wouldn't really feel like much at all. Then there's shadowing lovers. That feels a bit more like…"

I held up my hand to cut her off. I got the picture, and it definitely answered my question. "But why?"

She shrugged, reminding me of Matt. "Who can say really? When it comes down to it, we're using our own essence to fold someone else into the shadow world. It's possible it correlates to the level we would want to protect them, but I suspect it's much deeper than that. Sadly, a lot of what we do and why is still a mystery, even to ourselves. There's no science behind this, only instinct and inclination."

It sounded a lot like how Matt talked about using his powers. My thoughts strayed back to him in the other room. Was he still there?

Why was he there at all? Would he tell me the truth if I asked? I had a very strong suspicion the answer to that last one was "No".

"You shadowed Matt, didn't you?" I blinked at the sound of his name and looked at her. She smiled knowingly. "I'd like to say I saw it all on my own, but apparently, I can be dense with things like this. Gabriel's actually the one who pointed it out."

"Gabriel Xiander has been here?"

A malicious smile curled on her face. "He won't be pleased at all that someone figured that out. He's actually been here several times to check in on how things are going. It seems he could relate."

I looked at her, confused. *Why, in Nyx's name, would the son of an original be interested in some lowly students?* "Relate to what?"

"Pining after someone who doesn't have a clue."

I shifted in my chair. Matt wouldn't like this.

"It's okay, Alexi. I'm glad to see he came around. Like I said before, you've been an exceptionally positive influence on him. Granted, when I assigned the rooms, I *was* hoping that you'd rub off on him. I just wasn't expecting it to be so literal," she added with a crooked smile.

My jaw dropped. This was *not* how teachers spoke with students.

The mischief left her face, and her expression softened. "I'm not sure how much he's shared with you, but he's had a very rough life. The world has not been kind to Matt. Admittedly, when I dropped him off with Jeffrey, I despaired that he'd ever find peace." She looked down at her hands. "It's hard to let go of the anger, especially when most of it's aimed at yourself." Seemed Gabriel wasn't the only one able to relate.

"Why did you do it?" The words were out before I could reconsider them.

She took a deep breath, and it came out a sigh. "At first, because I was told to. We didn't know better." Her gaze flicked up. "That's not an excuse, it's a fact. Namas was the only one of us who'd grown up in the supernatural world and he had his own evils to fight." She shook her head. "After a while, we suspected something was off. The orders became more aggressive, more final. By then, though, the damage was done. Then, of course, there's the whole matter of demons don't do well with heartbreak."

"I thought you loved Gabriel."

Her smile turned warm at the mention of her husband, then sad again. "I didn't always. My break up with Dorian, while mostly mutual, was not exactly pleasant. I fell into the darkness and had no desire to come back out. The darkness is a living thing that can reach back. Never forget that." Her look speared me to the chair. I'd never considered that my essence could hurt me. "The things I did are unforgivable, and the only person I have to blame is myself. I enjoyed being the Terror of the East. There was power in that. And I had the rage to carry it through."

I wanted to ask how she did finally come back, but chose a different route. "Backing up a bit. Dorian—as in—*Dorian Valens?* The greatest healer of our time?"

"Yeah. We actually went to school together—we all did. Except for Namas. I'm still not sure where he crawled out of." She laughed like it was an old joke.

Well, that was a surprise. I'd always thought the Regency had pulled the Shadows from around the world.

"I can see you thinking how preposterous that is. Agreed. To hear the Regency talk about it, power attracts power. Guess that's how they found us." It was weird listening to her so casually mention the organization that had oppressed the supernatural community for decades.

Then again, she'd just admitted her perspective on the entire thing was very different.

"Sounds like a mixed blessing."

"I suppose. Hey, do you mind if I ask you some questions about Matt? You don't have to answer, but I hope you will at least consider it."

I looked at her warily. "What *kind* of questions?"

"He still seems to struggle in class. I don't understand. I've seen him in a fight and he's a natural, yet in class, he's a totally different person. It's almost as if he's suppressing his own abilities."

I was inclined to agree with her, but then the full nature of what she said sunk in. "You've seen Matt fight?" I didn't care if I told Matt I would be more open to forgiving Vera, if she was complicit in that damnable fight club....

"He was fighting several supernaturals when I went to pick him up. I confess, I may have let it play out longer than I should have, but I was curious to see how he would handle himself."

"Oh."

Her gaze narrowed. "What did you think I was talking about?"

"Nothing. I was just surprised, is all."

"You and me both. He took out a Spiculo, a Sprite, and an Ick Demon. There's no telling what would have happened to that third-rate fire demon if I hadn't intervened."

I swallowed past a sudden tightness in my throat. Matt hadn't mentioned Oliver was a fire demon or what any of the others had been. Sprites were no joke and could put demons to shame for cruelty.

"Anyway, I wanted to know if he was doing better with shadowing outside of class. The classroom environment isn't really conducive to every type of learner."

"Yes," I answered honestly. "He shadows around the dorm all the time, though he never believes me when I tell him."

"Huh. What else?"

"He has a particular knack for shadow spells."

"That's surprising." She tapped a finger against her chin. "Why?"

She shrugged. "It isn't common that demons are good at both physical manifestations *and* spells."

"He is *very* good. He's already mastered portals and how to hide them." I considered her a moment. "My turn to ask a question. Did you convince some fifth year to loan him a Shadow Grimoire?"

She gave me a sheepish look. "It's actually mine, but I didn't think he'd take it from me. Am I right in assuming that he still hasn't forgiven me for abandoning him in a warded room?"

"Wow, you really did that? Matt told me, but I wasn't sure I fully believed it."

"It wasn't my finest moment, and it really was for his own protection. So I take that as a yes?"

"Definitely, but I don't think it's the warded part he's still upset about."

She snorted. "He seemed pretty pissed about it to me."

"You took charge of him and then left him *alone*."

It took her a moment, then understanding dawned. "Ah, I see. I'm not really sure how I can make that up to him."

"I'm sure you'll find a way," I said. And I had no doubt that she would. Vera Scry was a persistent woman if she was nothing else.

"Thanks for the vote of confidence." She rolled her eyes, but didn't seem totally put out. "One more question, then I'll let you go. How did you ever quiet his rage?"

"I kissed him." I clapped a hand over my mouth, but it was too late. She released a genuine laugh, and I started to understand how she'd accumulated so many allies, despite her notoriety.

"Relax, Roman, this room is warded. No one can hear anything we say." She stood. "I appreciate your honesty, and I'm glad Matt finally found a friend. Something tells me that's a first for him. You really are good together."

I gave her a shy smile. There was something to be said for someone recognizing our relationship outside of our four walls. "Thank you."

"I only speak the truth. I'm also pretty sure you're the only reason he passed his classes that first semester. If you ever have other questions, just call. Office hours aren't really my thing." She winked, then held out her hand. I passed her my phone, and she quickly keyed something. Her phone vibrated against the desk from where she'd set it earlier and she snatched it up, simultaneously silencing it. "There, now I'll know who's calling me."

I reclaimed my phone and pushed up from the chair. "Thanks for the uh... conversation."

"Anytime," she said, waving her phone.

With a smile, I turned to leave. If Matt was still around, maybe I could walk him to his next class.

"Oh, one more thing." Vera stood and walked around the massive desk to lean on it. "Gabriel wanted me to warn you. Demons can get a little... obsessed when we're into someone. It's normally pretty manageable if uncomfortable, but things get a little dicier when it's with another Shadow Demon."

I adjusted my backpack and frowned. "How so?"

"Remember how I said the darkness was a living thing? When our control slips, we can subconsciously reach out to the other person with our essence." She rolled her eyes and added, "It can make for some pretty uncomfortable situations. Not to mention how the line between fantasy and reality can get a bit blurred. So, you know, watch the lucid daydreams, unless you want to accidentally manifest your boyfriend or other things…" Her face reddened.

"I'm not sure what—"

Her phone rang, cutting me off. "I need to get that. I'll see you in class next week."

"Next week? Does this have something to do with Cara missing class?" I might have been inclined to think she'd just skipped, but she was the type of person to show up to class with the plague.

Vera's face pinched. "I really need to take this."

I nodded. No sooner did I turn to leave than she'd answered the call.

"What have you got? *Nothing* is not an acceptable answer," she growled.

My pace quickened, her blatant frustration chasing me out the door. With a sigh of relief that her ire wasn't directed at me, I shut the door behind me. As I walked back to the classroom, I wondered f Matt had ever experienced pulling at another Shadow Demon's essence. I certainly hadn't. Except the room was empty. Dejected, I made my way with dragging steps to my next class.

CHIMERA'S GRAVE

M

George Cartwright was a disgusting creature, and his goons were worse. Once again, I toyed with the idea of simply beating all of them to a pulp and calling it a day. The only problem with *that* was I still didn't know who this mysterious Thomas was or how he fit into everything. Until then, my options were limited to worming my way into their group.

It took a full week of staying after Battle Tactics, blowing off lunch with Alex—*twice,* and being late to class four times before I *finally* made headway. I wasn't great at lying to Alex about what I was up to, which left me doing something I hated even more—avoiding him. But it was that or risk spilling the truth and possibly getting him killed. The sooner I had what I needed from George, the sooner I could leave his foul sense of humor behind and return to Alex.

"So, what are we doing?" I asked as I joined Kyle and Travis at the end of the new fraternity row.

They shared a look, then said in unison, "Waiting." Their creepy smiles made my skin crawl.

I barely didn't shudder. "Cut the shit. I thought we were actually *going* somewhere." Given the meet-up spot, I was worried it was going to be a kegger. Given how long it had been since I'd done any kind of drinking, I didn't see that ending well for me.

"Quit your bitching." George joined us, his hair combed back like some old-school greaser and hands shoved into his jean pockets. "We're going somewhere all right. Taken me months to get the invite for this place. Real exclusive."

"You really got it?" Travis asked, practically beaming at George.

His mouth stretched into a toothy grin. "I really got it. Password, new location, and all."

"Fuck yeah! You're the fucking king!" Kyle shouted, pumping his fist in the air. A sentiment, Travis echoed equally enthusiastically.

I mentally rolled my eyes. The two were worse than leeches the way they sucked up to George; it was a wonder they hadn't bled him dry yet. Suddenly, George's words registered, and I narrowed my eyes. "Where *exactly* are we going?"

"I believe you're familiar with the place," George snickered without elaborating.

The unease in my gut grew. If I asked again, this time with more details, I risked being ejected from the group or being jumped by the three. Neither got me the info I needed. So I kept my trap shut and diligently trailed after him when he set off... away from the frat houses. With each step we got closer and closer to the edge of campus, my trepidation increased. I debated for the zillionth time if I might have better luck beating Thomas's identity out of the three, starting with George. Did I already know him? Was he in any of our classes? Was Thomas even his real name? Sadly, I didn't expect hitting George would provide any of those answers. Far more likely it would blow up in my face. The smart course would be to stick to the plan of infiltrating them.

Abruptly, I realized we'd officially left university grounds. Distant lampposts made bubbles of yellow in the night that didn't come close to touching our path. I glanced around for any kind of clue to help get my bearings without success. Then a large door came into view, illuminated by the saddest excuse of an overhead light I'd ever seen. The buzzing of the struggling bulb grew louder and revealed the door to be made of rusted metal, much like what you'd find on... a warehouse.

Alarm cleaved into my chest like a great axe, and I nearly tripped over my feet in my hurry to stop. This wasn't happening. No way had George gotten an *invitation* to the bruiser club. That wasn't how it worked. They recruited you. He might pick fights twenty-four-seven, but that didn't make him a fighter. Not like me. Cold that had nothing to do with the chill in the air slithered through my veins. *Like me.* They must have learned that I used to come here. Likely from Eric. Any chance that I might have been wrong went up in smoke the second George pounded on the metal door and a slot slid back to reveal a pair of yellow eyes.

"Password."

George opened his mouth and stalled. Then he whirled on Kyle and Travis, hissing under his breath, "Fuck, I forgot it."

"It wasn't written down?" Travis asked, earning himself a scathing look.

"No, I didn't fucking write it down, dumbass. It's against the rules."

Stupid rule, if you ask me," Kyle chipped in unhelpfully.

"It started with a C-H." He turned back to the door and waiting eyes. "Cherub's Noose?"

The yellow eyes blinked without answering, then the slot started to close.

Somehow, I kept my exasperated sigh to myself as I stepped past the trio of morons. The eye still visible zeroed in on me, and though I couldn't see anything else, I still registered their surprise. I may not have known the club was going to relocate, but I *did* know the cycle of passwords. "Chimera's Grave."

The door swung open, but my feet remained rooted while I fought the urge to vomit. Then hard claps on my back, coupled with cheers, forced me forward. Never had I expected to find myself in this horrible place again. Alex wouldn't forgive this. I closed my eyes and took a fateful step into the chaos. I was doing this *for* Alex.

George gave me an appraising look. "So Eric was right. You *have* been here before. Hey, Kyle, go find him. He said he wanted to know when we got here."

Knowing I'd been right about Eric being the one to approach them didn't make me feel any better. If anything, it made me feel worse. If Eric had seen me with these assholes, what else had he seen? Had he been the one watching me and Alex in the library? Did he know who Alex was to me? I tried to block out the trio's triumphant cheers and the blood lust filling the room so I could think. Then I heard the last voice I wanted to hear.

"Well, well, well, what do we have here?" That hiss could only belong to one person.

Reluctantly, I turned to face Neese. The wyvern—because I'd finally figured that out—did that weird slithery-walk thing until he was right beside me and far too close for comfort. "Looksss like our ssscraper has returned to usss after all."

"Hey, man. Kyle just went to find Eric." George angled his thumb at the crowd currently cheering around the ring.

"Ssso, who's fighting tonight?" Neese shifted his gaze to me and I glared back. "You look like you've healed up. Though you are sssmaller than I remember."

"We just came to watch," George whined.

Neese gave him a toothy grin that sent shivers down my spine. "Oh, you can, but sssomeone has to participate. Those are the rules."

George's brow furrowed. "Eric didn't mention anything about that."

"I didn't? Funny. Must have slipped my mind." Eric joined the group, looking every bit as imposing as I remembered, and gave me a sinister grin. "But, yeah, them's the rules."

I wanted more than anything to be back in the dorm with Alex, curled up on the couch and watching a boring movie. My heart ached for it just at the thought, but that didn't look like it was going to be happening anytime soon. George was a night forsaken imbecile, and they'd tricked him to get me here. The only upside was that if I was with George, then George wasn't looking for Alex.

I pulled my shirt over my head and tossed it at Travis. He nearly dropped it as I stepped forward. "You got what you wanted. I'm here. Who's it going to be tonight, Neese?"

It didn't seem possible for him to look any eviler. "I'm pretty sure Singe has been eager for a rematch since last time."

It would have to be fucking Carl. I'd have to be extra careful; I couldn't afford to get any marks on me if I had a prayer of keeping this from Alex. That meant not getting cocky and keeping my guard up. Given how much I'd improved in my abilities since the last time I'd been here, staying out of reach shouldn't be too difficult.

"Fine. When?" I asked, rolling my shoulders to loosen up.

"How about now?"

Without a word, I made my way to the center of the room with George and the others trailing after me, sounding so excited it made me nauseous. I doubted they'd be so excited if Neese demanded one of *their* hides. But then, this had never been about them. That much I knew. It was about getting me back under Neese's thumb, officially making me collateral in my quest to keep Alex safe.

"Yo, Singe, get your molten ass out here! Your favorite person is here to see you," Eric called out in his booming voice. The crowd erupted into a cacophony when I stepped into the ring. The golden goose had returned.

I eyed the perimeter warily while I waited for Carl. I'd be staying far away from that. Last thing I needed was electric shock on top of everything else. At last, the Fire Demon pushed his way into the arena. By now, the audience was practically foaming at the mouth, including my own unfortunate companions. My jaw tightened at seeing all the eager leers. I hated this place.

"Thought you'd never come back," Carl snickered, cracking his thick neck.

"What can I say? I missed your sparkling personality." I didn't really want to rile him up, but it'd be stranger if I didn't goad him at all. Everyone would expect me to live up to my former reputation. A task made doubly tricky because I couldn't afford to be reckless, couldn't risk returning to Alex covered in evidence of my broken promise.

The Fire Demon cracked flaming knuckles together. "I'm going to enjoy this."

"Just make sure you don't finish too soon."

The resulting chorus of 'Oohs' rippled around us and a column of flame shot from the top of Carl's head, followed by two more from his hands directed at me. I calmly shadowed out and waited for him to stop. This wouldn't last nearly long enough if he was already losing his temper. Another spurt of flame, this one lashing out like a whip. I sidestepped the misguided attack and shadowed again for good measure. The feel of after burn still fresh in my mind from our last encounter.

He abandoned the whip tactic and reverted to the columns. People around us shouted as the inferno got too close for comfort. Blood on their clothes was fine, just not actual burns or marks. They were here for other people's suffering, not their own. I shadowed closer to him while he focused on controlling the attack.

"Stand and fight, runt!" he roared, manifesting a club of fire. I dodged the wild swing and buried my fist in his gut. He grunted, and the flames sputtered as his concentration wavered.

"What's the matter, Carl? I would've thought you'd have practiced more after I whooped your ass last time." I spun and kicked his feet out from under him. He went down in a heap reminiscent of smoldering coal.

Many of the onlookers here would've kicked him while he was down. No doubt including my current choice in company. Carl may have been a terrible fighter with no control, but *no one* deserved to be beaten when they were down.

"Come on. Are you going to get up or are you taking a power nap?" I danced a couple of steps back in case he blew his top again. "Maybe you should change your name from Singe to Burnout."

"I'm going to incinerate you, you mouthy bastard." He recovered faster than I expected, and a stream of fire shot across the space, searing my side.

"Son of a bitch!" I bellowed. Besides the fact that it burned like hell, Alex was *definitely* going to notice that. Furious, I warped the surrounding shadows, cutting off his flow of oxygen, and extinguished him.

His jaw dropped as the flames abruptly guttered out, then released a grunt when my foot plowed into his side. He stumbled and tried to get his arms up, but without his fire to keep me at bay, there was no stopping me from wailing on him. It wouldn't take him long to recover and relight. Then he'd be a wild card, making it imperative that I kept him unbalanced.

Thankfully, I was a lot faster than even he realized. I landed blow after blow in a relentless fury, shadowing out at least half of the time. His forearms turned black, although I couldn't tell if it was from bruising or because that was all I could see. He still hadn't landed another shot when I gave him the final hit that sent him sprawling.

I stood in the center of the ring, panting more from rage than exertion. Sound gradually seeped into my awareness, followed by colors other than obsidian. The deafening roar pushed against the rafters. Someone snatched me out of the ring and I stumbled to a stop a few feet clear of the raucous crowd.

"When Eric told me you were the club's prize fighter, I didn't believe it. But damn! I've never seen anything like that. You were incredible."

"Why would you ever stop coming here?" Travis asked, looking a little high. He might be, for all I knew. I didn't really *know* any of them, nor did I want to.

I scanned the far wall until I found the stall where salves could be had and made my way over. To my surprise, it was the same witch as the last time, Misty. She eyed me just as appreciatively as before, and I barely restrained from sneering.

"Fancy meeting you again. Thought that fight with Granite would be the end of you. I guess you found someone else to play doctor with," she said with what I was sure she thought was a sexy smile that did nothing to eliminate my scowl. "Fine, have it your way." She reached for the familiar container of burn salve. Before she could hand it over, though, Neese joined us.

"No healing for the prodigal bruiser."

I looked up at him sharply.

He narrowed his slitted eyes and curled his lip. "Consider it the price of admission after your last terrible performance. As for you three, the deal stands. So long as he fights like he's supposed to, you can keep coming without stepping in yourselves."

I ripped my shirt from Travis and slipped it on, causing the burn on my side to flare angrily. I'd have to hide it as long as possible so it could heal more. That and come up with a reasonable explanation for when Alex inevitably discovered it.

George grabbed me by the neck and led us all over to the side. "Hear that, boys? We get to come back and Matty here gets to pummel everything in sight."

"Hey is that skanky witch here every week?" Kyle asked, nodding toward the healing stand.

Travis guffawed. "Oh man, she was practically begging for it."

"I'll give her something to beg for," Kyle responded, grabbing his dick through his jeans.

I did my best to tune them out. This was my worst nightmare. Neese had found a way to get me back in the ring, and George had unwittingly played right into his hands. There wasn't a chance in hell I'd get out as easily as I had the last time. And I had a sinking feeling that Neese would make sure I paid dearly for every fight I'd missed.

Travis shoved me, and I shot him a glare. "Easy, man. I was just asking if you'd ever tap that. She's obviously into you."

"Yeah, coming back might give you a shot at redemption," George chimed in. "She seemed pretty eager to *doctor* you up." They all snickered.

I didn't care what they expected of me. That was one line I wouldn't cross. Rejoining the fight club was one thing, but there were some betrayals you just didn't forgive.

CHAPTER 23

DREAM A LITTLE DREAM

A

I took my time packing up the books from my last tutoring session of the day, then headed into the early evening. With fall in full swing and winter fast approaching, the campus grounds were already swathed in darkness punctuated by strategically placed lamps. I trudged along the path in no particular hurry. Wasn't like there'd be anyone waiting for me at the dorm.

My chest tightened, but I ignored the ache. It wasn't like I could really be upset about Matt not being there, not when it was because he'd joined a study group. Though going nearly two weeks of only seeing him in Battle Tactics and Demonic History II and passingly in the dorm didn't exactly leave me thrilled.

Tempting as it was to stop by the dining hall, it wasn't the same without Matt. Dry cereal would suit my melancholy just fine. I adjusted my course to head for the dorm and tried not to think about how much I missed my boyfriend. Maybe I could convince him to have lunch with me, not that my last attempt had gone well. Finally in front of our door, I fingered the old-fashioned key. There had to be some way to get him to spend time with me that didn't involve him quitting the study group. When I opened the door, I blinked twice, not sure I trusted my eyes.

Was Matt *really* in the kitchen or had Vera's dire warning about lonely Shadow Demons hallucinating finally come to fruition? I stepped deeper into the room to get a better look at what he was doing, letting the door thump shut behind me. Judging by the jars on the counter, he was making a peanut butter and jelly sandwich. He pushed aside a plated sandwich and began another.

"About time you got back," he said without turning around.

I refrained from pointing out that he'd been coming back in the wee hours of the morning and put my stuff down. "Did your study group get canceled?" I asked, stepping up behind him.

He tensed, then let out a sigh as I rubbed my hands down the length of his arms. The defined muscles of his shoulders and biceps had me questioning if I'd already forgotten how he felt. Was it possible he'd started working out again? I dismissed the thought as I absently stroked his exposed skin. He'd have told me.

His hand clenched around the butter knife he'd been using, then he set it aside, his shoulders slumping. "I'm sorry. I know it takes up a lot of time."

"Nothing to apologize for. I'm proud of you for taking your studies so seriously." I leaned my head down until my lips brushed the shell of his ear and added in a low whisper, "I just hope it's worth it." He shivered and desire unfurled like a living thing inside of me. Night, how I missed him.

"It wasn't canceled. I just... I wanted to be here tonight." The admission made me giddy. Seemed I wasn't the only one feeling the absence. "I made you a sandwich," he added.

"I see that." I kissed lightly along the back of his neck, teasing the sensitive skin with the tip of my tongue and tiny nibbles, the scent of sage intoxicating.

He attempted to stifle a giggle and squirmed against me. "Someone's feeling frisky."

If I hadn't been hard before, I certainly was now. I dug my fingers into his hips and he groaned. "You aren't the only one who burns." Night, I needed this, needed him. I spun him around, eager for more, barely catching his startled expression before I claimed his mouth.

He melted against me, looping his arms around my neck and giving himself wholly over to the kiss. His moan filled my chest as he slid his fingers through my hair, urging me deeper. He broke off long enough to steal a breath, then resumed trying to steal mine while he ground his growing erection against my thigh.

I mindlessly reached behind him to clear the counter, shoving aside jars, plates, and bread, then slid my hands beneath his shirt and guided it over his head. No sooner was he free than he was scrambling to be rid of mine. My shirt hit the ground, and I hoisted him onto the counter, earning myself a surprised gasp that I promptly swallowed. "I've missed you," I said between kisses, working my way down to his neck.

"Alexi."

The whispered moan drove me wild. I glided my hands over his thighs and he tightened them around my hips. His eager response was almost better than hearing my name on his lips. I palmed his straining dick and his head dropped back with a sharp cry. My fingers tingled in anticipation as I coasted them along his sides. He flinched slightly, and I leaned back, fully prepared to tease him for being ticklish. But when I glanced down, my fingers hovered over the remnants of a gruesome burn that spanned from his hip to his ribs.

"What's this?" I asked, kissing gently along his shoulder to distract myself from overreacting.

"It's nothing." He took a moment to steady his breathing, which faltered when I nipped at his neck. "J-just a spell gone wrong."

"Why didn't you go to a healer?" I asked, doing my damnedest to keep my tone neutral.

"It's almost healed."

My jaw twitched as I fought the increasing urge to press for clarity. But as I scanned his face, taking in his pink cheeks and downcast eyes, I couldn't bring myself to compound his embarrassment. I trusted him to come to me if something was genuinely wrong. "Does it still hurt?" I whispered, barely brushing my fingers over the wound.

"No." The resulting flinch betrayed the lie, but if he wanted to pretend it was fine, then I could do that too.

I brushed my lips softly against his. "You'll tell me if I hurt you?"

"Yes," he breathed, leaning into me once more.

"Good," I growled, palming his ass to hold him in place and grinding against him.

He swore and attacked my mouth with a vengeance while he raked his fingers down my back hard enough to leave marks. I groaned into his mouth and did it again before encouraging him to wrap his legs around my waist. Then I shadowed us to the bedroom, where we landed in a tangle of limbs on the bed. The rush of him simultaneously touching every single cell in my body was a high I'd never tire of.

"That was... that was..." he trailed off, still panting for breath.

"Incredible," I finished for him.

"Yeah, that," he said, then captured my mouth, revealing a need that rivaled my own.

"What do you want, Matt?" I managed through hungry kisses and roving hands that spread a blinding ecstasy of sensation.

He bit my lip and tugged before setting it free. "Whatever you'll give me."

"Don't I always give you everything?" I crooned, kissing him slowly. He groaned in obvious frustration at the sudden change in pace while my own need rebelled violently against my insistence on hearing him voice his desire. "Tell me, Matt. What do you want?"

"I want you, Alex. I always want you." His eyes burned like the hottest flame. He reached for my pants, flicking them open without hesitation, then slipped his hand past the waistband to free my aching dick. He placed tender kisses at the edge of my mouth while he stroked me with a firm grip. "I want you inside of me. Fucking me until the only name I can remember is yours."

I released a strangled grunt and gently grabbed his wrist. "You have exactly five minutes to get ready."

He didn't waste time walking, shadowing directly to the bathroom. While he was gone, I finished stripping and took out the supplies, setting them within easy reach. When Matt returned, he too was naked, though his erection had flagged.

"On the bed." I waited 'til he'd laid on his back, then tossed him the lube. "Get yourself ready for me."

His eyes widened, and he swallowed. He might have been anxious, but his black eyes and plumping cock betrayed his interest. Without so much as a peep of dissent, he popped the cap and wet two fingers. He set the lubricant aside, and I plucked it up. His gaze flicked to me as I joined him on the bed, positioned between his wide knees for the best view.

"What are you waiting for?" I asked, giving my revived erection lazy strokes.

A flush spread across his chest and darkened his cheeks as he reached for his already clenching hole. Rather than rush, he took his time circling the quivering entrance before sliding his index finger deep with a high-pitched whine. He worked himself open with a chorus of needy moans that bordered on whines, his abs contracting as he pushed deeper and added a second digit. Then he moved to grab his leaking dick.

"No," I said firmly.

His hand froze, and he stared at me, mouth agape, fingers still plunged in his tight ass.

"I didn't say you could stop."

He dropped his free hand to the bed, where he clenched the sheets as he resumed stretching himself. His breath hitched as I scooted closer, then turned into a strangled moan when I wrapped a slick hand around his erection. His dick pulsed against my palm while his fingers thrust.

Sensing his release was near, I squeezed his base more firmly.

"Alex," he gasped.

"You ready for me, love?"

"Yes. Yes. Oh god, yes," he panted, already looking half wrecked.

I kissed the inside of each of his knees, then pushed them toward his chest. "Hold them there." He moved so fast to comply, I couldn't help but wonder if he'd shadowed and I'd missed it. I watched his chest rise and fall in time with his quick breaths while I opened one of the several condoms I'd laid out and rolled it on. I placed more kisses on the backs of his thighs and made sure he was truly prepped.

Matt's gaze tracked my every movement as I lined myself up with his wet hole. Then I pushed forward agonizingly slowly, and he stopped breathing. When my head breached the first ring of tight muscle, air rushed back into his lungs and came out in a keening moan. I gradually worked myself deeper with steady, shallow thrusts, even though I knew he could handle more and the measured pace was killing me. I ran my hands over his legs, enjoying how the coarse hair tickled my palms and made his legs flex.

"Tell me what you want." I stroked deep and stopped moving.

Matt looked at me with pupils blown wide. "Fuck me. *Please,* just fuck me."

Eager to please and not sure how much longer I could withstand this drawn out torture, I resumed thrusting, abandoning the previous slow pace and pounded into him. His neglected cock bounced against his stomach, leaving a trail of pre-cum behind. My thighs burned as I increased the punishing rhythm. I griped his thighs, both for support and to pull him closer.

His fingers turned white from griping his ankles so tight and he pulled his legs farther back, encouraging me to go deeper still. The chorus of his grunts filled my ears while sweat beaded on his forehead. Then he cried out, "Alexi!" His face contorted to the brink of pain and his body curled in on itself. His hole pressed against me, the muscle spasming and fluttering as he tried to expel me.

I groaned at the intensity of it and kept going. Then I realized he hadn't ejaculated. My thrusting faltered, and I was on the verge of checking on him when his body convulsed again.

"Don't stop. Whatever you do, don't stop," he gasped, his head digging into the mattress.

He "came" three more times before I relented and reached for his swollen cock. I'd scarcely wrapped my fingers around him when he bowed off the bed, releasing his legs, and his hole clenched like a vise. I groaned deep down in my soul as he milked everything I had and then some, then collapsed beside him, barely retaining the wherewithal to lose the spent condom.

We laid like that in silence as we caught our breath and let our bodies cool. I glanced at Matt and debated whether to tell him how much I'd missed him these last two weeks. Part of me worried this time, this moment, was fleeting, and that I was wasting it. We should be talking, spending *quality* time together. Another part argued that getting lost in passion was an excellent way to spend time together.

Smiling, I rolled onto my side and traced the definition of his torso, spreading the smears of release along his abdomen. His eyes fluttered open as his chest expanded with a deep breath that he released in a contented sigh. I leaned in to give him a sweet kiss. "How are you feeling?"

He closed his eyes and hummed.

I chuckled. "That good, huh?"

"So much better than good." He opened his eyes, his easy smile shining in their crystal depths. "I've never orgasmed so many times. I didn't even know it was possible for a guy to do that without ejaculating."

I laughed again and rested my head on my arm. "Oh, it's possible. I'll explain the science of it to you later."

"So it's *not* magic," he said with a cheeky grin, then gave an exquisite stretch before sinking back into the mattress. "Speaking of magic, how are you even functioning right now?"

"Pretty sure if I closed my eyes, I'd pass out."

"So why don't you?"

I shifted my gaze from studying the rise and fall of his chest. "I'm not ready to stop looking at you." Pink blossomed on his cheeks. I caressed his jaw, leaning down for another kiss. He sighed and leaned into the touch. "I have a question for you," I said as I resumed tracing his torso.

"Hmm."

"Are you working out again?"

His eyes flew open, and he shifted away. "No. Why do you ask?"

I shadowed to the bathroom to grab a damp towel, then used cleaning him up to stall for time. Once I'd resettled, I met his worried gaze. "Because you've gained some definition." I wanted to chase down the sudden wariness hiding in his eyes, but I also didn't want to jeopardize our evening, either.

He licked his lips and swallowed. "Is that okay?"

"Did I sound like I was complaining?" I smiled and wrapped an arm around his waist, sliding him closer until he nestled in the curve of my body.

"Okay," he said with a nervous smile. "Now, I have a question for you."

"What is it?" I laughed, nuzzling his neck.

"Your eyes. Earlier they went black like when we shadow, but you weren't shadowing anything. Or maybe you were, and I was too distracted to see what," he added with a more devious grin.

"That took longer than I would've expected."

He twisted beneath my arm to face me better. "What do you mean? What is it?"

"It's a manifestation of our true nature and our true desires," I said simply, thinking back to Vera's own awkward explanation.

His eyebrows furrowed as he considered my response, then shot up in understanding. "Have mine ever done that?"

"Yes." I was tempted to leave it at that, but if I expected honesty from him, it was only right that I return the favor. "I have a confession to make." He narrowed his eyes and I let out a sigh tinged with guilt. "You actually do it all the time. I... might have been using that against you." I winced in anticipation of retribution.

"Really? How?" Matt's open curiosity once again defied my expectations.

"Yeah. As a matter of fact, the first time you did it was the night you convinced me to stay. It's why I decided to give us a chance." I placed a kiss on his shoulder for emphasis.

"Oh." I couldn't tell if the information was being well received or if he was about to be really upset. "All the time?"

I smiled. "Kind of."

He placed a hand on my chest. "Alex."

"Yes?"

"Alex, I..." Struggle twisted his face, and he didn't finish.

I cupped his cheek once more and gave him a tender kiss, our lips sticking together until the distance pulled them apart. "I love you."

His conflicted expression softened. "Alexi," he sighed as he snuggled into my neck.

I wanted to ask him about his use of my name-name instead of the nickname he used for me. Twice in one evening was surely remarkable. But there was something fragile in this moment and I didn't want to break it. I squeezed him tight and enjoyed just having him near.

It felt like forever before I finally felt him drift off, almost as if he was intentionally trying not to sleep. My sleep was much longer in coming. I wanted to relish every microsecond we had together. Gradually, my breathing slowed as exhaustion worked its magic.

Matt jerked violently, wrenching me out of a deep sleep. I shifted to give him room, but the space only let his flailing get more extreme. The sheets tangled around him, strangling his movements and mine.

"Matt. Matt. Stop. You're okay." I hastily freed an arm and switched the lamp on. The yellow light illuminated a wild-eyed Matt.

Terror flooded his blue eyes as they searched the room. The soft glow of the lamp dimmed, fading despite the new bulb. Then I realized the night itself was being pulled from all corners of the room. I looked back at Matt to find his eyes were solid black. Fear clutched my heart.

"Matt. Wake up. Matt! It's not real. Whatever you think is there, it's not. Matt, please!" I begged, as the darkness got closer and the air thinner. The very night pulled at my essence, and Vera's warning flashed in my mind. I tried again to get Matt's attention, but wherever his mind was, it was far from here. It wasn't until I grabbed his face that he reacted.

He blinked once and the encroaching darkness stalled. He blinked again and his eyes flashed of blue. A third blink and suddenly air poured into his lungs as if he'd been underwater for hours. Then he turned his panicked gaze to me. "What happened?"

"I think you were having a nightmare," I said, trying not to sound too relieved. "Tell me about it? What was happening?" I stroked his cheek in an attempt to ground him, but my anxiety returned when his eyes lost focus again.

"They were hurting you," he whispered, barely loud enough to be heard over my thundering heart.

"Who was hurting me?" I asked, confused.

His focus immediately sharpened. "No one." He shook his head and averted his gaze. "It was just a crazy dream."

I considered telling him that crazy dream had come alarmingly close to killing us. Instead, I brushed his hair back. "Matt, look at me." When he refused, I grabbed his chin and ordered more firmly, "Look at me."

Begrudgingly, he lifted his gaze, revealing the fear he was trying so hard to hide.

"I'm right here. I'm fine. I'm safe." At the last word, his face finally softened. He curled into my chest and I wrapped him in an embrace, determined to never let him go. He wriggled a hand between us so he could rest it on my heart, and that was how he fell back asleep.

I continued to rub his back and failed to dispel my growing worry. My beautiful Matthew was terrified of something and I felt powerless to help. What could I do if he wouldn't let me in? I wrapped my hand around his and fought off sleep for as long as I could. But it was for naught.

When I awoke in the morning, he was gone. The sheets were stone cold and there wasn't a trace of him anywhere in the dorm. Even his bag was gone, though it was too early for him to be in class.

CHAPTER 24

POOL FOR BEGINNERS

M

After the third night of nightmares, I gave up trying to sleep with Alex. It was bad enough listening to his screams in my sleep, but lying to him when those dreams inevitably woke me up was worse. Trying to sneak out *after* he fell asleep didn't do any good either. Since I'd rejoined the bruiser club, exhaustion had become my permanent state of being. The ache in my chest doubled. He didn't deserve the constant lies, but the truth would only get him hurt, or worse, killed.

I carefully closed the dorm door and slipped quietly into my room, bypassing the kitchen despite the gnawing hunger in my belly. It was well past midnight, and I didn't want to risk a stray noise waking Alex. Safely ensconced in my room, I sagged against the door. But not even the weariness weighing me down could tempt me to seek sleep.

Memories of the most recent nightmare threatened to creep up, overlaying my barren room with a horrific image of Alex covered in blood and crying for help. I squeezed my eyes shut and violently forced them back down as I mentally chanted, "It's not real. It's not real." When I reopened my eyes, the image was gone. My shoulders slumped as I took in the empty space. We still called it my room, but it didn't feel like it. My *place* was on the other side of the dorm, back in bed with Alex.

For a moment, I considered tempting fate and just as quickly dismissed it. I was one intense nightmare away from spilling everything, consequences be damned. It wasn't worth the risk. My gaze fell on the sketch pad Jeffrey had given me eons ago. I grabbed it and a couple of pencils, then headed back to the living room. After a quick glance at his door, I started sketching Alex the way I imagined he looked right now. Snuggled deep beneath the comforter, hair in wild disarray, lips parted ever so slightly.

The mindless task worked its magic, and I settled into a kind of trance that both kept me awake and too focused to think about the dreams. When I finally looked up, the page was almost completely covered and hours had slipped. Mercifully, it was Wednesday, so I wouldn't have to go to the club tonight.

I let out a sigh and rested my head on the sketch pad. I missed Alex so much. Not just the kisses and killer sex. I missed my *friend*. I took a deep breath in a vain attempt to shake off the melancholy thoughts. At least it was late enough now that it wouldn't be strange to be on campus. I tucked the sketchbook safely beneath my mattress before grabbing my backpack.

The rest of the week went by in a blur of misery. Thursday's fight turned into *fights* and thanks to my lack of sleep, it was a total shit show. Everything hurt, even the parts of me that *hadn't* gotten hit. Normally I'd look forward to the weekend, but George had developed an irritating knack of monopolizing all of my free time. Then the impossible happened—George went home for a family event. Suddenly free, I was determined to enjoy my reprieve by spending as much of it as possible with Alex. I just had to figure out how.

By the time Saturday morning arrived, I was no closer to an answer. We couldn't risk an intimate outing at the coffee shop and no way were we going to the library. I was still desperately wracking my brain when Alex walked through the main door. Confused, I looked towards his room and back at him. He'd been in there; I was sure of it. How had he left without me sensing it? I sat there at a loss as he waltzed into the kitchen and began preparing an early lunch.

"Don't have anything better to do today?" he asked in a deceptively neutral tone, turning to glance at me.

I flinched inwardly. "I thought we could spend it together."

Guilt flashed across his face, then his eyes hardened and he turned back around. "Then I guess you should have said something sooner. I already have plans."

I sat in silence, not sure if that was actually true or not. Then he wrapped his sandwich to go. Disappointment wrapped around me and tightened until there was only pain. I couldn't even be mad; I deserved this. He chunked the food he'd put together into his backpack like it had offended him, then slung the strap over his shoulder and stalked toward the door.

"Alex." I don't know what possessed me to call out. Him being mad and avoiding me was probably for the best.

He stopped, tilting his head to listen without looking directly at me.

"What are you doing tonight?"

His shoulders sagged, and he was silent a moment before finally admitting, "I'm not doing anything."

"We should go out."

"Out?" he asked, finally meeting my gaze. I never wanted to go out.

"Yeah, somewhere different," I said with a spark of hope. "I've got a place in mind."

"I should be back around four." With that, he walked out of the dorm, leaving me with nothing better to do than wait for him.

I alternated between sketching and catching up on past due homework, while I kept a close eye on the time. Finally, it read four... and no Alex. I struggled not to assume the worst, that somehow, despite

George's absence, Alex had been discovered and wouldn't be coming back. By the time five o'clock rolled around, I was seriously considering going to look for him. There was just one problem: he hadn't told me where he was going.

The door opened, and I paused in my pacing. Alex looked from me to the table covered in notes, then shut the door. "Um... hey."

"Hey," I replied, for want of something more inspired.

He set his bag down. "So, someplace different?"

"Yeah." I took a hopeful step toward him. "Ever play pool?"

A smile twitched on his lips. "No."

"Then I think it's about time you learned."

His grin stretched to fill his face, lighting the entire room. "That could be fun."

"Come on," I said, leading him back into the hallway. "If we get in before seven, there's no cover." He eagerly followed, peppering me with questions about the game and where we were going. As we walked up to the pool hall, though, his wariness returned.

He eyed the peeling paint and crooked neon sign. "This doesn't really look like my scene."

"Well, your scene is the library and you need to get out more. Besides, it looks worse than it is on the inside." I nudged him in the ribs, then walked into what, in fact, was a total dive bar. "Relax, have a drink."

He stalled in the entrance. "The last time you said that, it didn't end well."

I rolled my eyes and dragged him inside. Fortunately, the place wasn't overly crowded this early, and I spotted an open table toward the back. "Do you really foresee that being a problem here?" I asked, flagging down a waitress.

She eyed us with a grin and sauntered over, swaying her hips to emphasize her barely there skirt. "What'll it be gents?"

I gave my best play-nice smile, not at all appreciating the once-over she gave Alex. "Two beers for me and my friend."

"You're really good at that," Alex said once she'd gone.

"What do you mean?" I asked, grabbing us a pair of pool cues.

"She's completely smitten. We're going to get amazing service," he added, staring at the cue I gave him.

I shrugged. "I've found a smile can go a long way if you want decent service."

The waitress reappeared with excellent timing, dropped off our drinks, and moved on to check on other nearby patrons.

"Right, take a drink so you can stop looking so weird and come over here."

He eyed the beer like it was a grenade that could explode at any second, then took a drink. "Not bad. Not as good as that fruity beer, but not bad either."

"Glad you approve. Now get over here before someone tries to take the table because we're not playing."

He set the beer on a nearby high-top and joined me at the end of the table. "Now what?"

"Mimic what I do." I positioned the cue between my fingers and held it level.

He leaned down to imitate the posture.

I shook my head. "No. Look at how I have both of my hands, not just the leading one. When you strike, it needs to be in one smooth motion. This game is about finesse, not power." It would have been easier to stand behind him and correct the errors that way, but I really didn't trust myself or what it would look like. We may not be on campus, but that didn't mean we were safe. "Drink some more of your beer. It's getting warm."

Huffing, he grabbed the bottle and made a big show of polishing it off.

I gestured for our waitress to bring us another round and repositioned. "I'll break so we can work with a real layout." The cue ball made a loud crack as it smashed into its brethren. The balls rolled in every direction, with two dropping loudly into the pockets.

"I feel like that was impressive," he said, looking clueless.

I smiled. I kind of liked the fact that he was impressed, even though he didn't know why he should be. A walk around the table revealed I'd sank two opposites. "Okay, it's still open. Do you want to be stripes or solids?"

He frowned. "Is that a trick question?"

"No." I laughed. "Just preference. Because I got one of each, I'll let you choose."

His eyes danced with merriment. "Stripes."

"Then here's what you're going to do."

I walked him slowly through our first game. He was absolutely deplorable, but that didn't make it any less fun. We were halfway through another round when a familiar voice called over. I glanced up from sinking the eight to find Sam and Lucas walking toward us.

"Hey!" I shouted, while Alex stood patiently waiting to be introduced, steadily nursing his fifth beer. "Guys, this is Alex, my roommate."

He held up a hand in greeting.

"Alex, this is Lucas and Sam from my math class."

Sam clapped me on the back. "Haven't seen you here in a while."

"Yeah, studies have gotten in the way of a lot lately." I shot an anxious glance in Alex's direction.

"That's no excuse for blowing off your friends," Lucas said as he grabbed his own cue stick. "How long have y'all been here?"

"Not too long," Alex offered. "What about you?"

Lucas and Sam laughed and shared a look. "Long enough to know this is definitely *not* your game."

"I know. Why don't we play doubles? Loser buys the next round," I suggested.

Lucas narrowed his eyes at me. "Matt, you're a hustler. I know better than to play against you by choice."

"Yeah, but you've seen Alex play. It'll be like having a handicap."

They looked at Alex, who was giving me quite the sour face. I simply smiled and passed him a fresh beer. He drank it absently. They looked back at each other and I knew I had them.

"Deal," they replied in unison.

The table got reset, and Sam broke. I still had to coax Alex through a good portion, but by the second half of the game, the beers were finally working their magic and he was making somewhat decent shots. I dragged it out a while longer, then cleaned the table.

"I knew it!" Lucas cried after the second such game. "You tricked us. He's not a newb at all. When did you see us come in?"

I shook my head. "I promise, I had no idea you guys were here until you walked by. As for Alex, it's beginner's luck." I clapped him on the shoulder, nearly knocking him over. Alex was definitely tipsy by this point. Lucas continued to glare at me, suspicion rolling off of him, until the server arrived with the next round. Alex excused himself as we reset for the next game.

"You guys see those girls over there?" Sam said, indicating two young women a few tables away. One had long blonde hair and was wearing a pink top, while the other had short, brown hair that curled around her ears and was wearing blue. Both were shooting curious looks our way.

"What about them?" Lucas asked. "It's not like you stand a chance with either."

"You're an ass," Sam grumbled. "I know! You go, Matt. You always have luck with the ladies."

"What? No." I fervently shook my head, glad that Alex was missing this conversation.

"Pretty sure it has something to do with looking like some tortured puppy," Lucas mused.

"Shut up." I spied Alex coming back and inspiration struck. "Send Alex."

"What?" Sam asked in high-pitched disbelief.

"Yeah, he's terrible at talking to girls."

"But look at him. He could bugger the whole thing and they'd *still* go home with him. That's not even fair," Sam whined.

"What's not fair?" Alex asked.

I pointed at the women. "You see those two over there?"

He nodded in a fair imitation of a bobble head and confirming my hope that he was definitely tipsy enough to do this.

"Go talk to them."

Lucas and Sam looked borderline apoplectic. But they weren't about to go and this was a great opportunity.

"Why?"

They released groans of dismay in unison. I tried not to laugh as I leaned over like I was going to give him advice. "Because you need to blend in better and it'll make their night. Just go do it," I added louder.

He rolled his eyes and trudged over.

Watching Alex pretend to hit on women was the last thing I wanted to see, but it needed to be done. The women had the expected reaction to someone that looked like Alex approaching them. Even from over here, we could make out the giggles.

Lucas smacked me in the arm, and I laughed. "Just wait for it." Alex looked back at us with a lost expression and I snickered. "Told you."

"Oh gods, he has no clue what he's doing," Sam said in awe.

"Like it matters. Look at them, they're eating it up." Lucas wasn't wrong; the blonde was leaning in and the brunette was playing with her curls. After a while, Alex headed back to us. Disappointment flashed across the women's faces as he left them to their night.

"They were nice," Alex said, grabbing his drink.

"And?" Sam prompted.

"And what?" Lucas looked like he might strangle Alex.

"Please tell me you at least got *one* of their numbers," Sam said desperately.

"No. Why? Was I supposed to?" Alex looked at me questioningly and I hid my laugh behind taking a drink.

"That's it—for sheer shame. The next round is on you guys."

I smacked my bottle down. "Double or nothing."

"No chance. You and your roommate's 'beginner's luck' have already taken us to the cleaners. If that's what we're playing, then I'm out."

"Yeah, I think I'm done for the night, too. You're an expensive person to play with, Matt."

"You could always try not losing," I commented as we all said our farewells.

Back in the dorm, it was clear Alex was definitely still tipsy if not outright drunk. "I don't see why we had to leave too," he griped as he fixed himself a glass of water.

"Things can get a little rough there on a Saturday night. I'd hate to get into a bar brawl over something as stupid as someone spilling a drink." Or making a real pass at Alex.

He snorted. "Please. You'd love that. What are you doing?" he asked when he noticed me clearing the table.

"I'm going to show you how to play. Properly." I put the last chair in place and created a shadow billiard table. A spell later, and I didn't have to maintain it.

"Damn, you really have gotten good."

"Thanks," I said, creating a cue stick and indicating for him to do the same. "Set up like I showed you. We need to work on your form."

"Wouldn't this have been easier at the bar?"

"Not really."

He frowned and set up. While his playing had slightly improved, he really was terrible. I walked up behind him and reached around to fix the placement of his hands. "Little close, don't you think?" he asked.

I chuckled in his ear, and he shivered. "For the record, this is typically how most people teach their date how to play." I guided his cue, then had him reset. He was better, but still needed some additional direction. Once again, I leaned down to correct his positioning, enjoying the way his body fit against mine. This was much easier than trying to talk him through it.

"I think you're just messing with me." He giggled as I brushed my nose along his neck.

"Promise, just like this," I whispered. "You should see how people really play."

"What do you mean?"

"I'll show you. We'll play one game."

"Just one?" he asked.

"For now. Remember, it's about follow through," I added as he leaned his lithe frame over the phantom table.

He snickered. "Pretty sure I've never had a problem with follow through." His break was nearly perfect, albeit eerily silent. "How are we supposed to know who does what? They all look the same."

"Everybody's a critic. This is just for fun. Play until you miss." I waited until he made a few successful shots and his confidence increased. Much as I enjoyed hanging out as friends, there was no denying the desire growing inside of me. I wanted Alex in a way that sent heat coursing through my entire body. I walked up behind him once more and leaned down as he set up for the shot.

"That's a little distracting," he said calmly.

"That's the general idea." I slid a hand down the front of his thigh.

He scratched so badly I was concerned for the actual table beneath. "Shit, Matt."

I chuckled and removed the hand to take my shot.

"What was that?"

"I told you. People play differently than you think." I sank a couple, then missed.

"I think you're lying," he said, relocating to a spot at the opposite end.

I considered what he'd said about my eyes always going black and wondered if I could do it on purpose. All it would really take would be admitting how much I wanted to feel Alex beneath my hands, against my mouth, moaning...

Alex looked up and did a double take that resulted in another scratch. "Seriously, how am I supposed to focus with you messing with me?" He stubbornly went to try the shot again, and I shadowed behind him.

"You're not," I whispered, nibbling on his ear. He squeaked and his cue disappeared as I spun him around, then pushed him against the very real kitchen table. I claimed his mouth, and he eagerly returned the fiery need. "Alex," I sighed, removing his shirt without preamble. I missed this, missed him.

"What?" he responded breathlessly.

"Are you drunk?"

"No, maybe a little tipsy still, but that's all."

"Good." My mouth covered his once more while I slid my hands down his sculpted torso to undo his buckle. He moaned in anticipation and I forced him hard against me before moving my kisses lower. I pushed his pants down until his erection popped free, then licked him from base to tip before greedily swallowing him down.

"Oh fuck," he groaned, gripping the table until his knuckles turned white.

His moans of pleasure combined with the weight of him on my tongue was absolutely intoxicating. I freed him with a pop and mouthed his balls while my own erection pressed painfully against my zipper. But I couldn't be bothered to give my dick the attention it needed when that would require removing my hands from Alex. I teased the veins along his shaft and twirled my tongue around the tip. He shuddered as I sucked him down again, betraying how close he was. I pulled away. "You aren't going to tell me to stop?"

"Absolutely not," he gasped, tangling his fingers in my hair and guiding me back to his leaking dick.

I hummed in contentment as he controlled the bob of my head. When he let out a loud groan and tensed, I was more than ready to take everything he had. When he was done, he pulled me to my feet and captured me with a searing kiss.

"How are you doing, love?" he asked, palming my throbbing dick.

I choked on a groan at the same time my heart fluttered.

He squeezed my straining erection, then gentled his hold. "Tell me what you want, what you need."

"You. I want you so fucking bad."

"That so?"

"Yes," I gasped. Need bubbled in my veins, making me lightheaded and weak.

He grabbed my chin and forced me to meet his fierce emerald gaze. A hot poker of fear stabbed my heart. "Do you need a minute?" I shook my head, not trusting words, then he claimed me with a kiss so intense I forgot everything else.

We stumbled to the couch, leaving a trail of abandoned clothes. He pushed the coffee table out of the way and placed the couch cushions on the floor while I secured the condom and lube I'd hidden in here earlier. Alex plucked the supplies from my hand with a lascivious grin.

"Someone was optimistic."

"Hopeful," I corrected, as I pulled him down to the floor with me.

He kissed me deep, forcing my head into the makeshift bed, then moved on to lay a trail of open-mouthed kisses along my neck, chest, and stomach. I was shaking by the time he reached for my dick. "You are so hungry for it," he rumbled.

"Yes," I agreed eagerly. I'd been hungry—starving—plenty of times in my life, but never like this. I didn't even notice he'd opened the lube until slick fingers circled my hole at the same time he took me in his mouth. The intense sensation had me bowing off the floor. His free hand cradled my hip as he made a meal of me and sank his finger past my rim. My release danced closer. A couple more sweeps of his tongue, another press of his finger, and I'd come apart.

Alex relinquished my dick, and I let out a moan of frustration. "Not yet, love." I whimpered as he traced my freed dick with his lips. He added another finger, which slid in with almost no resistance.

I took deep gulping breaths, aching for more and already so close. He spread his fingers as he slowly thrusts them and I thrashed against the cushions. "Alex, *please*."

"You sure you're ready for me?" he crooned, peppering my chest with light kisses and tiny nips.

"Fuck yes," I gasped, and he chuckled. Too blind with lust, I didn't see him open the condom, but I heard it. Then he was pressing his head against my hole and I was positive I'd die if he tortured me with shallow thrusts. To my relief, once he'd breached the outer rim, he drove deep in one long thrust. I made a garbled sound, part gasp, part groan, at the combination of fullness and burn.

Alex's fingers glided gently along my jaw as I found my breath. "Still with me?"

Rather than respond, I hooked my ankles behind him and rolled us. It took some situating, but at last, I had him perfectly straddled. I gave an experimental roll of my hips and released a stuttering sigh.

"Night, Matt," Alex gasped, digging his fingers into my sides until his nails bit flesh. The hint of pain somehow grounded me and shot me into a whole other stratosphere. He released his grip and coasted one hand up my chest while the other encircled my erection. He gave me a firm stroke that I echoed with another roll of my hips. "That's it. Ride me. I want to see you fall apart."

I leaned back in search of that perfect angle, bracing myself against his upper thighs. He shifted his hand to the top of my dick and I thrust up to follow him before crashing back down with a grunt.

"That's perfect. Keep doing that."

I did. Again and again, getting lost in the incredible feel of Alex stretching me, owning me. My hands slipped, and I shifted them to the floor. As soon as his thighs were free, Alex thrust up hard and my head fell back in ecstasy. His hips pistoned off the floor, slamming into that spot I still didn't have a name for, but felt like pure fucking magic. Then, just like he wanted, I completely broke apart. With a grunt, I shot ribbons across his abs and chest. Alex gave a few more hard thrusts, then curled off the floor, holding me tight as he found his own climax.

I wrapped my arms around him and nuzzled his sweaty hair. This. This was all I wanted. The rest of the world—all the bullies and the bigots—could rot in hell. All I needed was Alex. *My* Alex. The light trail of his fingers along my back gradually brought me back down, grounding me in a way only he had ever managed.

"We should... we should get cleaned up," he panted against my chest.

I grumbled incoherently and held him tighter. Who needed to be clean? This moment was perfect exactly the way it was.

Sometime later, I blinked my eyes open to find Alex's emerald ones staring back. "Hey," he whispered.

"Hey," I replied with a sleepy grin. "Sorry. I must have dozed off." I combed my fingers through his hair, which was a wonderful mess, and gave him a gentle kiss that made my lips tingle. He was my absolute everything. I only wished I could find the words to tell him that.

"It's nice to see you acting like your old self."

Anxiety froze my limbs. I didn't want to think this had been a mistake, even though I knew better.

Concern darkened his eyes. "What's been going on with you?"

"Alex, please. Not tonight. I just want to appreciate being here with you." I stroked his cheek and hoped desperately he would agree. We'd found a small bubble of happiness and I wasn't ready to give it up.

He searched my face for a long minute before finally saying, "Okay, we don't have to talk about it right now."

I let out the breath I'd been holding and snuggled closer. "Thank you." He'd demand the truth eventually, and I prayed I'd be strong enough to keep it from him, but not tonight. Tonight, we were just us, like we had been before.

CHAPTER 25

CUTTING TIES

A

Matt was a bottomless well of frustration. First, I didn't see him for weeks, then he takes me out on a date. Pool was... interesting. I chuckled to myself as I replaced the last pillow on the couch. I'd never had anyone teach me how to do something like that before. Though I was still dubious about his methods. Matt was just secretly a scoundrel. Not that it bothered me in the least. I missed feeling the fire inside of him. It let me know he was alive, that he cared.

I finished moving the coffee table and paused. If Matt *did* care, then why had he refused to tell me what was going on with him? Why had he been so distant lately? His small request to drop the subject last night had seemed reasonable, but had done little for my worry. Was he preparing to leave Arminius like so many of our classmates and didn't have the heart to tell me? If I could just get him to confide in me, then we could work through things together. I would do long distance if that's what it took. Or... was it something entirely different? I sank onto the couch and closed my eyes against the headache forming.

"You sure you got enough sleep?" Matt teased from behind me. His hand rubbed along the curve of my neck as he placed a sweet kiss on the other side.

"I don't really think sleep was one of the things we did last night," I said with my eyes still closed. His resulting chuckle made my heart hurt. When had that beautiful sound become so rare?

"I thought the other things were pretty good too," he said, his voice low, then lightly bit my neck before soothing it with another kiss.

"That so?"

"Yeah." The heat in his voice sent corresponding waves coursing through me. Was it even possible to get enough of him?

I grabbed his hand. "Come here."

He didn't resist and walked around to face me, a playful smile tugging at the corners of his mouth. He really was quite the devil. I pulled him down and he came without hesitation. This was a wonderful side of Matt. He straddled my hips like he had the night before and leaned in to kiss me without having to be encouraged. I curled my fingers in his downy hair and arched into him, reveling in his slow, methodical exploration of my mouth.

"You know, I had a fantasy like this once," I said between kisses.

"Oh really?" He ground against me and I couldn't have stopped my moan if I wanted to.

"Yep," I said, snaring him again.

He broke off breathless and pulled his fresh shirt off in one fluid motion. I ran my hands over his chest and the niggling suspicion that he'd resumed working out resurfaced. Not that I was complaining. I flicked my gaze up to find him watching me appreciate the view. A few faint bruises caught my attention, but it was entirely possible that I'd done those last night. Not dwelling on maybes, I slipped my hands around to caress his back and he slid closer.

"And how's it measuring up?" he asked, his mouth returning to mine. My fingers dug into his back as I urged him on. I loved how he felt and how he responded to the slightest touch.

"No contest. Then again, it didn't actually get this far."

"No?" he asked playfully, rubbing against me again. I gasped, and he mercilessly did it again. "Wouldn't have anything to do with the fact that I suddenly showed up half-dressed out of my room. Would it?" He nipped my lip.

"How could you possibly know that?" I asked, my shock momentarily overriding the tide of ecstasy he was creating.

He gave me a truly wicked smile. "I'm pretty sure you're the reason I fell through the bed that night. Scarred the crap out of me too," he added, before stealing another kiss.

"How would I do that?"

"Easy really." His eyes went dark and the shadows in the room thickened. They reached toward us, not menacingly like when he'd had that awful nightmare, more like they wanted to be where we were. As they got closer, I felt a similar pull on myself, a need to be as close to Matt as possible, nudging me towards my shadow state.

I drew in a deep breath as the sensation vanished. "Oh, my."

"There was that... and this." He suggestively rolled his hips.

"Thought I managed to keep that to myself," I tried to say, though it came out more strangled than anything.

He laughed low and sexy as hell. "I told you, Alex, I pay attention, *especially* where you're concerned."

Unable to stand the torture any longer, I shifted so that he fell in the open space beside me and rolled to cover him. His mouth greedily found mine as he arched against me and locked his legs around my waist. "You have to be the most impossible person I have ever met," I said, digging my fingers into his thigh. He groaned and I could feel what control I was pretending to have slip away.

"It's never bothered you before." He punctuated the statement with a tantalizing kiss. No, it hadn't, but something else was bothering me now. The words were out before I could stop them.

"What's going on with you, Matt? What are you hiding?"

He pulled back so sharply I thought he'd taken my lips with him. He searched my face while confusion and anger warred for dominance on his own. Anger won. "Is this some sort of trap? Was that your plan? You'd ply me with sex and kisses to get what you wanted?" He pushed me away, and I fell against the armrest.

"What? No. I just want to know what's going on with you. I'm worried, Matt." Now, *I* was confused. Where was this coming from?

He sat up and yanked his shirt back on. "And you thought *this* was the best way to find out? You'd bait me and I would just tell you everything? Nyx forbid you actually just fucking ask." He stood abruptly, nearly toppling me off the couch.

"Bait you? *You* started this," I said hotly. "And I *did* ask. Multiple times."

"I'm not doing this with you." He turned and stalked off to his room.

I followed close on his heels. "Maybe if you would just talk to me, you wouldn't feel baited!"

"You can't use sex to get whatever you want, Alex. It doesn't work that way."

"What!" I shouted in furious disbelief.

He crossed the threshold to his room, slamming the door behind him.

"No, you don't." I reached for the handle to find it locked. Rage washed through me as I jiggled the handle uselessly. "Open the fucking door, Matt." I shook the knob violently. "Do it or *I* will!" I could feel him just on the other side. He was less than a foot away. The lock snapped beneath my persistence and I ripped open the door.

Just as I'd suspected, he was standing literally on the other side. He looked up at me, anger burning in his eyes and his jaw clenched so tight it was twitching.

"What the hell, Matt?" I stepped forward and ran into a wall so hard I staggered back. I scanned the opening, which, for all intents and purposes, looked perfectly passable. Except it wasn't—he'd put up a boundary to keep Shadows Demons out. My fury found new heights as my fist slammed against the spell.

He took a step back as if unsure the invisible wall would hold.

"Drop the fucking barrier," I demanded, pounding on the spell.

"Let it go, Alex. Just leave me alone."

I narrowed my eyes at him, silently demanding he drop the spell. Then inspiration struck. Just because I couldn't get in through the door didn't mean I couldn't get in at all. He must have realized the same thing, because he darted to the wall to keep pace with me, barely getting the rest of the boundary up in time to prevent me from simply shadowing right through the wall. I spent several frustrated minutes searching for cracks in the defensive barrier. My essence reaching out to feel for any gap, even a hole the size of a pin, would be sufficient. I found no such opening and returned with a vengeance to the open door.

He stood on the other side, looking more determined than ever and breathing hard. Putting up a spell like that so quickly could not have been easy. The flat of my hand smacked into the barrier spell and he jumped.

"If I can't get in, then you can't get out!" I yelled at him.

He simply stood there, staring back.

"Damn it, Matt, let me in," I ordered, but already I could feel my anger waning into hopelessness. This was it; he'd made his choice to keep me out. I didn't know what that meant, and that frightened me more than anything. I rested my head against the spell, surprised to find it was cool, like a heavy mist. "Please, Matt, drop the wall. Talk to me. Just let me help." I hated the sound of despair in my voice and didn't have the energy to look up. I didn't want to see how resolute he was in denying me. My hand fell, and I turned to lean against the spell, sliding to sit on the floor. "I'm not leaving," I promised quietly. There was only silence and the sound of my breathing. I sent out feelers so I'd know the moment the spell failed and resigned myself to wait.

At some point, I must have dozed off. My head snapped up in alarm and I fell backwards, the resistance of the spell gone. Panicked and not sure how long the spell had been down, I spun around, positive Matt was gone. To my surprise, he was sitting on the floor, leaning against the bed, completely passed out. My tortured angel looked exhausted. I couldn't even fathom the amount of energy or power it would have taken to sustain such a high-level shadow spell.

Distantly, I realized my feelers had created a perfect box around the room. I released them and bent to pick up Matt, then carefully laid him on the bed. "What can you not tell me?" I whispered into the quiet. For a moment, I considered letting him rest in peace—he certainly needed it—but I'd made a promise. I wouldn't leave. Part of me was afraid that if I let him out of my sight, I'd never see him again. So I crawled on top of the covers beside him and pulled him close.

I wasn't sure when I fell asleep again, but I knew exactly what woke me. Matt was struggling in his sleep, almost as if he was fighting for his life. His heart raced beneath my hand so hard it felt like it might give out. He mumbled something, sounding distressed. I leaned closer to make it out.

Suddenly, his eyes flew open, and he gasped for air, his whole body becoming a taut string that could snap at any moment. His hand covered mine, and he spun to meet my worried gaze. The panic in his eyes slowly receded. But anger quickly replaced the relief. He threw my arm off and swiveled his legs over the side of the bed.

"What are you doing here? I told you to leave me alone." There was anger and something else in his voice that took me a moment to recognize—fear.

"And I told you I wouldn't. Something is obviously wrong. Why won't you tell me what it is?" I asked, trying to remain calm as I shifted to sit beside him.

"Because I can't," he said, his voice raw and his body shaking.

"You can tell me anything, Matt. I'm still your best friend. If nothing else, I'm still that." I reached out to him and he flinched away from the contact, his shaking intensifying.

"Please, stop. Just... stop," he sobbed. He wasn't *just* shaking, he was crying.

Desperate, I took a stab in the dark. "Does it have to do with the dreams? We can fix those."

He shook his head violently from side to side, doing what he could to keep the growing sobs silent. "You don't understand."

"I might if you told me."

"I can't. I can't tell you, Ale—" He cut himself off. "I can't lose you." It wasn't the first time he'd said it, but this was the first time he'd ever sounded so hopeless.

I wrapped him in a hug before he could stop me. "You won't. I love you, Matt. Nothing will ever stand in the way of that."

The shaking stopped dead. He pressed the palms of his hand to his face and forcibly removed the evidence of his melt down. When he finally turned to look at me, a hollow anger that bordered on apathy filled his eyes. "You need to leave." The statement was quiet, but crystal clear without so much as a hiccup or waver.

"Matt," I said uselessly.

His eyes hardened, turning to unforgiving ice. "Get out, Alex."

I stood, feeling as if someone had scooped my insides out with a spoon. I paused in the doorway to look back. He sat there still as a statue staring at the floor, then he was gone in a blink of shadow. My heart shattered into a thousand pieces and I clutched my chest at the overwhelming agony of it.

I lay staring at the ceiling for hours until the pain of it faded enough that I could think again. How I'd actually gotten to my room was a mystery. Someone or something was taking my Matt from me. I had no idea what could have that kind of sway over him or if it was even something I could fight. There was one thing I did know for certain though: I *would* fight. Whatever it took, I wouldn't give up on Matt.

CHAPTER 26

BAD DECISIONS

M

It took days to figure out how to tie off the barrier spell so it wouldn't drain me dry. Unfortunately, the max I could get out of it before it failed was maybe five hours. If I could find a power source, I could make it stretch longer, days, maybe even weeks, like Vera had done. But I didn't have time for that. Much easier to wait until Alex was definitely asleep to return to the dorm. The image of his stricken face when I'd demanded he leave swam in front of me, obscuring the sidewalk leading to fraternity row.

I pushed away the painful memory as I caught sight of George. Per usual, Kyle and Travis flanked him. The horrid trio had their heads bent together, their voices lowered. Travis's gaze wandered past George, and he clocked me. Abruptly, the three went silent, but not before I caught a name—Thomas.

"You look fucking terrible, man," Kyle said, stepping away from the others. He clapped me on the shoulder and I shrugged him off. I really didn't have the energy for his lackluster banter *and* the fight later. Between not eating, sleeping, or talking to Alex, I was barely more than a husk these days.

"Still looks better than you," Travis snickered. Kyle punched him in the arm and George stepped in.

"What took you so long?"

I squinted at him, knowing damn well I was perfectly on time. "Sorry, won't happen again. Got caught up by some teacher I passed wanting to 'save me'," I said sardonically. They laughed as expected. Humorless twits. I shoved my hands in my pockets and aimed for an air of casual indifference. "Who's this Thomas guy? Heard y'all mention him a few times now. He a friend of yours? Seems strange I haven't met him yet." I snuck a glance to find Kyle and Travis sharing an anxious look while George appeared speculative.

"You know, I think it might be time for little Matty to meet Thomas," George said at last, eying me like a butcher weighing meat. He cut his gaze toward the other two. "What are you ass hats looking at? Let's get a move on."

Kyle and Travis had the wherewithal not grumble, but continued shooting me furtive glances the whole way to the fight club. George gave the password at the door and we slipped into what promised to be an exceptionally rowdy night. As expected, my name topped the roster. Upside to fighting so early in the night was that I could get it over with. Down was that there was a better chance I'd get tossed into the ring again.

I gritted my teeth, determined not to give George any reason to second guess his decision to introduce me to Thomas. If that took fighting twice or more in one night, then I'd give every round my all. Without a word, I passed my shirt to Travis, then walked over to Neese.

"About time," he said in his slippery voice. "You're facing a sprite tonight. His name is Titus. Don't fuck it up, kid." He pushed me toward the edge into what amounted to a waiting block.

I hadn't fought a sprite before. I couldn't help but think back to the sprite siblings at the orphanage. They'd look terrifying, but Christian had been small, almost fragile looking. Surely a sprite wouldn't be that bad. I'd handled worse.

The previous fight ended. Once they'd finished carrying out the unconscious fighter, I took my place center ring. A couple minutes passed by, filled with the familiar sound of spectators placing their bets, then the electric buzz of the barrier hummed to life. It hadn't been used in the previous fight, but then, I'd never seen it used for anyone but me. Neese, guarantying his pound of flesh.

I glanced over my shoulder toward the evil wyvern. The barrier was still in force, but no one else was in the ring. His toothy grin said I was wrong. Something slammed into my face and knocked me into the electric barricade. A sizzle filled my ears, and I leapt away just in time to avoid a crushing blow to my spine. Dust drifted into the air as I spun to find my opponent. Except there was no one there. I glimpsed a light mote no bigger than a penny and recalled how the siblings had transformed into points of light. Fucking sprites.

I shadowed out before he could force me against the ropes again and rematerialized farther away. This was going to be exceptionally difficult if I could barely see my opponent. I gathered shadow into the shape of a fly swatter. The crowd ate up the implied insult, and Titus finally made his appearance.

Titan would have been a better name for the guy. He was easily the size of Granite and just as broad. I swallowed. Hopefully, his size was an indication that he wasn't as good with his psychic abilities. *Those*, I painfully remembered from the when Scylla had forced me to the ground and sucked all the air from my lungs.

I took a step to avoid the roundhouse coming my way, only find that my left foot refused to leave the ground. Before I could think to shadow, the kick hit me square in the side, leaving sparks of blue magic to swirl in the air. I gritted my teeth and sank into the darkness.

Titus's next kick passed through me and the crowd erupted in boos. Bloodthirsty bastards loved it when I took hits, even more when I wailed.

I shook off the attack and grabbed his leg after it passed through me. It took more effort than it should have, but I managed to throw him against the electric barrier. Just because it was there to keep me in didn't mean I couldn't use it to my advantage. While he was struggling to regain his balance, I used his own shadow to reappear behind him. I locked an arm around his neck and clung for all I was worth. Unfortunately, I was nowhere near peak strength.

He elbowed me beneath my ribs hard enough to knock the wind out of me. I lost my hold, and he staggered forward, flailing out with a psychic push that knocked me toward the barrier. I skidded to a stop millimeters shy of the electricity now sizzling the hairs at the small of my back. broke free and staggered forward, using his abilities to knock me into the barrier myself. Not really sure how much I could actually take in my current state or what other tricks Titus might have up his sleeve, I used shadow to propel myself forward. The sooner this was over, the better.

As Titus rushed me, my biggest concern became a reality. Air was yanked out of my lungs. No matter how I gasped and gulped, I couldn't get it to stay. Stumbling to a halt, I held out my hands, palms facing each other. I ignored the bursts of color spotting my vision from lack of oxygen and formed the shadows into massive walls of darkness, then clapped my hands together. For a moment, Titus hovered in place, frozen mid-lunge. I dropped my hands, and he crumpled to the ground with barely a sound.

It took every ounce of willpower I had not to sag with relief as air found its way back into my lungs. I hated using my powers so much in the ring; last thing I needed was anyone realizing how strong I'd become. As it was, I was pretty sure George believed he was more powerful than me. I wanted to keep it that way.

At last, the barrier fell, and I could work my way over to the trio. When I'd fought during the summer, people had stepped aside, patting me on the back and congratulating me as I passed. Now, I had to push my way through the onlookers until I emerged on the other side in time to see Neese walking away from the others. It still rankled that they didn't have to fight at all.

I didn't bother asking if they were ready to leave. They never were. While the fights continued, I stole the opportunity to rest against the wall, letting the cool concrete ease some of my aches. Off to the side, Travis tried unsuccessfully to pick up the resident witch... again. I eyed the poultices and salves with envy, but Neese had made it clear that I wouldn't get so much as a bandage.

The witch glanced over at me while trying to avoid Travis's roving hands. She at least knew what was going on here. To her credit, she didn't seem to like it. Travis said something, and she laughed noncommittally, swatting at him. Schmuck couldn't take a hint if it bulldozed over him. Finally, George made his way back over to where I was sitting against the wall. I rolled my head to the side to look up at him.

He glowered at me, and I wondered what exactly Neese had said to him earlier. "You ready yet? I'm starving."

Kyle appeared out of nowhere. "Did someone mention food?"

"Little Miss Sunshine is a real piece of work," Travis said, joining us with a dramatic huff.

"You're probably not her type," Kyle said a little too helpfully.

"I know what her type is. The kind that wears a skirt," Travis said bitterly. I only barely didn't roll my eyes.

"Disgusting is what it is," George said, hocking a glob of spit that landed inches from my foot.

"Just because someone isn't interested in you doesn't automatically make them gay," I said, instantly regretting opening my mouth when George swiveled a venomous look on me. To my surprise, Kyle came to the rescue.

"She probably thinks you have a little pecker." Kyle laughed, and I let out a sigh of relief as George guffawed. Next time, I'd keep my opinions to myself. Travis hoisted me to my feet while simultaneously trying to slug Kyle and nearly clocking me in the process.

"Alright, bozos, let's get out of this dump." George opened the over-large metal door and I cast a surreptitious glance behind us. He better hope Neese never heard him talking that shit.

We wandered into the town proper to grab some food. Even starving, I could only finish half of my burger. I gave the rest of it to Kyle as a silent thank you for unintentionally saving my bacon. As we meandered our way back to campus, a neon sign turning off for the night caught my attention. I squinted to get a closer look, my vision still burning with the afterimage, and my heart constricted. The coffee shop. Longing for Alex welled up, making my throat tight and my eyes sting. I quickly averted my gaze and found George eying me. "What's your deal?" I asked defensively. Not even thinking about Alex was safe anymore.

"So you want to meet Thomas, huh?"

I shrugged. "Sure, why not? You guys talk about him enough." That wasn't entirely true; they didn't talk about him around me, at least, not on purpose.

"Then you should probably know a few things. Thomas is a pretty intense guy. He has brought it to our attention that there's an impostor in our midst; a disgusting creature that has been *contaminating* us with its presence." I held my breath and forced my expression to remain disinterested. This was it, the answers I'd been looking for. "If you were interested in helping, I think I could persuade Thomas to meet."

"Depends. What sort of disgusting creature? If we're talking boils, I'm out," I said with another shrug.

Kyle and Travis laughed so hard they snorted. George, on the other hand, had gone nearly purple, his eyes swelling with rage. "We're not talking about *boils*," he spat. "We're talking about one of our own masquerading like they're one of us, an abomination that needs to be taken care of. Permanently." He spat on the ground for emphasis.

Suddenly, my path was clear. If I could get this mysterious Thomas's approval to join the hunt, then I could ensure they were always looking in the wrong direction.

"Why the miserable thing hasn't taken its own life is beyond me. So that leaves us." George gestured at my heinous companions. Travis and Kyle leered.

My stomach rolled. Alex had never done anything to any of them, was hands down the best person I'd ever met. How could *who* he was be such an unforgivable crime in their eyes? I tightened my jaw and strengthened my resolve. Whatever it took, I wouldn't let them within spitting distance of Alex. "I could do that. What do we know?"

"Eager, aren't you?" George's searching gaze made my skin itch.

I shrugged again. "It's something to do." And there might even be a chance we'd stop going to that damnable club.

George resumed walking. "Suppose you're right. We don't know much. That's the biggest reason we haven't already found them. Thomas doesn't want us wasting his time and getting it wrong. We *do* know that they're at least a level ten, not easily intimidated, fairly intelligent, and good with orders."

I struggled to take deep breaths while panic strangled my lungs. All they were missing was that he was six-one, had dark hair, and green eyes.

Kyle walked up beside me. "You okay? You don't look so good, Matty."

My stomach heaved, and I forced the bile back, focusing on breathing slowly through my nose. "I think it's the burger," I managed, bending over just in case my last meal made a reappearance after all.

Kyle eyed the wrapper in his hand and quickly tossed it, wiping the grease off on his pants. George had stopped walking and was once again watching me curiously.

If I didn't pull it together fast, I was going to blow this whole thing. I took a deep breath and straightened back up. "Maybe it's whatever that damn pixie did to me."

George's face immediately lightened. "Why don't you call it a night, Matty? We'll catch up tomorrow. In the meantime, I'll talk to Thomas, see what he thinks," he said, then vanished, leaving Travis and Kyle scurrying to disappear as well.

Some friends. What if I really was sick?

Rather than shadow walk across campus, I took my time and ruminate over what I'd learned. George had confirmed pretty much all of my fears. The only mercy was that they didn't know who they were looking for or what they might look like. It wasn't much, but I'd take it.

When I arrived back at the dorm, all the lights were out. I left them that way and walked to my room in the dark. Hand on the doorknob, I paused, glancing toward Alex's closed door. One look couldn't hurt. In a heartbeat, I'd shadowed across the living room, then hesitated. What if he was awake? I cautiously shadowed my head through the door. Darkness greeted me, along with Alex's slight snore. I walked the rest of the way in and tiptoed to the bathroom. Fortunately, it wasn't closed. I created a mock door of shadow and laid it over the opening. Then I reached inside and flicked on the light. I winced at the click of the switch and darted an anxious glance toward Alex. Reassured I hadn't woken him, I thinned the shadow door to a thin veil, careful not to brighten the room too much.

Even in the faint light, I could make out Alex's perfect features. By some miracle, his hair was behaving and, for once, not angled in every direction. His hand slid out from the cocoon of covers towards the edge of the bed, as if he could sense me standing there.

Night, I missed him. I didn't even feel like a whole person anymore. The urge to go to him, to trace his beautiful face, to run my fingers through his hair increased until I could hardly stand it. I wrapped my arms around myself, lingering a moment longer, then shadowed straight to my room. I fell onto the bed, too tired to even attempt the boundary spell, while silent tears streaked down my cheeks.

CHAPTER 27

BROKEN PROMISES

A

I stared at the back of Matt's head in our Demon History II class. There was no telling if he was passing or even doing the assignments. Still, he was here, which was something, and more than I could say for the dorm. What I couldn't figure out was why he kept leaving the bathroom light on in my room. And why not stay if he was already there? It had to have something to do with his nightmares, which undoubtedly had something to do with whatever he didn't want me to know.

The professor dismissed the class with a wave and I lurched to my feet. I pushed past some slower movers in my rush to catch Matt before he could pull his usual disappearing act and nearly ran into him. His sharp gaze snared mine and my heart skipped. Then it darted to something behind me and he shadowed out, avoiding the crowd altogether. I looked over my shoulder in search of what had made him bolt. When I realized George and his goons weren't far, I snarled. Tempting as it was to demand answers about why my boyfriend was spending so much time with them, I didn't want to hear what they had to say. I wanted to hear it from Matt.

I all but sprinted to Mysterio College and, for what might have been the first time, was actually grateful for Battle Tactics. It was a sorry state of our current affair that I was actually looking forward to sparring. Considering how long it had been since he'd last touched me, any excuse to touch was a good one.

In a surprising twist, Vera waltzed into the room. Her gaze swept over the assembled students and I couldn't help but notice that yet another two were missing. Who the hell dropped a class two-thirds of the way through the semester? Then a possibility occurred to me—maybe it hadn't been by choice. My glance slid to Matt. Given how many classes we had together he'd missed, he was likely flirting dangerously with expulsion. At Vera's heavy sigh, I returned my attention to the front of the room.

"Today, we'll be using multiple training rooms to allow for ample space to spread out. I'll be checking on each group periodically to offer guidance and advice. You'll be in your usual pairings for sparring. Depending on how much... correction is needed, we'll be mixing up the groups next class." She crossed her arms and stared at the class. "Well? What are you waiting for? Go."

Her demand got the class moving with purpose and in short order, I found myself in the farthest training room with Matt, Ellie, Louise, Ronald and Yaren. I stood across from Matt, where he still had yet to meet my eye. Better at fighting or not, he'd have a bloody hard time holding his own if he refused to look at me. "You ready for this?" I asked, in an attempt to get his attention.

He finally glanced up from his study of the floor. His eyes glinted darkly with anger and something else. Hesitation? Fear? Why would he be afraid of me? He was substantially better at sparring than I was, if for no other reason than he was perfectly okay hitting someone. Finally, he shrugged and looked away.

I clenched my fists and fought the urge to yell at him to get over himself, to let me in. But I'd done that already, and it hadn't done an ounce of good. With no kind of warning or formal start to the match, I surged forward.

His eyes widened in alarm, and he shadowed out of reach.

I growled and spun to face where he would likely manifest. At least one of us had been paying attention in class and it sure as hell wasn't him. When he reappeared, my swing was already in motion.

He barely caught the hit before it could land and promptly followed through with his own. His fist collided with my jaw before I could even register mine had been stopped.

"Really? The face?" I snarled.

Matt looked at his hand in horror and jumped backward out of reach and kept jumping. Despite the growing ache in my jaw, I didn't relent. He could avoid me all he wanted outside, but here, he had no choice but to face my wrath head on. The sensation of someone shadowing prickled my skin, and I gripped the shadows around Matt without mercy. Shock exploded across his face, no doubt at discovering he couldn't shadow away from the hold. His demeanor slowly shifted to something akin to panic as I unleashed and he struggled to parry my attacks. Yet despite my ferocity or the shrinking distance, he didn't strike back.

The door to the classroom opened and closed, signaling Vera's arrival. "Good form, Ellie. Remember, keep your senses open so you can tell when your opponent is about to move. Yaren, try to take this seriously."

As her voice got closer, my frustration with my own sparring partner increased. Even with Matt solely playing defense, I'd yet to land a single blow. I redoubled my efforts and our motions became a blur. Then he caught my fist once more and froze. My gaze slid past where he held my hand captive to meet his. To my surprise, his eyes were black, though he'd given up attempting to shadow a while ago.

"Alex," he panted, his voice strained.

Undeterred, I shifted gears, and he caught me again. "Damn it!"

"Alex," he said again, his voice shaking.

Suddenly, worry eclipsed my frustration. I reassessed his body language. Something was wrong. I looked at where he had hold of my arm, but he wasn't holding it like he was preventing an attack, more like he was hanging on for dear life.

"Alex, I can't." This time, I recognized the tone—desperation.

I spied Vera approaching out of the corner of my eye. "I'll get you out of here, Matt."

His eyes flashed blue, and I glimpsed a spark of hope. My poor Matt was breaking.

"I'm sorry about this." I shadowed out and grabbed him in a headlock from behind. He didn't fight me, but I caught the moan when I touched him, sensed his essence bleeding into mine. That was bad. Really, really bad. Already, I could feel the pull as he reached out to the shadow world subconsciously for help.

Vera must have as well. She adjusted her course to make a beeline for us.

I looked at her and fought to keep the mounting panic from my voice. "Something's wrong."

She took one look at him and didn't hesitate. "Get him out of here." A portal opened up beside us, as big as I was tall.

I eyed it warily.

"Go," she hissed, "before anyone else notices that he's warping every shadow in here."

I didn't wait for her to tell me a second time. I pushed him through the portal and followed. It deposited us just outside of the college.

"Alex—" Whatever else he'd intended to say devolved into one pained sound. The surrounding shadows warped and twisted with a life all their own in direct defiance of the morning light.

I glanced toward our dorm clear across the lawn and down at Matt sagging against me. He looked like he was desperately trying to pull himself together and failing miserably. His eyes flashed rapid fire between blue and black. Much longer out here and we'd have significantly bigger problems than our lack of communication. I took a deep breath and grabbed his hands. The shifting stopped, landing squarely on black.

I walked us into the shadow world and raced to the dorm. We emerged on the wrong side of the door and Matt shadowed us through. I wasn't even fully materialized when his mouth closed over mine. The intensity of it forced me the rest of the way into the physical world. My shoulders dug into the door as I crushed him against me. I'd been terrified that day he'd told me to leave that he'd finally changed his mind about being together. But whatever this was, it proved that he still wanted me.

His fingers dug into my sides and I couldn't tell if he was trying to push me away or urge me on. It didn't matter. His mouth was still hungrily on mine and I was too far gone to stop. I pushed us away from the door to get to the bedroom. We made it halfway when he started pushing back. I tried to shadow us there, and he used the same trick I had earlier to keep us rooted. Fine, neutral territory it was.

The couch slid away from our less than graceful fall. It wasn't until I was holding the shredded remains of his shirt that I realized my own clothes were equally in tatters. I violently shoved the coffee table further out of the way. This wasn't about being tender or sweet. Something deeper had hold of us, a fire that left no room or breath for questions. No chance to voice doubts.

I pulled him close against me, desperate for the skin-to-skin contact I'd been denied these last few weeks. He groaned and wrapped himself around me. This was going to be rough, and I didn't care. I needed more of him. I needed all of him.

"Matt," I moaned between kisses. "I love you. I can't... I don't..." There was no way to finish that. I couldn't live without him. It was a truth deep down that wouldn't let me give up on him. I worked my way along his neck and shoulder, gripping him like he might vanish at any moment.

He arched into me and tangled a hand in my hair. "Alexi," he moaned.

I scrambled for our supplies, but barely had a chance to roll on the condom and apply lube before he drove himself onto me. The world went white. It felt frozen in place and I thought I might pass out from the sensation. Neither of us moved, and I worried that Matt actually had. He shuddered and everything shattered. Matt was mine, body and soul, whether he could admit it or not.

With a growl I didn't even recognize as mine, I drove into him, pistoning my hips until the world fell away. Matt met me thrust for thrust, his intense heat fluttering and pulsing around me, while he raked his nails across my shoulders. Not even climaxing could satiate the need dominating us.

I shuddered through a third orgasm that threatened to disintegrate me and collapsed beside Matt. Despite feeling wrung out, there wasn't a doubt in my mind that we could keep going. I was dubious if that was an upside or a downside to being a demon. Once my heart rate and breathing returned to normal, I glanced over at Matt. His eyes were closed, but he was definitely still awake. He still hadn't said a word since he'd cried my name hours ago.

Hours!

I sat bolt upright, a move my spent body immediately protested. "I can't believe you got me to skip my classes."

He cracked his eyes, revealing a pair of perfect blue crystals, a hint of merriment swimming in their depths. "You should play hooky more often," he responded with a short laugh.

I raised an eyebrow. "Is this what you do when you're skipping class?"

"No," he said simply. I didn't think he was, but the sadness in the answer implied that there was something else. But I expect asking to result in answers.

I slid down beside him, rolling so I could hold him more easily, and placed a gentle kiss against his lips. Even after our marathon, he reacted, tilting my hips closer and leaning into me. My stomach grumbled, and he smiled against my mouth. I pulled away with a groan. "We should probably eat something."

"Certainly, sounds like it," he replied playfully, a small smile tugging at the corners of his mouth.

"Are you hungry?"

"Not really."

"Liar. When is the last time you ate something?" I asked, sliding my hand over his sides, unable to deny how prominent his ribs had become since the last time I'd seen him.

He shrugged. "I haven't been able to eat." His choice of words concerned me. I'd seen how much food Matt could make disappear; he was always hungry.

"Bet I can fix that." Hope shone in his eyes and my heart broke. I glanced towards the kitchen. The phone and takeout menu were both in there, but I was petrified if I got up he'd vanish.

"I won't go anywhere," he said quietly.

I looked back at him, not sure if I dared to take him at his word.

"Besides, I'm too tired to move," he added with a devilish smile, closing his eyes as if feigning a nap. He squeezed my hand, though I hadn't realized he was holding it. "I promise," he whispered.

Waiting wouldn't get us fed, so I shadowed to the kitchen and ordered entirely too much food. In a moment of bravery, I slipped into my room to grab some lounge pants and the comforter from my bed. When I returned, Matt's fake nap had turned into a very real one. I bundled him beneath the blankets and settled beside him. He stayed curled up until a knock at the door. He blinked, as if surprised to find that he'd fallen asleep.

"Food's here," I said in explanation, standing up.

"In case you forgot, I'm still naked down here," he said snidely.

I smiled back at him. I most definitely had not. "Then I guess you should stay quiet," I said, tossing the comforter over his head. I could just make out his faint chuckle as I opened the door.

"All of this for you?" the delivery guy asked in disbelief.

"No," I replied calmly. Matt snickered behind me, and the guy's eyes widened knowingly.

"Got quite the evening planned, eh?" he asked, wiggling his eyebrows suggestively as he passed me the bags.

"Who said it was just the evening?" I returned. "My partner is very hungry after... our day." Matt's snickering was nearing outright laughter. When was the last time I'd heard that sweet sound?

"Don't do anything I wouldn't do," he added with something bordering on a leer.

I gave him my most sinister smile. "I'm sure I will."

Matt finally erupted into all out giggles beneath the comforter. The poor guy didn't even register what I'd said until I closed the door on his shocked face. The second the latch clicked into place, Matt threw off the comforter, gasping for air between bursts of laughter.

I brought the bags over and arranged their contents on the coffee table. "You doing alright?"

He struggled for air. "Have I ever told you that you're really funny?" He wiped tears from the corners of his eyes as he finally sobered and eyed the spread. "That's a lot of food for one person."

"I'm hoping you'll share." I passed him a fork and an entire carton of beef lo mien.

"I told you I wasn't hungry," he said bluntly.

I stroked the side of his face. "Yes, you are. Now eat."

He looked into the carton with a longing that broke my heart. There was no way he wasn't starving. "You're the one who should eat. You're getting too skinny."

Weren't we the pot calling the kettle black? And did my ears deceive me, or was that a note of concern? I wasn't about to argue with him, though. I leaned forward and grabbed a carton at random that turned out to be chicken and broccoli. He watched me as if making sure I would actually eat while still not having taken a single bite himself.

"I'll make you a deal. I'll eat, if you do."

He looked from my container to me and then back at his own. He let out a deep breath, then slowly swirled some noodles and took a bite. I mirrored the action, and he took another. After a few bites, he stopped checking to see if I was still eating. I finished mine and nibbled on some rice while he continued to devour container after container. It reminded me of when we'd first met and he always eating.

I leaned against the couch and went for broke. "I'm going home next weekend."

He turned at the declaration and the noodle he was slurping tossed broth on his nose.

I chuckled and wiped the sauce away. "The Harvest Fair will be in town. It's usually pretty interesting. You should come with me, get out of this place for a while."

He swallowed his latest bite and actually seemed to consider the proposal. "I guess I could see what I can do." It was more than I had dared hope for.

"It'll be nice. We'll go somewhere that we won't run into anyone or anything relating to school. Almost like a mini vacation." I smiled and mentally crossed my fingers.

"No one from school, huh?" he mumbled, more to himself than me. Then he took a deep breath that came out in a tremendous sigh. "Whoa, I'm stuffed." He eyed the devastation he'd wrought. Of the vast quantities I'd ordered, only three small cartons had survived. He glanced at me nervously.

I cupped his face, gently turning it so he was looking at me, and he met my gentle kiss with one of his own. "I love you," I whispered. This whole day had proven to me he wasn't nearly as far away as I'd feared. Maybe there was hope for us yet.

"Alex, I..." Emotion shimmered in his eyes. A longing that reminded me of the sketch he'd done. "I think it'd be great to see your hometown." He leaned in again and the feel of his mouth against mine was pure ecstasy.

We disintegrated into cuddles and kisses until at last we both drifted off. When I awoke hours later, he was gone. My heart fractured into a thousand pieces at seeing the empty space where he should have been. Not again.

I curled into a tight ball and cried myself into oblivion. Had I just imagined the whole thing? It had been so vivid, so real. Matt, my Matt, had returned to me for a few glorious hours and now it was like he'd never been here at all.

In my misery, I lashed out at the cartons on the table, except they were gone. In their place was a single piece of paper. I wiped my face and tried to focus. It was too dark to make it out properly, so I shadowed the lamp on, revealing a sketch and two words.

I picked up the page and held it up to the light. It was a picture of me sleeping with "*I'm Sorry*" scribbled next to it. So it hadn't been some dream. Matt had been here, and he'd left—again—even though he'd promised not to.

CHAPTER 28

THOMAS

M

y inability to stay away from Alex was going to get him killed. It didn't matter that he was like life itself to me or that even an hour in his company could restore my spirits. If I couldn't stay away long enough to eliminate the threat, I'd lose him... for good. Even knowing that, I couldn't stop myself from considering his invitation. The danger was in Arminius, not in his hometown.

Alex's home. I'd get to see the place—the people—that had made Alex, well, Alex. I'd give anything to see that. Decided, I quickened my pace. If I was going to go, I'd have to really show up until then. Sadly, that included being more engaged at the fight club. I suppressed a groan as I approached the usual meeting spot.

"You look better," Kyle said, eying me skeptically.

"What's that supposed to mean?" I crossed my arms, not appreciating his sudden interest in my appearance.

Travis walked up behind me and grabbed my shoulders. "Ease up." He released me and moved around to get a better look at me. After suffering his gaze for several seconds, he snapped his fingers. "I've got it. You look like you got laid."

I scrambled to hide my surprise, but judging did my Travis and Kyle's smirks, I was doing a piss-poor job of it. Was I really so transparent, or did I just look that bad before?

Travis's gaze narrowed abruptly. "It wasn't that witch from the club, was it? Because you said you weren't interested." He bared his teeth at me in a snarl and I rolled my eyes.

"Trust me, I'm not the reason she's not interested in you. Besides, she's not really my type."

He pulled his shoulders back and puffed out his chest. "What the hell is that supposed to mean?" It was an empty bluster. We both knew I could put him down without even trying. Still... I'd seen smarter people make stupider mistakes. I braced myself in case he took a swing after all. Getting into a scuffle with Travis might not be the wisest thing, but I was in no mood for his antics. Abandoning Alex in his nest of blankets had felt like cutting off a limb, and the wound was still fresh.

"He's saying you're an ugly ass. Now stow it. Thomas is expecting us." At George's interjection, my head snapped around. It was about time I got to meet this mysterious figure. He sneered at me. "That's right, little Matty, the big boss is intrigued enough to want to meet you. Best not to keep him waiting."

Travis and Kyle shared a look and shrugged, then ambled away from fraternity row... in the *opposite* direction of town.

I did a much better job of stifling my surprise this time. I'd suspected "Thomas" might be in charge, but hadn't been able to confirm it without raising more suspicion than it was worth. And bonus: if we were seeing Thomas now, then that meant no fight club for me tonight. I felt downright smug as I moved to follow the duo.

I'd only gone a few steps when George grabbed the front of my shirt and yanked me to his face. I mentally berated myself for letting my guard down and smothered the overwhelming impulse to tear him apart.

"You better not embarrass me, gutter rat. I went out on a limb for you." He shoved me back without giving me a chance to offer any empty reassurances, and I gained another useful tidbit. Whoever this guy was, he frightened George. He glared at me, then spun on his heel.

I jogged to catch up and fell in step. When they finally slowed their brisk pace, we were in a part of campus I'd never been, if we even *were* on campus anymore. The surrounding buildings resembled the stone of the main entrance. But where that was shiny and warm, the stone here was worn and blackened. Not even the foliage seemed to want anything to do with it beyond a smattering of stubborn weeds. One word came to mind: desolate.

"Where are we?" I finally asked, as I peered through a crumbled wall into the maw of an equally derelict building.

George held out his arms. "This is old fraternity row."

"Why does it look empty?" I asked, taking in the choking vines slowly pulling apart the ancient masonry.

"Because it is," Travis offered unhelpfully.

Kyle picked up a broken piece of stone and chunked it into the night. "We pretty much have the run of the place."

"Why?" I asked.

George rounded on me. "You sure are asking a lot of questions."

"Excuse me, if I don't want to wander off into some vampire blood cult," I snapped, getting in his face. I didn't even know if that was a *thing*, but it did the trick.

George resumed walking as if nothing had happened. "Something happened here during the Uprising.

I frowned and searched my knowledge of recent events, limited as it was. "You mean the Shadow War?"

George's face twisted with a snarl. "Leave it to that bitch to get a whole war named after her."

I wisely bit my tongue and refrained from pointing out that the war was actually named for the whole group and not Vera specifically.

"*Anyway*, like I was saying. Something happened here. Something bad. The witches won't go anywhere near this place."

I wanted to ask what had happened, but I'd already asked too many. Undoubtedly, Alex would know. If we ever got through this, I'd have to ask him. We continued picking our way through the ruins until we came to the building at the end of the row. Massive columns rose into the sky to end in broken edges. Their missing halves littered the ground in yet more broken pieces all around the entrance. I'd been in some pretty sketchy places in my life, but even *I* thought this place was a dump.

"Are you coming?" George snapped.

I scurried up the crumbling steps, dubious that they wouldn't disintegrate beneath our combined weight. Of all the rotten places to have a hangout, these assholes would find the rottenest. Not that I was truly surprised. People like George inevitably found themselves on the fringes where there were fewer people around to judge their depravity.

George and the others confidently worked their way through the rubble, and I followed sedately in their wake. The inside didn't look to be in any better repair, though magical orbs clung to the walls offering ambient light that nothing to illuminate the foreboding dark. The deeper we ventured, the more my skin crawled. Something about this place wasn't right. But beyond present company, I couldn't imagine what that might be.

Kyle peeled away from the group. "I'll let Thomas know we're here."

"I already know." The disembodied voice seemed to come from nowhere and everywhere all at once. I contemplated shifting the darkness to illuminate him, but doubted the others knew that was even something that could be done.

"Do you always have to do that?" George asked, sounding more like a whiny brat than the leader of a gang determined to hunt down and murder my best friend.

The voice laughed without humor and stepped into the light. Its owner was older than I'd expected. He could have been a teacher, and he definitely wasn't a Shadow Demon. He came closer and a sense of familiarity washed over. Try as I might, though, I couldn't place the short, dark beard and soldierly face. His gaze narrowed to a predatory slit. "You certainly took your time."

George angled his thumb at me. "The recruit was gawking at the front door."

"Recruit, eh? We'll see about that." He walked leisurely around us, his gaze picking apart every detail like he was dissecting rats in a lab instead of young men. "What makes you so sure that he's not the one we're looking for?" The man's gaze snapped to George.

"I'm not an idiot, Thomas. We vetted him. Nothing weird or nothing," he spluttered. "Plus, I'm stronger than he is."

"You have a very high opinion of your power. Come here."

It took me a second to realize Thomas was addressing me. I shoved my increasing anxiety down and took a step forward. I'd certainly faced opponents far more imposing than this guy. Sure, he had wide shoulders and looked like he could take out a stone wall by himself, but that wasn't what had me worried. I couldn't shake the growing sensation that I should *know* him.

"What's your name, boy?"

I gritted my teeth and ground out, "Matt." His eyes drilled into me until I added, "Matthew Duncan."

He raised a bushy eyebrow. "Matthew. Interesting." Despite the assessment, he sounded bored. "So, *Matthew*, what makes you think you can help with our little... quest?"

"I'm observant and better at going unnoticed than your current—" The term lackeys came to mind, but I didn't expect that would be well received. "Recruits," I finished instead.

Thomas considered me without blinking, then pointed into the distance. "You see that wall over there?"

I followed the path of his finger. A light blared to life, revealing a wall adorned with pictures of people from Battle Tactics, as well as classmates that hadn't returned for the fall semester. Some of them had giant X's drawn across them, including present company. I squinted at the X-ed out image of myself. It was an unusual shot from the side and a little blurry, as if I'd been moving when it was taken. I eagerly sought the only picture I cared about, praying there was already an X on it.

Alex's picture was significantly better than mine, boasting a stunning shot of his emerald eyes and a half smile on his lips. But no X. My heart seized, and I fought to keep the reaction from showing on my face. I shifted my gaze higher to see who else was on the chopping block, but my focus got snagged by someone unexpected.

Above the photos was a picture of Vera herself. She wasn't sporting the amiable smile I'd become familiar with, though. No, she was absolutely terrifying in full battle regalia and charging forward. The picture was too far to tell, but I'd bet good money that her eyes were the color of midnight. She might have even been shouting some sort of war cry, but it was hard to tell with the dagger sticking out of her face.

I swallowed my trepidation and forced my voice to remain neutral. "George mentioned y'all were looking for someone in class. But he was a little vague on the details."

Thomas shot George a nasty look before walking over to the wall of photos. It seemed appropriate to follow, but I made sure to stop in front of a photo a suitable distance from Alex's. "Not just *someone*. We're looking for an abomination of nature. Something that cannot be permitted to exist in this world." Spittle flew from his lips to pepper the image before him. He regathered himself and glanced at me as if to gage my reaction to his outburst. "We've been able to cobble together a few clues, but admittedly, we *are* much farther from our mark than I would like."

"What do you know?" I asked, giving him a level stare in return.

He waved a dismissive hand, but I didn't miss the tightening around his eyes. "As far as *demons* go, they'll make the top ten for sure. We suspect they've perfected the art of passing. Undoubtedly, how they've remained undetected for so long." He tilted his head and added in a more musing tone, "Moderately attractive."

"They eliminated Travis, right out the gate," Kyle snickered, only to be silenced by what sounded like Travis hitting him in the gut.

I didn't turn to look, far more focused on Thomas and his witch hunt. "What else?" I prompted, needing to know just how much they had.

He gave me a curious look. "Graceful, a natural at movement. Fluid. Like a..." He paused, as if debating how much to reveal. "Like a dancer."

Travis snorted. "You mean queer." The others laughed, but Thomas didn't.

"This stain must be wiped from the earth. Do not belittle the severity of this with your inconsequential labels." His intensity silenced the others and sent a shiver down my spine.

"How can I help?" I could have thanked Nyx herself that my voice didn't shake. Thomas' smile turned evil.

"Let's see how *observant* you are about your classmates. Perhaps you *can* be of use in eradicating this contamination of the blood."

"You're friends with Roman, right?" George asked, stepping up and yanking Alex's picture off the wall. "He's an odd one, for sure."

My stomach sank. I wasn't sure I could answer without retching right there on the floor. "Alex?"

"Yeah, what do you know about him?"

I shrugged, painfully aware of how closely Thomas was watching me. "For starters, I'm stronger than he is. He's a total bookworm. Even got him to tutor me last semester. It comes in handy knowing an egghead."

"Well, I guess that's one strike. If you're stronger than he is..." My heart slowed as the marker George held hovered over the picture of Alex.

"What about other people? Who does he spend time with? If you catch my drift." Kyle asked, and I could have killed him on the spot.

"We don't really talk about girls," I said, barely managing not to snarl.

"Oh?" George stared at me like he was second guessing my usefulness. "He never brings anyone back to the dorm or anything?"

"I haven't seen him bring anyone around. But who can say?"

"He's in ballroom, right? Who voluntarily signs up for that?" Travis asked with a grating guffaw. My murder list was getting longer, and I was increasingly more alarmed at how much they knew about Alex.

"Yeah... It's weird alright, but I think he might know something the rest of us don't. The chicks in that class practically drool every time he comes around. It's a little disgusting honestly," I added with maybe a hair too much conviction.

"And he hasn't brought any of them to the dorm?" George insisted.

What the hell was wrong with these people? Who *cared* who he brought to the dorm? "I think he's hung up on someone else."

"Who?"

"I already told you, we don't really talk about girls. He's odd for sure, but nothing special." It was the first outright lie I'd told all night, and I prayed no one would catch it.

George sucked his teeth and pinned the image back. He did not add a red X, however. Apparently, it would take more than my word to clear Alex and I already felt like I'd run a gauntlet.

"Got anything to drink?" I asked to direct their focus away from the fact that my composure was seriously cracking.

Kyle and Travis let out a whoop and waved for me to follow them. As I ventured after, I heard Thomas catch George. I slowed to listen, but didn't dare look back.

"Your little friend better not disappoint. I grow weary of your failure," Thomas said gruffly.

"Ease up, old man. We'll find your poser."

At the whisper of shuffling, I quickened my pace. George brushed past me as he followed his goons. I chanced a glance over my shoulder to see Thomas glowering at all of us like he'd rather skin us alive than trust us to find who he was searching for. His glare itched between my shoulder blades long after I was out of sight.

As I followed the trio back outside, my resolve strengthened, along with my conviction that I knew Thomas from somewhere. But where?

About the Author

S Bolanos (she/they) is a genderqueer author and the founder of Chaotic Neutral Press LLC. They believe in love, equality, and the Oxford comma. As a member of the Inclusive Romance Project, S can support and connect with other creative minds.

She is proud of their Cuban heritage, and currently lives in Texas, a startling eight miles from everything, as the saying goes. Their two Labradors, Mr. Darcy & Lizzie, along with their Boxer-mix, Elinor (Dashwood), keep them plenty busy with cuddles, kisses, and never-ending demands for more walkies. S adores their supportive husband who's invaluable when it comes to working out sticky plot points. When not playing with her three dogs or spending time with her incredible husband, she's probably agonizing over edits or escaping into her latest fantasy.

She enjoys creating worlds that feel as real as they are fantastical, and doesn't shy away from the darkness that makes the light so much brighter. Readers can look forward to many stories within the same universe that reach into the past and stretch all the way to the future.

WEBSITE: Booksbysbolanos.com
TWITTER: @Booksbysbolanos
INSTAGRAM: @sbolanosbooks

Special Treat

Scan or click the image below for the War on Darkness playlist at Spotify!

Want to stay in the loop with all the latest and greatest? Sign up for the newsletter and an opportunity to become an ARC reader!

Booksbysbolanos.com/newsletter

Keep reading for a sneak peek at the final installment for the War on Darkness!

ABSENTE OMNIA SEMPER NOCTE

DENHAM

ALEXI

My hope that Matt would accompany to the Harvest Festival in my hometown shriveled with each day that went by without so much as a glimpse of him. It officially died as I packed my bag. Perhaps the time away from each other was for the best. Maybe I'd even extend my stay beyond the weekend. All of my assignments were completed and there were no pending projects. Missing a few days of class wouldn't hurt.

The fact that I was contemplating skipping classes—intentional-ly—was enough to give me pause. It also reminded me of how I'd *unintentionally* played hookey with Matt the week prior. When I'd invited him to go with me. For all his enthusiasm about seeing my hometown, he'd vanished faster than water in a desert. Not even the sweet picture of me sleeping made up for the lackluster apology scrib-bled next to it or the fact that he'd left in the first place. What he was apologizing for anyway? Leaving? Being an ass? Lying about wanting to come?

I nearly ripped the zipper of my bookbag off its track as I slammed it home with a little too much force. A glance at the clock on my nightstand confirmed what I already knew—time was up. He wasn't coming, and no amount of stalling would change that. Tears pricked at the back of my eyes. Would he even tell me we were over or would he keep ghosting me until I got the hint? I willed my eyes to dry as I carried my bag into the living room.

"Good, you're still here," Matt said, appearing out of nowhere. His gaze flicked from me to the stuffed backpack. "You still going home?"

I fought to keep my glimmer of hope at seeing him from flourishing. If he truly wanted to go, he'd have been here this last week. "Um… yeah," I said, hating how raw my voice sounded. Was this it? Had he planned to wait until the last second to break up with me so that he wouldn't have to deal with the fallout? I braced myself for the inevitable, carefully keeping my gaze fixed on the carpet, so he wouldn't see the hurt threatening to swallow me whole.

"Still want me to come?"

My head shot up. "What?"

He took a tentative step closer, that same hint of sheepishness to his features that I'd once found so endearing. "I'd like to go to the Harvest Festival with you. That is, if you'll have me."

"Of course," I said too quickly.

Despite my over eager reply, the biggest grin I'd seen from him in a long time stretched across his face. Then, a tide of words flowed out. "When do we leave? Where exactly are is Denham? How are we going to get there? What's a fair like? I've never been to a fair before. How long does it last? Do I need to bring anything? How many people will be there?"

I held up my hands to stem the rush, unable to hold back the laughter at this unexpected energy. "One at a time, please."

His mouth snapped shut with an audible bubble sound while the rest of him appeared to vibrate in place with the force of keeping his questions restrained.

"Okay, one question."

He took a deep inhale that puffed his chest, then let it out in a burst. "What's Denham like and how are we getting there?" He winced. "Oops. That was two."

A laugh burst out of me, bringing forth the tears I'd been fighting before.

Panic flashed across Matt's face as I dropped my bag and doubled over in my fit. "What? Did I say soething wrong? I know I should have been here sooner. But I had a thing I had to take care of and—"

I held up a hand once more to stop his babbling. I barely even cared that he said "a thing" instead of whatever he'd actually been doing. He was here. He wanted to come with me. And he was *excited*. "You didn't say anything wrong. I just... missed you," I said as I straightened and wiped my eyes.

A light pink stained his cheeks. "I-I've missed you too."

My heart soared. He didn't want to break up. I cleared my throat and picked up my bookbag again before the emotion had my crying... again. "Denham is nice, if quiet. Like most small towns, everyone knows everyone. As for how we'll get there, I made a portal."

"Really?"

"Yep. It's on the roof." I neglected to mention that it had taken nearly everyday since I'd invited him to make the damn thing *and* get it to stay open. Much as I'd have liked to keep the portal for future visits home, I wasn't sure it was quite worth all the effort to keep it maintained. Abruptly, I realized we were staring at each other and smiling. "We should get going if we don't want to miss supper. Do you need to pack anything?"

He smirked and reached *into* the couch. When he pulled his hand out, he held a small duffel bag.

My eyebrows shot up. "How long has that been there?" And did I need to check the rest of the dorm for other "hiding places".

"I've... uh, been packed for a few days." His smile slipped. "I didn't mean to cut it so close."

I searched his face, but the answers I wanted weren't there. "The important thing is that you *did* make it. Now, let's get out of here before my mom calls to ask where we are."

Matt brightened and slung the duffel across his body. Without warning he stepped forward and planted a chaste kiss on my lips, then dashed to the door. "What're you waiting for? Let's go, slow poke. I could use a break from this place," he said, though that last bit was more to himself.

My head spun as I situated my bookbag on my shoulders and moved to join him. Who was this person? He bore no resemblance to the Matt I'd been forced to endure the last couple of months.

Unbridled joy danced in his eyes as he flashed me a wide smile and reached for the door. I flattened my palm on the door to keep it closed and his eyebrows pinched into a V. "What—"

I cradled his jaw, cutting him off with a kiss. It was truly a shame we didn't have more than the lingering press of lips, but if we waited much longer to leave, my mother would start calling. "I love you, Matt," I said, then opened the door. We smiled at each other, neither of us making a move to leave. My heart felt like it might burst as I waited for him to say it back.

"Alex."

"Yeah?" I whispered, anticipation making my voice thin.

Wickedness darkened his crystal blue eyes. "Race you to the top."

He took advantage of my stunned state to turn and bolt. I shadowed to catch up while the door slammed shut, automatically locking, but didn't shadow again. Our feet pounded against the lush carpet that absorbed the sound of our frantic race. We careened around a corner, nearly taking out one of our RAs, pushing and shoving each other to get to the stairwell first. We burst onto the rooftop, laughing and panting for breath. Matt caught my gaze and we shared another smile. Then he straightened and looked around at the flat—noticeably empty—roof.

"Uh... Where is it?"

I gestured to the side of the maintenance room.

Matt looked from me to the innocuous wall, then a knowing smirk spread across his face. "You cloaked it." The pride in his voice filled my chest with a warm glow. He held out his hand for mine. "Well, what are we waiting for?"

I wrapped my fingers around his and led us through the portal. The cool mist of the barrier brushed over my face until it encompassed my entire body. Then the infinite darkness of the Shadow world gave way to bright sunlight and a crisp autumn afternoon. A light breeze ruffled my hair as we stood at the edge of a forest with nothing but open field between us and Denham. I took in Matt and his expression of awe, I knew I'd made the right decision not to put the exit by my house, or even better, in it.

"That's..." He dropped my hand and took a step forward before stopping to look back at me. "That's Denham?"

I walked up beside him and wrapped an arm around his shoulders. "Sure is. And if you look over there," I pointed to our right where you could just make out the ferris wheel and some low-lying buildings, "that's the fair."

"It looks as big as the town."

I chuckled and squeezed him close. "Denham is small even compared to Sieben Hügel. But the Harvest Festival Fair is actually for all the surrounding parishes."

"Parishes," Matt repeated like he was tasting the word. Then he wrinkled his nose. "Why does the UK have to have such weird naes for everything?"

I snorted. "You mean the *right* names? You, know, since the UK was here *before* the US."

He rolled his eyes, but leaned into me. We stayed like that for a few minutes, soaking up the sunshine and appreciating the view. Then Matt tilted his head back to look at me with half-lidded eyes and whispered, "I really like it here. Your home is beautiful." He stretched his neck and I met him halfway for a kiss sweeter than cotton candy.

Seconds from turning him and deepening the kiss, my phone rang. I groaned and Matt chuckled into my shoulder. "Hello, mother," I said without checking the caller ID.

She sniffed indignantly. "Don't 'mother' me. Have you left the university yet?"

I glanced at Matt failing to smother his grin. "We're actually at the edge of the forest. Should be there in fifteen to twenty minutes."

"We? Matt decided to come along after all? That's wonderful, sweetie! I can't wait to finally meet this boyfriend of yours."

"He's my friend too, Mom," I countered, cringing at her loud enthusiasm.

Matt leaned toward the phone. "Looking forward to meeting you too, Ms. Roman."

My heart exploded, or maybe it froze. Whatever it was doing, it definitely wasn't beating anymore. Matt had basically labelled himself as more boyfriend, in public, to another person. Granted, it was my mom, and there wasn't really anyone around to witness it, but it was also the first time he'd acknowledged our *relationship* extended beyond friendship out loud.

"Lexi. Honey. Are you still there?"

"Huh? Yeah. I'm still here. We'll be there soon." I glanced at Matt, who's lips were twitching in a repressed smile. He knew damn well what he'd done.

"Excellent. I'll make sure the guest room has fresh linens. See you soon. And don't dally!" she admonished before hanging up.

Matt raised an eyebrow. "So, guest room, huh?"

BOOKS SUPPORTED BY

CHAOTIC NEUTRAL PRESS

One Kiss Changed Everything

Four years ago, Mitch and Andy were inseparable. But even the best of friendships can't weather every storm.

When Andy comes out as gay to the only person he trusts, he doesn't expect to have his heart broken.

Now in their final year of Ulwich Prep, they find themselves once again in the same orbit. While they both appear to have moved past what happened that night, looks can be deceiving.

Mitch needs Andy more than he's willing to admit. He still harbors guilt about his response to his best friend coming out. Through a twist of desperation, Andy becomes Mitch's tutor.

As bad as he needs the help, though, all Mitch can think is that this is his chance to make things right. He won't go another four years without Andy.

A Mythical Desires Universe Series

Gregor Lyndon became a public safety officer to help people. Greg thought he left his family's legacy of canonized heroes that rescued maidens from dragons. What he can never get away from is his family's ability: the power to take down a dragon with one killing blow.

Xavior Brantley has lived a somewhat reckless life for a dragon. He's been an explorer, an investigator, traveled to parts of the world that individuals have barely ventured. When he became bored, he turned to public servant work. A transfer to a local headquarters makes things a lot more interesting when he meets Greg and discovers the secret of the Saint George Knight.

The Saint George Chronicles is a spicy/slow burn gay dragon shifter romance with a HFN. The Mythical Desires Universe is a queer-centric world where myth and legends exist alongside advanced science and technology.

Bitter and depressed after a bad breakup, Serafin moves towns to escape his old life, only to find when he arrives that his brand new home is haunted by an oddly handsome ghost.

Charming, confident, and mysterious, Darius is both alluring, & impenetrable. As Serafin learns more and more about his ghostly inhabitant, he has to fight his feelings, but with every day that passes he finds it harder and harder.

The question always on his tongue:

"Could I ever love a ghost?"